Mission to Kill

A Garcia Girls Mystery

LIZBETH LIPPERMAN

This is a work of fiction. Names, characters, places, brands, media, and incidents are either the product of the author's imagination or are used fictitiously, and any resemblance to actual persons, living or dead, business establishments, events, or locales is entirely coincidental.

For more information, please direct your correspondence to:
The Story Vault
c/o Marketing Department
364 Patteson Drive, #228
Morgantown, WV 26505-3202

MISSION TO KILL
A Garcia Girls Mystery
All rights reserved.
Copyright © 2015 by Elizabeth R. Lipperman

http://www.lizlipperman.com

ISBN 10: 1517289904
ISBN 13: 978-1517289904

Cover Design by Kelly Crimi
Interior Book Design by Bob Houston eBook Formatting

Published by The Story Vault
Website: www.thestoryvault.com

Dedication

To my sisters, Lill Magistro, Mary Ann Nedved, Dorothy Bennett, as well as Theresa Pollack (who died way too young.) Without you, I couldn't have written this book centered around the loving relationships between the Garcia Sisters. I love you all so much.

Acknowledgements

To Dan, my children, Nicole and Brody, Dennis and Abby, and my grandchildren, Grayson and Caden and Ellie and Alice, who never cease to brighten every day for me.

To my amazing agent, Christine Witthohn, who is my biggest cheerleader and task master. I couldn't do this without her.

To my critique partner, Joni Sauer-Folger, and to my beta readers, Sylvia Rochester and Chris Keniston, all talented authors themselves, for making me a better writer.

To Versel Rush, an awesome attorney who has guided me through the legal system of a small town in Texas through all my Garcia Girls books and who has become more than a loyal reader to me. I so appreciate the friendship and the coaching.

To Lauri Barge for all her help with this story.

To all the rest of my amazing family—numbering in the 200s—who epitomize a fun-loving family. You are the reason I know so much about unconditional love and can write about it.

Chapter One

Hello, Sis. Miss me?

Kathryn Garcia turned sharply before dropping the tray of instruments, unable to stop the scream that bubbled from her throat. The speculum clattered loudly on the marble floor, and she jumped back to avoid getting hit in the shins when it bounced her way.

Nancy McGuire rushed in with two other doctors behind her. "Dr. Garcia, are you okay?" the nurse asked.

Kate swallowed hard and stared into the corner where her sister Tessa was leaning against the wall, picking at an imaginary piece of lint on her sleeve. "The tray slipped out of my hand." At least that was half the truth. Admitting the other half—that her dead sister was standing in the room, grinning like she'd just pulled off the biggest prank in the history of mankind—was out of the question.

Taking a deep breath, Kate faced the others and tried to smile. "Guess I tripped over my own two feet."

She stole a quick glance Tessa's way before donning a pair of gloves. Then she bent down and began to pick up the metal instruments. Making eye contact with her boss and mentor, Joseph Solano, she shrugged, wondering if any of them could see Tessa but not stupid enough to ask. They'd load her on the looney train faster than a lion on the tail of a hyena if she told them she was looking at her dead sister. "Bet you didn't know I was such a klutz when you hired me, Joe."

"Oh yeah! I've seen you in action the past few years, remember?" He tried to act upset but the amusement in his dark eyes gave him away. "Guess you'd better get her another tray, Nancy." He winked at the nurse on the way back to his own patient.

"Welcome to Vineyard OB/GYN, Kate," Greg Keller said with a warm smile. "I knew you'd fit right in."

Kate glanced up at her associates, noticing how green his eyes looked today, complementing the lime green button down under his lab coat. Too bad he had a wife and two beautiful little girls. "Hope so."

"Here, let me take that back to the autoclave," Nancy said, reaching for the tray.

"Thanks." Kate handed the instruments to the nurse and waited until she was alone before allowing herself another peek back into the corner. She caught her breath when she realized this wasn't just a bad dream. Her deceased sister Tessa was leaning against the wall, taking it all in with a smirk on her face.

Have you played doctor with that younger guy yet?

Kate's heart skipped a beat. She ignored the question and got right to the point. "Why are you here?"

Beats the hell out of me.

An uncomfortable chill crept up Kate's spine as she tried to make sense of it all. Tessa had been murdered a few years back and only showed up when one of the Garcia sisters was in trouble. The last time she'd graced them with her presence had been the year before when their oldest sister Maddy was charged with murder.

"There's nothing going on in my life right now. In fact, it's downright boring at the moment. And although I love seeing you, even though you scared the crap out of me, I'm pretty sure I don't need you." Kate hoped her sister didn't pick up on the uneasiness in her voice. That was exactly what their oldest sister Maddy's reaction had been before she'd found the obnoxious drunk in the back cell at the jailhouse with a huge hole in his chest and her Glock lying next to him.

Just like I told Maddy, I have no control over when the dudes up there—she pointed to the ceiling—**send me back to Vineyard. And I never know why, but trust me when I tell you, there's always a good reason.**

Kate narrowed her eyes. "If I'm remembering correctly, the last time you showed up, it was because you got caught trying to put the moves on St. Pete, and his wife wanted you out of the way." She chuckled. "You always did have a knack for pissing off other women. I'm sure you've been up to your old flirty ways."

Tessa huffed. **Even if I did re-stir that pot a little, there's always something going on with one of my sisters when I show up. The last time I was here Maddy damn near ended up in a jail cell. The fact that I'm standing in front of you now means you obviously need...**

Both Tessa and Kate turned toward the door when Greg Keller walked back in. With his curly blond hair falling to just above his ears and a smile that screamed mischief, her associate could sell just about anything on TV and make you want to buy it. Four years older than her, Greg had been a resident when she was a med student, and they'd dated a few times before discovering they were much better friends than lovers. Greg had ended up marrying the daughter of a local politician, and Kate considered both he and his wife Cyndi close friends now.

If you haven't already gotten under the sheets with this guy, something's seriously wrong with you, girlfriend. Look at those dimples. If he were Pinocchio I'd be sitting on his face begging him to lie to me.

Kate glanced up at to see if he'd heard Tessa's last remark. She was relieved to discover his expression hadn't changed. Either he didn't see the ghost, or he was one hell of an actor.

"Just checking to make sure you really are okay, Kate." His eyes were filled with concern.

Although he'd never met Tessa, Kate had shared the story of her older sister's murder over a beer one night. But she hadn't mentioned that her sister's ghost still made an occasional appearance. She bit her tongue before she said anything that might make him suspicious.

"I'm good. Really." She waved him off. "Now, don't you have something more important to do than babysit me?"

He studied her for a moment before replying, "You always did know how to bring out my protective side."

She tsked. "Yeah, right! Are you forgetting how you used to goad me into those stupid beer chugging contests before we grew up and became real doctors? You would've sold me to the devil if it meant watching me beat some redneck to win a pitcher of beer—which you always horned in on, by the way. Protective side? I think not." Playfully, she punched him in the arm before nudging him toward the door. "Go. Nancy mentioned that Mrs. Jamison was coming in today. You'll need a lot more caffeine flowing through your veins before you deal with her and all her imaginary emergencies."

"Damn! I forgot about that. I'll need something stronger than coffee." He turned back to face her. "Hey, before I forget, Cyndi wanted me to ask if you were available for dinner on Saturday night. The girls are spending the night at her folks' house. Said you could even bring a plus one."

"Like I have time for a plus one. You and Joe are like slave drivers here. I've done so many Pap smears, I'm beginning to think you guys must have advertised a two-for-one sale as soon as I signed on. Geez!" She tried to make light of the fact that there was nobody romantic in her life right now, but like she'd said, who had the time? She couldn't hold back a grin, remembering something Tessa had said at her last appearance about keeping a man fully charged and out of sight for whenever one needed to get laid. Called it the Dustbuster theory.

"Consider all those Pap smears as paying your newbie dues. I did so many when I first joined the practice I probably could have done them with my eyes closed." He grinned. "Come to think of it, I probably did one or two like that back in our drinking days at Southwestern." He gave her a mischievous side grin. "And about that plus one—my friend Josh is always asking about you. I could invite him to dinner Saturday."

"Get out of here, Keller. You know I don't do setups. Besides, your friend Josh thinks just because I'm a doctor familiar with the human anatomy that it gives him a free pass to mine."

Some men are like finger paint. One squeeze, and they're all over you.

Kate bit back a grin and focused on Greg. "Your friend's roaming hands aside, I'm perfectly capable of finding my own date. Tell Cyndi to set an extra place."

"I can't wait to see what kind of loser you show up with. Remember, I'm the guy who has to listen to you complain about all your dates. Cyndi and I had a good laugh over that last one. And who could forget the one who lived with his mother and called her every half hour?" He chuckled. "Oh yeah, you know how to pick 'em, alright. I'm looking forward to your next gem." He ducked out of the room before she could come up with a comeback.

As soon as the door closed behind him, Kate slapped her head. Why did she go and open her big mouth like that? She hadn't had a second date in over a year, and there certainly wasn't a Dustbuster on her back wall for the occasional booty call. But she should've seen it coming. Greg had been working her like that since she was a medical student and he was the resident over her. All it took was a dare, and she'd bite. *Damn!* You'd think she would've wised up by now.

"Don't even think about telling me that I walked right into that one, Tessa." She turned to the now empty corner. "Tessa?" Shrugging, she hoped the ghost's disappearance meant that nothing in her life had prompted the appearance after all.

She was finally living her dream and didn't need help from above, although it was almost laughable to think of her sister and heaven in the same thought. Tessa, always a loner, had been the middle Garcia sister. Of all the girls, she'd been the one to receive the good looks. As far back as Kate could remember Tessa had boys from three counties lining up at their door. She'd also been the one to use that beauty to her advantage and hadn't been above doing whatever it took to get what she wanted, making more than a few enemies on the way.

When Tessa was murdered a few years back, it was their sister Lainey, only two years older than Kate, that Tessa had chosen to grace with her other worldly presence, which was weird in itself since the two sisters had been estranged and hadn't spoken in over nine years. Somehow, they had set aside their differences, and after Lainey was able to reveal secrets about the other sisters that only Tessa could have known, she'd finally convinced her siblings that she really was talking to a ghost. And exactly like it had been all their lives, the sisters had bonded together to find Tessa's killer, even though the list of potential suspects who hadn't shed a tear over Tessa's demise was mind-boggling.

Once that was accomplished, they'd assumed Tessa would go off into the light—or wherever the soul goes after death—and that would be it. When she appeared the last time just like she'd done today, Maddy hadn't taken it seriously until she was framed for the murder of a prisoner on her watch. That had pretty much convinced them that, as incredible as it seemed, their smart-mouthed middle sister had sort of become their guardian angel.

Which was exactly why Kate couldn't stop thinking about ghostly Tessa showing up today.

Her life was perfect. Almost a year ago, she'd been recruited by the top OB/GYN practice in Vineyard when she'd finished a two-year residency in obstetrics at Southwestern in downtown Dallas. She'd met Dr. Solano her senior year in medical school, and they'd clicked. When his father had retired several months before she'd completed her residency, he and Greg had worked extra hours filling in to avoid hiring someone else until she was ready.

Yes, she was blessed. She had a job she loved right here in the small town where she'd grown up, and her three sisters close by. They'd always been best friends and still were, which made her even more nervous about seeing Tessa. Was one of her siblings in trouble? Was that why she'd shown up today?

Pushing those thoughts from her mind, Kate concentrated on the four hours she had left before she could go home. Tomorrow was Wednesday, high-risk pregnancy day, which was always so busy, and then Thursday, her favorite day of the week since the office closed at noon. On the third Thursday of the month, she, Lainey, and Deena volunteered at the Mission of Hope in downtown Vineyard serving hot lunches to the city's down and out citizens. She looked forward to this for two reasons. Not only did she get to spend the day with her two sisters at the Mission, as it was known, but also there was always time to go shopping or to a spa afterwards with Maddy joining them when she could get away from the police station. Plus she'd grown fond of some of the street people and loved the way their eyes lit up when they spied the sisters on the serving line.

She'd even talked Dr. Solano into allowing her to use the office one Thursday afternoon a month to minister to the homeless women, most of whom sold their bodies on the street to pay for their drug habits. Nancy had immediately signed on to come in on her afternoon off to help. Convincing the women to have a checkup had been a daunting task at first, but word that it was safe had spread quickly throughout the homeless community, and before long, the lines were so long, she and Nancy had occasionally had to work into the wee hours of the night to see them all. And with Greg and Joseph Solano's help, they'd convinced several of their colleagues in the Vineyard medical and dental community to offer some degree of pro bono help as well.

The Mission had been a mainstay of the city since she'd first volunteered in high school and was run by a family friend who had found himself homeless after coming home from the Gulf war with PTSD and a heroin addiction. With the help of her stepfather, who paid for the man's rehab and then gave him a job in the family furniture business, Benjamin Yates had finally gotten his life together. Not only had he pulled himself out of the rut he'd dug for himself, but he'd also run the business for Kate's stepfather while he and her mother took time off to explore the country, one city at a time, in their RV.

The first thing Benny had done when he had enough money was to buy an old abandoned warehouse in the town square and open the soup kitchen to pay it forward, much to the dismay of the Chamber of Congress who tried every legal maneuver they could think of to close down the kitchen. Kate had been forced to give up her days at the Mission when medical school and the years of training had gobbled up all her waking hours, but it was the first thing she'd reestablished once she'd become a full-fledged obstetrician. Benny was like the older brother she never had, and she loved the time she was able to spend with him.

Yes, life is good, she thought as she glanced around one last time to see if her sister had returned. Staring at the empty room, she let out a relieved sigh and began preparing for her next patient.

*****

That old saying that "time flies when you're having fun" popped into Kate's head as she pulled off her latex gloves, said goodbye to her last patient, and headed to her office. No way would seven Pap smears in three hours ever be considered fun, but being that busy had at least made the day go faster.

In her office, she went straight for the chair and sat down, plopping her feet up on the desk. A quick stop at the health club on her way home and about an hour in the Jacuzzi jumped straight to her rest-of-the-day check list. Leaning back in the chair, she admired the way her sister Deena had decorated her new office. The second oldest of the Garcia clan had quit college her junior year and married Mike Hernandez, a loser whose womanizing ways should have been a red flag. But Deena had been smitten, and no amount of sisterly warnings convinced her to dump the guy. After Mike was killed last year, Deena had quit her job at the nursing home and gone back to night school to finish her degree in interior design.

She'd begged Kate to let her practice on the drab space that used to be Greg's office and had turned it into it into a warm environment that immediately put the patients at ease. Gone were the hard-back chairs that reeked of doctor's office, the awful plastic figurines of the female anatomy and pamphlets about everything womanly that had lined the walls. In their place were two comfortable navy blue chairs across from Kate's desk and colorful pictures of waterfalls gracing the walls, giving the room a feeling of serenity to even the most uptight patient. Deena had also turned one corner of the office into a fish tank.

Joe Solano had been so impressed, he'd immediately hired her sister to redecorate the entire building. It had been Deena's first paying job and had caught the attention of all the patients. She now had a thriving business without having to spend a dollar on advertising.

The intercom on Kate's desk buzzed, and she picked up the phone.

"Kate, there's a guy on the line who says he's a lawyer and needs to talk to you," the receptionist said.

"Thanks, Carla. Put him through." A flutter of apprehension snaked up her spine as Tessa's face popped into her brain.

After taking a deep breath, she said, "This is Dr. Kathryn Garcia."

"Are you the Kate Garcia who volunteers at Mission of Hope?"

"I am. How can I help you?"

"I'm Conrad Winters of Winters and Delgado in Houston. We're the attorneys of record for the estate of Horatio and Paulina Santiago."

Kate scrunched her eyebrows, wondering why a lawyer was calling her at the office. Was someone suing her? And who were Horatio and Paulina Santiago?

Before she could ask, the man continued, "We've received word that their daughter Emily was killed in El Paso last week." He paused as if allowing the news to sink in. "Two years ago, Horatio and Paulina died in a tragic plane crash, and with the exception of an endowment to Houston Memorial to build a new cancer wing, Emily inherited everything, including Santiago Oil Refineries."

"What does this have to do with me?"

"Please allow me to finish. The private investigator hired by the estate found Emily living on the streets in Vineyard not long after the death of her parents. When I flew down to complete probate and transfer everything to her, she chose not to use any of the funds at her disposal. A good thing since one of the provisions of Horatio's will was that no funds be distributed until she was completely drug free. At the time, Emily wanted nothing to do with her father's money or the weekly drug tests required to begin receiving stipends, but she did allow me to execute her own will, naming you and Mr. Yates as beneficiaries."

"I have to interrupt you again, Mr. Winters, because I think you're wasting your time. I've never heard of Emily Santiago."

"You probably knew her as Emily Ruiz. She sometimes used her mother's maiden name instead of her legal one because she and her father had an antagonistic relationship at best."

Kate gasped. "There must be some mistake, Mr. Winters. Emily Ruiz died three months ago. An overdose, I believe." She wasn't sure what was more shocking, that Emily had left everything to her and Benny, or that she may have died twice.

"Your information must be incorrect."

"Sir, I identified the body at the morgue myself." Kate closed her eyes and rubbed her forehead as if to push away a migraine. The police had found her phone number in Emily's tattered jacket when the woman's body was discovered in the woods behind the Square, and she'd been called in to make the positive ID. Even though she'd viewed the body months before, the image of sweet Emily lying on that flat metal slab in the county morgue still haunted her. Emily, who had been so hopelessly addicted to meth and anything else that would take her out of the world she lived in, at least until the next fix—an heiress?

"There is no mistake, Dr. Garcia," the lawyer continued. "I'm looking at the police report right now. Emily apparently got her life back on track and left Vineyard to start a new one. Unfortunately, she was in line at the El Paso National Bank when a robbery went terribly wrong, and both she and the security guard were shot and killed."

"But I saw her body—"

"Since you and Mr. Yates are the only beneficiaries of her estate, I'd like to set up a time to sit down with the two of you and go over the technicalities," he said, ignoring her protests.

As he continued to talk, the sound of a cough from inside her office distracted her. Opening her eyes, she stared directly at her dead sister, who was now standing across from her desk with an I-told-you-so look on her face.

She swallowed the lump in her throat. She and Benny had counted on a quick burial with no questions asked. The last thing they needed right now was an investigation into Emily Ruiz's death.

Chapter Two

"**H**ow does this Friday sound? I've already talked with Mr. Yates, and he can be available any time after two that afternoon."

The lawyer's voice snapped Kate out of her own thoughts. She hesitated briefly before answering, "Mr. Winters, this has to be a mistake. How does a woman show up in El Paso three months after she died in Vineyard?"

"I'm sure there was some kind of dreadful mistake made in the case of the body you thought was Emily's."

Kate thought back to that time. She'd met Emily Ruiz eight months earlier during her first week back at the Mission. Despite the woman's tattered clothes and serious lack of hygiene, she'd made a connection with Kate almost immediately. It was hard to imagine the thirtyish, drug-addicted, rail-thin woman, who made her living on the streets, as an heiress. But even though her appearance may have been shabby, Emily had been anything but that on the inside. No matter how strung out the woman had been, Kate remembered how she'd always taken the time to visit with the other poor souls at the soup kitchen.

But Kate had also known there was a darker side to Emily. Known she'd do anything for her next fix. And when the homeless woman had shown up at the clinic after hours one night, just when she and Nancy were getting ready to go home, they'd had a peek into how dark her world really was. She'd been beaten so badly by a john, her eyes were mere slits, and she'd been bleeding profusely from a vaginal tear so traumatic it had required five stitches. Not to mention the eight stitches it took to sew up the two inch gash on her face that still had the imprint of a ring.

Despite their pleas to let them take her to the emergency room, Emily had refused. In the end, Kate had convinced her to spend the night on the couch at her apartment, afraid of the possibility of a massive infection if she allowed her to return to her home under the bridge on Bell Street. Emily was gone by the time she'd awakened the next morning—probably searching for a fix. Although both she and Nancy had tried to find her at known homeless hangouts in Vineyard, the woman had disappeared.

Until the night Benny had called, frantically begging her to come to the Mission.

When Emily's body had been found in the wooded area behind the Mission less than a day later with Kate's business card in her tattered jacket pocket, she'd been called to the morgue to identify the body.

At first the police suspected the homeless woman had been beaten to death, but Kate had produced the medical records that proved the facial trauma had been over a week old. Toxicology results a few days later confirmed she'd died of an overdose of cheese heroin, the street name for the potent heroin mixed with an over-the-counter drug used for insomnia. A combination both cheap and toxic.

Since the police had found no missing persons reports for an Emily Ruiz, and no one had come forward to collect the remains, Emily had been classified as an unclaimed dead body. Under Texas law, her body would have been buried in a potter's field, cremated, or donated to medical research, but Benny had stepped up and paid for a simple burial in the town cemetery. Kate had been back to the grave several times since then, knowing Emily had no one else who cared.

"So, will Friday afternoon work for you?" the lawyer asked, interrupting her day dreaming.

Kate grabbed the rest of the week's schedule from her desk, and quickly scanned it. She only had two patients coming in that afternoon. "I can be available after three thirty."

"Excellent. Why don't we say four o'clock? I've already contacted Charles Prescott and Associates. He was kind enough to allow me to use his conference room for this. I'll call and confirm the time and apprise him of your concerns about the mistaken identity of the homeless woman. Are you familiar with the location of his practice?"

Kate stifled a giggle, tempted to remind him that he was talking about Vineyard, not Houston. Everyone was familiar with all the locations here, and if she guessed correctly, the entire town would know about this lawyer's four-hour drive from Houston before he turned off Interstate 45 and made his way up Highway 114 to Vineyard. "Yes, I am. I'll see you there at four."

After she hung up, she remembered that her sister had reappeared and quickly turned to see if Tessa was still standing in the corner.

I told you there was a reason I was sent back here, the ghost said. **But I can't figure out how you're involved.**

Kate shrugged, not ready to tell anyone the secret she shared with Benny. "I know you were listening when I told him this was all a mistake and will get straightened out in no time. So, I guess this means you can go back into the light and stir up more trouble up there." Kate tried to make a joke of it all, but in truth, she was more than a little unnerved by the phone call.

Wonder how much money you're going to get? Tessa asked, making her way to the navy blue chair and plopping down. **Who was this Emily person anyway?**

"Just a homeless woman I was fond of. It's ludicrous to think she somehow rose from the dead and ended up in the middle of a shootout in El Paso." Kate blew out a breath and leaned back in her chair. "Think I should call Colt?"

Colt Winslow was the sheriff of Vineyard and married to their older sister Lainey. If anyone could make sense of it all, it would be him.

Call Maddy and run it by her first. She may tell you not to get involved.

"Good idea." Kate scribbled a few notes from the conversation onto a notepad, then picked up the phone and dialed the police station. Her oldest sister was a full-fledged cop now and would be able to tell her what she should do, if anything.

"Vineyard Police Station."

"Jeannie, this is Kate Garcia. Is my sister there?"

"No, she went out with Rogers on a domestic call about an hour ago. I expect her back shortly, though. Is there a problem, Kate?"

"Probably not, but I wanted to talk to her before I went to Colt with something."

"Colt isn't here, either. Do you want to talk to Landers?"

"No," Kate said way too quickly. She hadn't seen Danny Landers since she'd come back to Vineyard after her residency, but she was pretty sure he was still mad that she'd used him to get information when Maddy's life was on the line. "I'll just call—"

"Hello, Kate," the familiar voice said. "Are you calling to see how you can screw me over again?"

She felt the blush creep up her face. She and Danny Landers had been best friends since kindergarten. Then when they'd reached high school, he'd started looking at her differently, stammering and acting goofy every time he was around her. When he'd finally built up enough courage to ask her to the homecoming dance their sophomore year, she knew she'd broken his heart when she'd declined. But how could she go on a date with a boy she'd considered a brother almost all her life? A boy she'd shared her intimate secrets with—or at least as intimate as secrets could get at that age. She hadn't wanted to lose that friendship, but after she'd turned him down, he'd gone out of his way to avoid her.

"Everything isn't always about you, Danny," she said, slamming her hand to her head for the lame response.

The truth was, she regretted that what she'd done when her oldest sister was looking at jail time had gotten him into trouble with Colt, but in her heart she knew she'd do it again if she had to. They'd been able to use the information she'd stolen from his desk to eventually get the charges against Maddy dropped. "I wanted to talk to my sister about a woman who died three months ago."

"Who?"

"It's probably nothing. I'll talk to her when she gets back."

"Is this about the homeless woman who was found behind the Chinese restaurant on the Square a few months back and somehow has miraculously risen from the dead?"

She caught her breath. "How do you know about that?"

He laughed. "Ranelle at Charlie Prescott's office called Jeannie to find out what was up."

"I should have guessed. But yes, it is about that. A lawyer from Houston called to tell me that a woman with the same name was killed in a bank robbery in El Paso. Apparently, she had money and named Benny and me as her beneficiaries."

"Whoa! You sure someone isn't jerking your chain?"

"He's coming Friday to talk to us."

"Where are you now?"

"At the office."

"Stay there. I'm on my way over to get details. I want to have them ready for Colt when he gets back from Gracie's horse competition."

As soon as she hung up, she reached for her purse and pulled out her compact.

The last time that boy saw you, you were in skinny jeans and a silky blouse that showed off your assets. You'll need more than powder and lip gloss to top that.

"Who says I'm trying to look good? Besides, he's still really pissed about what we did to him when Maddy was in trouble. I'm just freshening up, that's all."

Yeah, and I'm not really dead. She waved her hand. **Lighten up, Katie, and invest in a new push up bra to go under those scrubs, or you might find out that the only one interested in your boobs is the person doing your mammogram.**

*****

Benjamin Yates had been sitting in the leather chair for the better part of an hour, still in shock over the phone call from the Houston lawyer. It was hard to believe they were talking about the same woman. The Emily Ruiz he'd known was an addict. She'd been living under a bridge, so drugged out he'd found her lying in her own waste.

He remembered that day like it was yesterday. He'd picked her up and carried her to Kate's apartment, thinking Doctor Kate would know what to do. Together, they'd sobered her up, and Kate had gotten into the shower with her to hold her up. After throwing away the filthy clothes Emily had been wearing, Kate had given her one of her own outfits. He'd hoped Emily would take better care of herself after that, and although it had taken a long time to gain her trust, they finally had. Teeth damaged by years of abusing meth were attended to, and they'd gotten her into a methadone program to bring her down off the drugs. She'd eventually let Kate give her a physical exam and put her on birth control.

Benny had been feeling proud of himself—especially when Emily began to take an interest in her own hygiene again and showed up two or three days a week at the Mission.

He knew she still walked the streets at night, but he'd hoped for a better future for the lonely woman he'd taken under his wing.

That had all changed one night in the kitchen at the Mission. A night he had tried so hard to forget.

"Are you okay, honey?"

He straightened up at the sound of his wife's voice, then forced his shoulders to relax. "I'm still thinking about a phone call I got earlier. Some lawyer in Houston called to say that Kate Garcia and I are the beneficiaries for the estate of a young homeless woman we befriended."

Wendy Yates's eyes lit up. "Oh my God! Why didn't you tell me? I've been agonizing over how we were going to pay for Lori's braces." She sat down in the chair opposite him. "How much money is it?"

He shrugged. "I don't know, but I wouldn't think the man would make a special trip to the Dallas area if it wasn't substantial."

"Holy cow! And he said it was a homeless person who left you the money?"

A flash of guilt coursed through his body. He would have to be very careful what he told her. He nodded. "Apparently, the woman died in El Paso."

"Do I know her?"

He shook his head. "Her name was Emily Ruiz. According to the lawyer, she got caught up in a shootout between a bank security guard and two armed robbers." He stopped before he blurted out that the woman he'd known by that name had died three months earlier. Until he was able to make sense of it, there was no reason to get his wife involved.

"Wasn't that the name of the woman who was found behind the Square a few months back?"

So much for keeping that a secret. "I thought it was. Guess we'll just have to wait and see what the lawyer says. He's driving to Vineyard on Friday."

"This is the answer to our prayers," she said before standing up and clapping her hands in glee. "Come on. Lori's having dinner at Shelby's house tonight, and I've made your favorite—steak and gravy. Maybe we can celebrate afterwards before she gets home." She wiggled her eyebrows in a comical way, then turned and ran to the kitchen.

But he didn't move. He couldn't stop thinking about Emily. How could she have turned up in El Paso when they'd buried her four months ago in Vineyard?

The El Paso police had to be mistaken. He was one hundred percent sure the body in the woods behind The Mission had been Emily Ruiz—AKA Emily Santiago.

After all, he was the one who had put it there.

*****

Kate powdered her nose and put on new lip gloss, feeling foolish even as she did it. What did she think that would accomplish? Like a little makeup could turn Danny Landers into her best friend again? For a nanosecond she even entertained the idea of stuffing gauze under her boobs for a little push-up action as Tessa had suggested.

Where was Tessa, anyway?

She jumped when the receptionist opened the door and popped her head it.

"Dr. Garcia, Officer Landers is out here and says you're expecting him."

She licked her lips and nodded. "Send him in, Carla."

Danny must've been right behind the young receptionist because he was there before the woman even had time to turn around. "So this is where you hole up every day?" He whistled as he twirled around to take in the room. "A far cry from that old treehouse in my backyard where you used to make me pretend I was sick so you could doctor me back to health." He sauntered over to one of the chairs and settled in, his eyes never leaving hers.

"Do you want coffee? Or water?" she asked during the awkward pause.

"No thanks. Just had lunch."

He leaned in and rested his elbows on her desk, giving her an up close and personal look at his blue eyes. She wondered why she'd never noticed how Paul-Newman blue they were before.

"Tell me what's going on so that I can give Colt a heads up when he gets back. How are you and Benny involved with a dead woman from El Paso?"

She'd been taking his inventory and was embarrassed when he noticed and smiled. She scolded herself for acting like a school girl on her first date. This was Danny Landers, and although her sisters had joked that he'd had a crush on her since junior high, he was still the same guy she'd known all her life. And the same nervous rookie cop she'd tricked over a year ago to help her sister. He'd always had that mop of dirty blond hair and dimples that sucked you in when he smiled. So why was she suddenly so unnerved sitting across from him?

"All I know is that the person they say was killed can't possibly be the homeless woman I knew because I personally identified her at the Vineyard County Morgue three months ago. She might be Emily Ruiz Santiago, but she's not *my* Emily Ruiz."

He leaned back in the chair, and she had to force herself to look away. When did he get so damn cute? When she'd spoken to him earlier, she imagined him being the same immature boy she'd grown up with, the one who could make her laugh even when she was so mad at him she wanted to kill him. This new version—looking pretty hot in a police uniform with a gun strapped to his hip—threw her off her game.

"Maybe you'd better start from the beginning," he suggested.

For the next fifteen minutes she told him everything she could remember about Emily Ruiz, including how badly injured she'd been the night she was beaten by one of her customers.

"And that was the last time you saw her?"

Kate lowered her eyes before again making eye contact. Danny had a knack for knowing when she was lying. "That happened on Sunday night. I'd hoped to see her on Thursday when I volunteered at the Mission, but she didn't show up. I figured she was still recuperating from her injuries. Saturday night you guys found her body." Mostly true. She'd just left out the part about Benny calling her hours before the police did.

"I remember. The coroner said she'd had so many drugs in her system there was no doubt about the cause of death. We'd investigated one other cheese overdose in the county and helped with a couple of other cases in Karpell." He reached across the desk and turned the picture of her two nieces around. After studying it for a minute, he looked up. "I would've thought you'd have married some big-time doctor by now with kids of your own. Last I heard, you were dating a neurosurgeon."

"Religious differences." Knowing he'd checked up on her at least once in the past made her heart skip a beat. "He thought he was God. I didn't."

Danny's eyes crinkled the way she remembered when he was tickled. "Yeah, well. I can see how that would create a problem."

"What about you? Are you in a relationship?" she asked before she could stop herself. The possibility of him being her plus one at dinner at Greg's house on Saturday sounded better with each one of his dimpled smiles.

And why not? He'd always been able to make her laugh, never allowing her to take herself too seriously. She could use a little fun in her life right now, especially after the grueling six years she'd spent post medical school.

"Guess you could call it that. I've been seeing Miranda Walters for a few months." He captured her stare. "You remember Miranda? She was a few years older than us and lived around the corner? She just moved back into town from Laredo and works for the District Attorney's Office now."

She tried hard not to show her disappointment at that bit of news. Miranda was the same age as her sister Lainey and used to come by the Garcia house every now and then. She remembered her as being very popular and never wanting for male attention.

"Miranda's a lawyer?"

"And a pretty good prosecutor from what I hear," he replied.

A twinge of jealousy danced in Kate's head. "You'll keep me updated on this Emily Ruiz thing?" she asked, standing up and dismissing him before she said something stupid.

He nodded. "My guess is that it's a case of mistaken identity. At any rate, we'll get it cleared up." He stood up, allowing his eyes to travel her body and causing a flurry of heat to skitter up her back. "You look a whole lot different in those scrubs than you did that day you wore those tight jeans and sexy red blouse and got me into trouble with Colt."

She stepped closer. "Danny, you have to know I would've done anything to help my sister."

He put his finger to her lips, causing little shivers to race up her arms. "I'm just saying I had a hard time getting that image out of my head, and I'm more than a little disappointed you're wearing scrubs and a lab coat."

Before she could react, he tipped his hat and exited, leaving her standing there with her mouth open, thinking he would've made a *really* nice plus one.

Chapter Three

The rest of the week seemed to crawl by until finally, it was Thursday. Kate rushed to get the last patient seen by eleven-thirty and finished the paperwork in record time before grabbing her purse and heading out the door herself. She was looking forward to seeing her sisters at the Mission followed by lunch and a day of pampering. She hadn't yet told her siblings about Tessa showing up, hoping that the ghost's appearance had been some kind of fluke.

She loved Tessa and had always been closer to her than the others had, but her surprise visit from the afterworld signaled the possibility there might be trouble down the road for her or one of her sisters. Things had been going well since she'd joined Joe and Greg in the practice, and she preferred they stay that way.

Another reason she was excited about volunteering at the Mission today was because she was anxious to talk to Benny about Emily and the phone call from the Houston lawyer. After the burial on the outskirts of town, with only she, Benny, and Miriam, Emily's friend from the homeless community in attendance, Kate had tried to put her out of her mind. She'd done all she could to help her, but sadly, the pull of the frail woman's drug addiction had been too strong.

Sitting at a red light, she let out a squeal when Tessa suddenly appeared in the passenger seat.

You need to work on that startle reflex, kiddo. Tessa twisted around and flipped off the driver in the car behind them when he laid on his horn after the light changed.

"Geez! Give a girl a little warning next time." Kate shot her sister's ghost a sideways glance. "And why are you still here, anyway?"

Tessa shrugged. **Guess we'll find out tomorrow when the lawyer shows up.** She clapped her hands together. **I can't wait to see the rest of the gang today. How are my sisters doing?**

Kate pulled into a parking spot in front of the Mission. "Lainey's still headlining the six o'clock news on the weekend, and she's got her hands full the rest of the week now that the new grapevines are finally beginning to produce at the vineyard."

Tessa gasped. **Are you telling me we're close to making wine again at Spirits of Texas?**

Kate stifled a grin, nodding as she watched Tessa doing the dead version of the happy dance. She'd owned Spirits of Texas with her second ex and had worked hard to make it a success. When she'd died, she'd willed her share—and subsequently the entire vineyard—to Lainey with the stipulation that it would eventually be turned over to Gracie, Tessa's eight-year old daughter. But Tessa's killer had set it on fire, and Lainey had been forced to start from scratch, importing all new vine cuttings from Palermo, Italy.

"Not from the new vines. Lainey's importing grapes like you did, and she's promised to let us be the first to taste the initial batch of wine next week." She leaned back in the seat and faced her dead sister. "Maddy is carrying on a long distance romance with that cop from San Antonio who helped her when she was accused of murder at the beginning of the year."

And Deena?

"After Mike died, she took a leave of absence from the nursing home and spent a few months trying to make sense of it all. How can you live with a guy for that long and not really know him?"

Mike was always an asshole. Everyone in town knew—except Deena, that is—that he'd do just about anything to get laid, including screwing over his sister-in-law. I'm not surprised it finally caught up to him.

Kate opened the door and got out. "Asshole or not, Deena loved him, but his death made her realize it was time to decide what she wanted to do with the rest of her life. After she quit her job at the nursing home, she figured it was now or never to take a shot at interior design. She's actually making a living at it and having a blast." Kate opened the door and slid out. "You coming?" she called over her shoulder.

Oh, I wouldn't miss this for the world. I get to see my siblings, and I haven't seen Benny since my funeral.

As soon as Kate walked in, she spied her sisters at the front, chatting animatedly with two of the homeless women. When Lainey spotted her, she waved for her to come over.

Approaching her older sisters, Kate used the time to study them. Of all the siblings Lainey looked the most like Tessa, but she didn't dare mention that to her. Although the two sisters had resolved their differences after Tessa was killed, Lainey hated that people still compared her to her older sister who had made enemies with just about everyone in town before she died.

Tall and slender with jet black hair cut in a stylish bob that hit just below her ears, Lainey looked every bit like the journalist that she was. Although she enjoyed doing the weekend news, she'd given up a gig as the talk show host in Savannah and an opportunity for a more prestigious job in Florida to hang around Vineyard after Tessa's ghost had begged her to find her killer. But it had reaped way more benefits than just the satisfaction of working with her sisters to solve the crime when she'd married the town sheriff, whom she'd been in love with since junior high.

And who had previously been married to Tessa, which had caused the nine-year rift between the two sisters in the first place.

Deena, three years older than Lainey, had cut off her long dark French braid when she was widowed and decided that besides a totally new outlook on life, she needed an entirely different look. A short pixie cut brought out the sparkle in her dark eyes. As part of her new makeover she'd gone all in on a diet and exercise regime and had already gone down two sizes.

"Hey, guys, what's up?" Kate asked when she reached them.

Lainey nudged the homeless women closest to her until she was standing directly in front of Kate. "Tell her what you just told me, Irene," she prompted.

The slightly overweight, fortyish woman who had once been a nanny and now made her living panhandling on Main Street turned to Kate. "Rumor on the street is that the woman they found behind the Mission may not have been Emily Santiago, after all. I heard Louie from the Crab Shack tell someone that the actual dead woman was a childhood friend of Emily's from Houston who ran away from an abusive husband and came to Dallas."

"Where in the world did Louie hear that?" Kate asked, definitely interested now. If that were true and the real Emily had been living in El Paso all along, why would she and Benny have been named as her benefactors? And then there was the mystery of the friend who had supposedly stolen Emily's identity? Why would someone go to all the trouble to do that, only to live on the streets and die a pauper's death? It didn't make sense.

But the lawyer had been pretty adamant about the dead woman in El Paso being the real Emily.

Irene shrugged. "Don't know. Louie thinks the woman who'd lived under the bridge on Bell Street may have been a criminal, too."

The other homeless woman tsked. "Louie has always been a blowhard. I bet he made that crap up." She tugged on Irene's arm. "Come on. It's getting crowded. We need to find a table while we can."

After the two women walked away, Deena hugged Kate. "How are you holding up with all this drama?"

Kate looked surprised by the question. "I'm fine—unless you count the fact that I desperately need to find a date for dinner at Greg and Cyndi's next weekend."

Lainey tilted her head. "Why is that such a big deal? You must know a lot of eligible doctors."

"Not one I want to break bread with at my friend's house. Greg can be merciless when it comes to his teasing."

"So, go alone. It won't be the first time you've done that."

Kate frowned. "I can't. I opened up my big mouth about bringing a plus one when Greg goaded me."

So, if he had asked you to jump off a bridge you would do it?

Kate twisted around as Tessa walked up.

Oh my God! Deena looks fantastic. She must be getting laid, finally.

"Why does everything always have to be about sex with you?" Kate tried to sound disgusted, but the truth was, Tessa made her laugh.

Because when you ain't getting any, little sis, it's a big deal. Trust me, nobody gets it on up there. She pointed upwards. **And heaven doesn't come with a Walmart for batteries. A girl's left to her own devices.**

"Please tell me you're not talking to who I think you are." When Kate nodded, Lainey narrowed her eyes. "Why is she back this time?"

"She thinks I may be in trouble."

I never said that. I just mentioned that someone close to me apparently needs my help. Tessa grinned. **Like it or not, I've been chosen as the new angel in charge of my family's well-being.**

Kate turned back to her living sisters. "According to her, she's always going to show up when one of us is in trouble. So, since I'm doing great, it must be one of you guys."

"Oh, Lordy! I finally got my life going in the right direction." Deena paused. "Where is she?" When Lainey flipped her thumb to her left, Deena took a step backwards.

I don't bite, Deena, Tessa said indignantly. **And I have no idea which one of your pretty little asses is in trouble.**

Benny walked over from the kitchen, drying his wet hands on the already dirty apron before he gave Kate a hug. "Hey, Doc, can you stay for a few minutes after lunch?"

Tall and stocky, the ex-Marine still wore his slightly-graying hair in a buzz cut and was built like an NFL defensive tackle. After he'd returned from Afghanistan and finally kicked his heroin habit, he'd promptly gone back to the lifestyle he was most comfortable with and ran the Mission with the same zero-tolerance mindset as the military.

"Only for a minute. We're having a sisters' day at the spa after we finish up here. I need to talk to you, too."

Just then two men walked up to Benny. The taller of the two extended his hand. "I'm Ryan Kowalski, and this is my partner, Jerome Woodson. You must be Benny. We've spoken on the phone a few times."

Benny reached out and shook their hands, but it was obvious he had no idea who they were.

The guy named Ryan laughed. "We're the dentists who have been donating time to help with some of your people."

Kate stepped forward. "Oh yes. I'm Kate Garcia. It's a pleasure to finally meet you in person. We can't thank you enough for providing free dental care to the Mission community."

She followed his eyes as they trailed down her body and back up again, her feminine pride wishing she'd chosen something a little more provocative than her jeans and the oversized sweater.

"Ah! Had I known you looked like this, I would have made it a point to meet you a lot sooner."

Kate smiled at the compliment. "And these two lovely ladies are my sisters."

After the introductions, Benny surveyed the completely-filled room and nodded to his assistant to close the doors. In a perfect world every person down on their luck would have the opportunity to come in and eat, but as difficult as it was to watch people being turned away, Kate knew there was no other way. Besides not having enough food, there was a limit on how many people were allowed in the building at one time. The last thing they needed was the Vineyard Fire Department shutting them down for violating code. Those unfortunate enough to come late would have to try the soup kitchen closer to Bell Street.

Benny turned to the new arrivals. "So are you just checking out the place, or did you have questions?"

Ryan shrugged. "We're actually here to help you serve lunch. We have an afternoon golf game scheduled and decided it was time we got to know some of the people we've been seeing. Since we're both fairly new to Vineyard, it's an added bonus that we'll get to meet some of its more attractive citizens." He made a special point to greet all three of the sisters, making eye contact with Kate a few seconds longer than the others.

That boy definitely uses that line—along with that killer smile that showcases his pearly whites—to score, Tessa said as she walked around the newcomers to check them out. She stopped behind Ryan. **This one can eat crackers in my bed any day.**

Kate took a moment to size them up herself. She remembered speaking to Ryan several months earlier right after she and Nancy had called on some of the health care professionals in the city to recruit pro bono work for the less fortunate street people. She'd learned Ryan Kowalski and his college roommate had moved to town a little over a year ago and had set up practice in the renovated railroad depot on the outskirts of town. Both had graciously agreed to her proposal and were the reason some of the homeless people in the room were now walking around with cleaner teeth and fewer cavities.

Standing around five-eleven, Ryan wore his light brown hair in a professionally coifed style cut just above his ears. She couldn't decide if his eyes were green or gray, but they crinkled in the outer corners when he smiled. His aqua-blue golf shirt with the name of his practice above one breast and his perfectly pleated jeans showed off a tiny waist and an even better backside. Although not drop-dead gorgeous, Ryan Kowalski was the kind of guy her mother would classify as "clean cut" when she was pointing out potential suitors for her daughters.

His partner, Jerome, resembled a typical computer nerd with his tan Dockers and a darker tan golf shirt. He stayed behind Ryan, his wind-blown blondish-brown hair falling over his forehead and his bespectacled eyes giving her the impression that he'd turn and bolt if she said boo. He kept twisting the wedding ring on his left hand as if to send a message that he was off limits.

Like anyone would go for him over his much more attractive partner, Kate thought before deciding that was a little harsh. The ring twisting was probably just a nervous habit rather than a ploy to ward off aggressive females.

She pegged him as being extremely shy and vowed to make him feel comfortable, at least while they were serving lunch. Ryan, on the other hand, was definitely a mover and a shaker and was already in the corner schmoozing with Deena and Lainey.

Him, she'd have to watch out for.

Benny waved to the crowd before turning back to the group of volunteers. "I'm serving my famous stew today, and the natives are getting restless. Let's cut the chatter and get down to business." He walked around to the food line with the others following suit.

Kate positioned Ryan between Deena and Lainey, sure he would be a distraction next to her. Having the happily-married Jerome beside her seemed safer and would probably prove to be more productive in the long run if she wasn't constantly being reminded what a hunk the taller dentist was. She'd already gotten a whiff of his citrusy aftershave, and given her lack of romance over the past year, she couldn't trust herself with him that close.

There was an unusually large number of participants at the Mission today, probably because word had hit the street that Benny was serving up a crowd favorite. Kate recognized several of the women from the clinic and addressed each one personally as she handed out the cornbread.

Until she spotted the man next in line.

The first time she'd met Ernie Jackson she'd taken an instant dislike to him. With his scraggly beard that even now housed specks of dried food—and possibly critters—and brownish hair that begged for a dollop of shampoo, Ernie looked much older than his forty-some years.

Irene had mentioned a while back that in a rare moment of lucidity, Ernie had confided that he'd once lived on Swiss Avenue, the ritzy section near downtown Dallas. That was before the schizophrenia had landed him on the streets. Beyond that, no one knew much about him.

Although he was a man of few words, when Ernie did open his mouth, it was usually to talk to the people in his head or to preach something religious. He spent his days panhandling and dumpster diving for meals behind the restaurants on the Square.

Because she'd heard rumors that the street women were terrified of him, Kate had managed to keep her distance so far. She didn't know if the stories about him were true or not, but only last week, Miriam had told her that Ernie had assaulted an older homeless woman simply for standing too close to him.

When he walked through the line toward her, Kate noticed that his usually red face was now pasty-looking with a few droplets of sweat forming on his forehead. As he got closer she saw his pained grimace, and her medical instincts kicked in. When he was directly in front of her, she made the mistake of leaning toward him to ask if he was all right and immediately paid the price.

Stepping back, she couldn't keep from wrinkling her nose. Along with his usual foul odor from being inside the dumpsters, the man reeked of feces. No way anybody sitting anywhere near him would be able to eat.

She was about to walk over to Benny to suggest they find a place away from the others when Ernie's eyes rolled back into his head and he fell to the ground. The plate hit the concrete flooring with a loud thud and splattered stew all over him and everything around him.

Kate rushed out from behind the counter just as he went into violent convulsions. "Call 911," she screamed, bending down beside him and turning him on his side so he wouldn't aspirate as the white foam spewed out from the side of his mouth. Loosening his clothes, she waited for the convulsions to stop, wondering if he was on an anti-seizure medication.

When the EMTs arrived, Ernie gave one final jerk then stopped breathing. Quickly, she turned him on his back, checked his pulse, and began chest compressions. Up this close, it was all she could do not to throw up over the smell.

"We got it, lady," the first tech out of the ambulance said as he bent down to assess the situation. Quickly, he grabbed a breathing tube and a scope from his bag.

"I'm a doctor," Kate said to the other tech as he ran up with his bag. She stopped the chest compressions while she checked his carotid. "Still no pulse. Take over here and I'll insert that." She motioned to the other tech. "Get a line in so I can give him drugs," she commanded.

The tech handed her the breathing tube before pushing up Ernie's dirty sleeve, now dripping with stew. When the endotracheal tube was in place, she attached an Ambu bag to it and began squeezing it.

"I'm in," the medic said before taping the IV needle to Ernie's arm. Then he switched places with Kate to allow her to push the emergency drugs directly into the IV tubing. With the entire room watching, she and the EMTs worked feverishly for over twenty minutes to no avail.

"Let's get him into the ambulance," Kate commanded, grabbing the Ambu bag from the tech. "You drive."

On her knees now, Kate glanced up at her sisters who were watching with horror on their faces. "I'm not sure how long I'll be. Deena, will you drive my car over to the spa? Then when I'm able to leave you can pick me up."

When Deena nodded, Tessa moved up to stand between her two sisters and shrugged. When Kate's eyes moved from her dead sister to Benny, she expected to see him reverting to his marine persona and taking charge of the situation.

She was surprised to see that he hadn't moved from his position in front of the stew pot, and his face registered total shock at what was happening in front of him.

Then she noticed the tears streaming down his face.

*****

She waited in the rental car across the street from the Mission, impatiently tapping her short fingernails on the steering wheel. She wished she could have long, painted nails like other women, but she didn't have the time nor the inclination for things like that. Besides, the men with the power to bring her down a notch would see it as "girly", and that would never do.

She'd arrived in Vineyard two days earlier and had spent most of the time searching for the one man who now had the power to erode her position in the family business.

Ironic that she'd been fighting for equality all these years and had never even heard of Ernest Jackson until last week. Realizing how badly he could hurt her, she'd gotten here as quickly as she could. When she'd located him, she'd been repulsed by his appearance.

My God! She'd watched the man climb into the garbage bin outside a Chinese restaurant and emerge with old food.

And he'd devoured it like it was a filet mignon instead of discarded Cashew Chicken or some equally disgusting scraps.

She'd made up her mind right then and there that she'd do whatever was necessary to keep him from screwing up her life. She'd waited too long for validation, and no trash-eating bum was going to take it away from her. Not now.

Just then she heard sirens and watched an ambulance pull up to the soup kitchen. Two medics ran into the building. She waited fifteen minutes before the men emerged, carrying a stretcher with a patient that looked to be about six feet tall. A closer look showed a young woman running beside the injured person inflating and deflating a bag over his face. She didn't have to be a doctor to know the guy wasn't breathing on his own.

When they lifted the gurney up and pushed it toward the back door of the ambulance, the patient's hand slid out from under the sheet and hung limply at his side. She caught her breath when she recognized the plaid shirt as the same one Ernest Jackson had been wearing when he'd entered the building.

Intrigued now, she watched the EMTs load him into the vehicle and race down the road. Rear view lights disappeared when the ambulance turned down the street at the corner, and she couldn't stop the smile from spreading across her face. Throwing back her head, she laughed out loud.

Maybe this would be easier than she'd thought.

Chapter Four

The ten minute ride to Vineyard Community Hospital took forever. When the ambulance finally pulled up to the emergency room entrance, Kate had already pushed several meds into the man's veins to no avail. Things weren't looking too good for Ernie when they wheeled him into a room and attached the monitors.

"What do we have here?" the young doctor who had rushed into the room asked.

"His name's Ernie Jackson. He was standing in the food line at the Mission of Hope and began seizing," Kate explained.

The doctor glanced up and made eye contact with Kate. "How did you get involved?"

"I volunteer there on Thursdays, Mitch. Right before he collapsed, I noticed he was looking a little pale and starting to sweat."

"Is he epileptic?"

Kate shrugged. "I'm not sure. Nobody really knows much about him, except that he's schizophrenic and probably doesn't take his medicine. The convulsion lasted about eight minutes, and then he quit breathing." She stepped back to allow the doctor to deliver the charge that would shock his heart.

When the monitor still showed a straight line, the doctor motioned for the nurse to recharge the defibrillator. "How long did you do CPR before you got here?"

"About twenty minutes total," she replied, knowing where he was headed with the questions.

"Clear," he commanded before he delivered the second charge to Ernie's chest, again with no results. After checking the man's pupils, he said, "Fixed and dilated. I'm calling it." He stole a glance at the clock on the wall. "Time of death—one fourteen."

As the nurse shut down the machines, Kate felt an overwhelming sense of sadness wash over her. How pathetic that Ernie Jackson had no one but a roomful of perfect strangers with him when he'd taken his last breath. She thought of Emily, who had also died with no one who loved her nearby and said a quick prayer of thanks for her own loving family.

"Kate, what happened?"

Recognizing the voice, she turned to face her brother-in-law, the sheriff of Vineyard. Before she could repeat what she'd just told the ER doctor, she noticed Danny Landers behind Colt.

"He convulsed and died at the Mission," she explained, finally taking her eyes off Danny and focusing on Colt. "How did you find out about it so quickly?"

"Lainey called. She was pretty upset."

"Yeah, things got intense for a while." Kate snuck another glance Danny's way and was immediately sorry when she discovered him staring at her. "Hey, Danny," she said, feeling foolish for being caught looking.

He nodded a greeting.

Colt rubbed a hand across his forehead as if chasing away a migraine. "It doesn't sound like foul play, but I still need to fill out a report. I'll hang around and see if I can talk to the EMTs and the doctor who pronounced him." He turned to his young detective. "Will you give Kate a ride back to the Mission?"

"The kitchen will be closed by now. Can he run me over to the new spa that just opened off Main Street? I had Deena drive my car over there, thinking she could pick me up here when I was finished. It would save her a trip if Danny takes me."

"No problem. I forgot today was the Garcia sisters' day out. Have fun and tell Lainey I should be home for dinner on time."

"Will do."

She remembered back to when Colt left Texas A & M to come home to Vineyard after his dad was killed by a drunken driver. After helping the police find the man responsible, he'd given up his veterinarian studies to take care of his widowed mother. Soon after, he'd gone to night school while he worked as a deputy, and four years ago, he'd been elected sheriff of Vineyard. She was proud to call him part of her family.

She stood on tiptoes to kiss his cheek before turning to Danny. "Ready?"

He stepped closer to her then led her into the hallway toward the exit. "Looks like you've had more excitement this week than you've had in a while. I almost expect to see you blink twice. You know, like we used to do when we were kids and one of us was in trouble."

She laughed at the reference, one of many eye signals they'd developed as they took on the world back then. "I'd forgotten about that."

"The last time I saw you so serious was when you pushed me out of the apple tree in my backyard and thought you'd broken my arm."

"You deserved it," she said, frowning at him. "If I remember correctly, you said I smelled like a French whore."

He chuckled. "You did."

She tried to look indignant but had a hard time holding back her amusement. "I only borrowed a few drops of Maddy's perfume. Bet you wish I had a little of that on right now," she said, leaning over and sniffing her sweater that reeked of the dead man. "And how would you know what a French whore smelled like, anyway?"

He opened the passenger door of the police cruiser and waited until she slid it. "Wouldn't you like to know?" he teased before he shut the door and moved around to his side.

"Does Miranda wear French perfume?" She slammed her hand to her mouth. "I'm sorry, Danny. I have no idea where that came from?"

His eyes twinkled with glee. "If I didn't know better, Kate, I'd think you might be a little jealous."

"Of Miranda? No way. I'm glad you've found someone who makes you happy. She was always nice to me when she came to our house with my *older* sister," she said, immediately chastising herself for emphasizing the older sister remark.

What is wrong with me?

"She is more experienced," he said, sneaking a sideways glance her way. "So, exactly what spa?" he asked as he pulled out of the hospital parking lot.

"The new one that just opened on Murray Street. Go down Main and turn left at the light. It's called Healing Waters, and it's supposed to be the perfect release for all your stress. God knows I could use that after a day like today."

"Do you actually get in the water, or do they just massage you with it?"

"I've never been there, but Lainey has and said it's absolutely fantastic. The pool is filled with hot sea water."

"Where in the hell do they get sea water in Vineyard? Sounds like a scam," he said, turning the cruiser down Main Street.

"Of course there's no sea water in Vineyard, you goofball. They use volcanic clay and sea salt imported from Hawaii, and then add seaweed to detoxify the body, soul and spirit, according to the brochure. Before you leave they massage you with hot oils to generate tranquility. Unfortunately, all that pampering doesn't come cheap."

He turned to her. "So where's your bathing suit?"

She couldn't stop the blush that crawled up her cheeks.

His eyes crinkled in the corners. "You're skinny dipping?"

She finally recovered and replied, "That's the best way to get rid of all the tension from your body—or so they say."

"How much does a guy have to pay to join you?"

She knew he was teasing but still, she felt the warmth again on her face. "Way more than you make as a cop," she teased back, hoping to steer the conversation somewhere other than him being naked in a hot tub with her.

"Might be worth saving up for. Eating at restaurants only when they have a special going on could just pay off," he joked, pulling into the parking lot at Healing Waters next to another police car. "Here you go, Kate. Looks like Maddy's already here. Say hello to your sisters for me."

"Thanks, Danny." She got out of the car and watched him back the cruiser up and head up the main road toward the police station. The idea of Danny Landers being her Dustbuster popped into her head again, making her wish he did have enough money to join her in the hot water—wearing only his birthday suit.

*****

Relaxing in the pool with her sisters was the perfect way to end a stress-filled day, even if the water wasn't really healing seawater as advertised.

"God, I could stay in here forever," Maddy said, closing her eyes and leaning against the side of the pool.

"Unfortunately, Colt will have my head if I'm not back at the station by four."

Just get Lainey to give him a little extra bang for his buck tonight, and all will be forgiven.

"Tessa!" Kate exclaimed.

"Oh dear God, don't tell me she's back," Maddy said, before waving in the air. "Hey, Sis, what are you doing here?"

"She says one of us is in trouble," Kate answered for her sister's ghost who was now in the water with them, clothed but not getting wet—which was disturbing in a way she couldn't quite explain.

"Which one of us?" Maddy asked cautiously. She furrowed her brow, probably thinking about the last time Tessa showed up. A masked man had been at her mother-in-law's house holding a gun to her daughter's head while she slept. Before it was all over, Maddy had been framed for murder.

"She doesn't know, but she thinks it has something to do with that woman who was killed in El Paso and named me in her will. Personally, I think one of you went and screwed up, since I know I haven't." Kate was not as confident as she tried to sound since in the past, Tessa had only appeared to the one in trouble.

The thing I've always loved about you, Kate, is your smart mouth. Makes me proud.

"Why would you need her for that? Sounds pretty cut and dry," Lainey said, breathing in the steam from the bath before pointing to the other side of the pool. "Hey, isn't that Ramona

Larson over there? I heard she's having twins." They all turned in that direction.

"I thought pregnant women weren't supposed to be in hot tubs," Deena said, moving closer for a better look.

"Technically, this isn't a hot tub," Kate answered. "And it's the really hot water that's discouraged during pregnancy because it can be damaging to the fetus."

"Only last year her husband filed for divorce. Guess they made up," Deena commented.

She would've been lucky to be rid of that jackass, Tessa said, shaking her head. **One night he got all liquored up and told the entire roomful of people at the bar that he'd installed strobe lights in his bedroom to make it look like she was moving during sex.**

Kate couldn't help it and laughed as she told her sisters what Tessa had said.

"The man would wake up one morning missing a few critical parts if he were my husband," Maddy said. "Ramona's with Jennifer Robbins, who looks like she's about to deliver any day now. Lots of pregnant women in Vineyard," she observed. "Must be something in the air."

The only two things in the air that can get a woman pregnant are her legs, Tessa wisecracked.

"Thank God for legs in the air," Kate said, "or I'd be out of a job." When her sisters looked confused she remembered she was the only one who could hear Tessa and repeated what the ghost had said.

When the laughter died down, Maddy turned to Kate. "Was that Danny Landers I saw dropping you off?"

"Yeah." She shook her head. "Why is it that when you finally start flirting with someone who's been flirting with you all your life, they suddenly stop."

"Ah ha! He's playing hard to get," Lainey said. "That's the fastest way to get a woman's libido stirred up."

That and a brand-new Jaguar. Tessa licked her finger and drew an imaginary number one in the air.

"So, are you saying you're going to make a play for Danny?" Deena asked. "I always did like that boy."

"He's dating Miranda Walters," Kate replied, surprised that saying it out loud made her a little sad.

"Last I heard Miranda was all over town with the new dentist. Ryan something or other," Maddy said.

"We met him, by the way," Kate said. "And he's pretty hot. But Danny told me himself that he was seeing Miranda."

"She always was a cougar," Lainey said. "Remember the year she took Johnny Rosenthal to the senior prom when he was just a freshman?"

If you'd spent one night with Johnny out on Inspiration Point, you'd know what his appeal was. The boy could do tricks with his tongue.

Kate held up both hands. "Stop! That's way too much information. Why am I not surprised you sampled him, Tessa?"

"My younger sister could also have been called a cougar in her time," Maddy said. "And just for the record, I heard Johnny was pretty good in the sack." She glanced in the direction of the ghost. "So, back to why she's here in the first place. What does she have to say about it?"

Tessa only shrugged.

"One of the few times our sister has nothing to say. She has no clue but thinks we'll find out tomorrow when Benny and I have that meeting with the lawyer from Houston."

"Forgot that was tomorrow," Maddy said. "Oh, I meant to tell you. I fielded a call today from an El Paso policeman who's working the dead woman's case. He's coming to town in the morning to gather information about the other Emily. I'm sure he'll want to talk to both you and Benny."

When the chatter turned to their mother and her latest adventure with their stepdad in the RV, Kate found her mind drifting back to the meeting tomorrow. With a little luck, they'd discover this was all a mistake and that the real Emily was buried in the cemetery behind the Mission. But no sooner had she thought that when a warning bell sounded in her head, and she found herself dreading tomorrow and her meeting with the lawyer. Tessa had said it herself. She was sent here for a reason.

*****

Dammit! How could I have been so careless?

He paced the room, running his fingers through his hair, trying to figure out how he was going to get out of this one. When he'd gotten the call about the woman being killed by bank robbers, he wondered how he could he have been so unlucky? Emily Santiago was supposed to live out an invisible life in El Paso."

Until now he'd been so careful, vetting each victim meticulously. The reason his operation was so successful was because he had personally hand-picked each one. So how had he screwed up so royally with Emily Ruiz Santiago?

He nearly jumped when his cell phone vibrated in his shirt pocket. After checking the caller ID, he declined the call. He knew why they wanted to talk to him—knew what they were capable of doing to him because he'd messed up.

Somehow, he had to make it right. His continued good health depended on doing it sooner rather than later.

Chapter Five

Kate was in the middle of a Pap smear on her last patient for the day and gasped when she noticed Tessa in the corner. You'd think she'd be used to seeing her sister's ghost pop up at any given time by now, but she was especially anxious today.

In less than thirty minutes she'd be on her way to meet with the Houston lawyer about Emily Santiago—it was hard not to call her Emily Ruiz—and she was more than a little on edge.

"Everything okay?" Nancy asked as she gave her the swab.

"Yes." Kate finished taking the sample and handed it back to the nurse.

Dr. Kate Garcia at your cervix, Tessa deadpanned. **Has a nice ring, don't ya think?**

Kate ignored her and concentrated on finishing up. After snapping off her gloves, she walked around to face her patient. "Everything looks good, Alisha. We'll have the results back in a few days, but I'm not anticipating anything out of the ordinary. Unless there's a problem, I'll see you back here in a year."

"Thanks, Dr. Garcia." The woman climbed down from the examining table and followed Nancy back to the dressing room.

When Kate was alone—except for Tessa—she said, "Are you here because you're going with me to see the Houston lawyer today?"

Damn straight I'm going with you. That old joke about lawyers is true. If their lips are moving, they're lying. I would never leave you alone in a room with one. I've always regretted that I didn't get a chance to teach you everything I know about dealing with the assholes of the world before I died, baby girl, so I feel like I need to protect you. Besides, we have to find out why the good people up there—she pointed to the ceiling—**sent me back.**

For some reason, although that caused Kate's heart rate to escalate, in some twisted way it comforted her. No matter what they discovered at Charlie Prescott's office today, knowing that when one of the Garcia girls was in trouble, all five of them would band together to work it out eased her mind a little.

She scolded herself for worrying about it in the first place. What could possibly happen there? Worst case scenario, they'd find out the Emily they knew wasn't really who they thought she was. So what? There was no way the cops could possibly know what really went down that night.

Still, she felt lucky to have the loyalty and camaraderie of her sisters, including Tessa. Her dead sister may have not been the sweetest Garcia to walk the earth, but she'd always been there for Kate, both financially and emotionally when she was broke and disillusioned about medical school.

After saying goodbye to her coworkers, she grabbed her sweater and walked to the car. Halfway there, she turned to see if Tessa was behind her. She had a moment of panic when she realized she wasn't, until she spotted her already inside the car.

It must be nice having supernatural powers, she thought as she unlocked the door and slid into the driver's side.

Nervous?

"A little, but I keep telling myself how stupid that is. I've done nothing wrong, that's for sure, and I hardly knew the woman.

That's what they all say, Sis. Tessa turned sideways. **You sure you didn't screw up somehow in the office and cause her death?**

Kate frowned. "Of course not, although she was beaten up pretty badly the week before she died, and I was the one who treated her. Besides, the coroner said she overdosed on several different drugs."

That's a relief. Maybe you'll find out she was super rich, and you can quit your day job and eat bonbons all day.

"Does anyone really do that, and what the hell is a bonbon anyway?" Kate giggled before getting serious again. "The Houston guy said her parents had money, but I doubt there's much left. She was homeless, for God sakes."

You're probably right. At any rate, I'm looking forward to staring into Charlie's eyes, Tessa said. **I trusted**

that old coot with my finances, and he nearly screwed Gracie out of her inheritance after I died. If it hadn't been for Colt calling him out on it, he probably would have succeeded.

"Money makes people do strange things," Kate said, more for herself than for Tessa. Squirming in her seat, she was unable to stop the ball of fire that ignited in her gut as their destination loomed ahead. It was racing to volcanic proportions.

Why am I so nervous? She blew out a long, slow breath and pulled her Honda into the parking lot at the law offices of Charles Prescott and Associates.

Halfway up the steps, she whispered to Tessa, "I'm glad you're with me." Then she took a deep breath and opened the door.

The first person she saw was Benny sitting in the corner of the waiting room sipping a steaming cup of coffee. He looked more nervous than she did, if that was even possible. After declining her own cup from the receptionist, she gratefully accepted a bottle of water before bending over and kissing Benny on the forehead. For some reason her mouth was uncharacteristically dry right now.

Sitting down beside him, she said, "Let's hope this is all a formality, and we can get out of here soon."

He tried to smile but failed miserably. Visibly shaken, the man nearly jumped out of his skin when Charlie walked out and greeted them.

"Mr. Winters is already in the conference room waiting. He's asked me to sit in on the meeting and act on your behalf. Do either of you have a problem with that?"

I do, you asswipe, Tessa said, getting up and walking toward him, her face twisted in anger.

Both Kate and Benny shook their heads.

"Then let's go on back and get this started. Do you need anything before we do?"

Again, both of them shook their heads, then got up and followed him down the hallway to the conference room. Kate did a quick one-eighty to make sure Tessa was behind her. She was.

As she entered the conference room, she noticed two men sitting at the table. The younger of the two was so busy reading the file in front of him, he didn't even bother to look up or acknowledge them. Sitting to his right at the head of the long, dark oak table a man, whose picture she was sure would show up in the dictionary if she looked up the word lawyer right now, glanced up and nodded a greeting. Fiftyish with salt-and-pepper hair—more salt than pepper—the Houston lawyer wore a classic three-piece dark gray suit, even though the local temperature was expected to reach the low nineties that day.

Pewter-colored spectacles sat on the end of his long, slightly crooked nose, which suggested it may have been broken at one time, making Kate wonder if the man had ever been a boxer. Sporting a gold wedding band on his left hand, he closed the file he'd been examining and greeted them.

That's when Kate noticed his eyes. They almost matched the metal frame of his reading glasses and were now moving from her to Benny and back to her again, before he extended his hand. "I'm Conrad Winters. I know you must be confused by all this, but hopefully, together, we'll be able to solve the mystery behind Emily Santiago's death."

He motioned for them to sit before pointing at the younger man across from him, who hadn't taken his eyes off Kate once he'd finally looked up. "This is Detective Ross Perry from the El Paso Police Department. He flew in a few hours ago, and I've asked him to sit in on our conversation. Maybe he can help us make sense of it all."

Ross Perry looked to be in his late thirties, and although he wasn't wearing a wedding band on his left hand, the tell-tale outline on his tanned finger told a different tale. Either he had just recently divorced, or he was living out the old "when the cat's away" thing. He saw her looking and quickly slid his hand beneath the table. She decided it was the latter.

Although he was seated, it was obvious he was at least six feet—maybe even taller. He had a nice enough face—although nobody would ever call him handsome—with a dimple in his chin deep enough that it made her wonder if it went all the way through to the inside of his mouth. The plaid cowboy shirt he wore, coupled with the Stetson on the table beside him, suggested he was probably born and bred Texan. She would've bet a week's paycheck that he was wearing boots made from snakeskin or something similar, and she had to restrain herself from peeking under the table.

Charlie Prescott took the seat next to the lawman and was careful not to make eye contact with Kate.

Look at him, Tessa said, plopping down beside him, catty- corner from Kate. **The chicken shit won't even look at you.**

"Okay, let's get started," the Houston lawyer said. He opened the file in front of him and slid a picture across the table toward Kate. "Is this the woman you positively identified at the Vineyard morgue four months ago?"

Kate picked up the glossy and stared, unable to stop the sharp intake of breath that followed. The last few weeks of Emily's life had been hard on the woman, Kate knew, both physically and mentally, as was evidenced by the deep lines on her face. She hadn't expected that the drug-addicted woman she knew as Emily Ruiz would look exactly like the one in the picture Winters had passed to her, but she was totally unprepared for the striking differences.

The young woman staring back at her from the five by seven was standing in front of a church, dressed in a polka dot sundress and showing off a petite figure with nice curves. Her shoulder length brown hair was highlighted so perfectly, it had to be the work of a professional. Curling toward her wrinkle-free face, it brought out the dark haunting eyes, now crinkled with laughter.

This was not even close to the Emily that Kate knew, especially since the last time she'd seen the woman, she was banged up so badly, she'd been almost unrecognizable. Her face had been so swollen from the vicious attack by one of her clients that she could barely open her blackened eyes.

Years of heavy duty heroin use and living on the unforgiving streets of downtown Vineyard, not to mention making money the only way she could, had taken its toll more than Kate could have even imagined. She felt a pain in her heart for the petite woman who had once been a happy and vibrant Christian.

Going to church no more makes her a Christian than standing in the garage would have made her a car, Tessa said, causing Kate to catch her breath once again after discovering her sister standing behind her, now looking over her shoulder at the picture.

How weird is it that we were both thinking the same thing?

Kate took another look at the photo, leaving her with no doubts that despite the differences, the woman in the sundress was indeed the woman she'd last seen naked on the cold metal slab in the morgue.

She glanced up at Winters. "Although Emily had changed quite a bit since this picture, I'm positive I'm looking at the same woman whose body was found in the woods behind the Square." She handed the photo to Benny, who looked about to cry. "See if you agree with me."

Reluctantly, he began to study the picture. After a few minutes, he confirmed Kate's identification. "This is definitely the woman we knew as Emily Ruiz." He shoved the photo away as if he couldn't stand to look at it another minute, making Kate wonder what that was all about.

Something's going on with Benny, Tessa said, also picking up on his strange behavior. **I'm getting bad vibes**

**about all this, like he knows something he isn't saying. We
can't let anything happen to him, Kate.**

Replacing the picture back in the file, Conrad Winters
looked at the El Paso police officer. "Detective Perry, could
you tell us what you know about the woman who was killed
during the robbery?"

Perry glanced around the table before opening his own
file in front of him. "We don't have much. We know she
rented an apartment on the east side of town a little over eight
months ago. The neighbors said she kept to herself and never
caused any trouble." He shuffled the papers, then slid another
photo across the table. "Recognize her?"

Kate positioned the photo of a man and a woman
drinking beer on the hood of a car so that Benny could view
it with her. After a few seconds, both of them shook their
heads.

"To my knowledge, she's never been at the Mission
before," Benny said. "Who's the guy?"

"We've been unable to find out that information. We were
hoping one of you would recognize him from Emily's time
here in the area." Perry passed one more picture across the
table toward Kate. "This is another shot of the woman. Take
a good look just to make sure your first observation was
correct."

At first glance, Kate thought the woman on the table in
the El Paso morgue could have been the Emily she once
knew, but the more she looked, the less the two women
resembled each other. This woman appeared to be a few
years older and a bit taller. Although she wasn't heavy by any

stretch of the imagination, she was definitely stockier than the petite woman who'd barely been able to walk when she came into the office the night she'd been beaten. With tattoos covering both arms, and long, dark hair that was pulled back off her forehead, the El Paso woman showed some resemblance to the Emily she knew but not nearly enough to say for sure.

Kate brought the picture closer to her face to study it. After a few minutes she looked at Perry. "The Emily Ruiz that Benny and I knew had tattoos as well, but she also had a very distinct mole above her upper lip. I convinced her to have it removed and had already made the appointment with a local dermatologist who was willing to do it gratis, but she died before the appointment." She turned to Winters. "May I see the picture you have of Emily again? And if you have one of her at the Vineyard morgue, I'd like to see that one as well."

"Just picked these up from the police station before coming here," the lawyer said, handing her the original church picture and several taken during the autopsy. "I do remember that mole, now that you mention it."

After examining them, Kate was positive she was right. "The mole is clearly shown in both these photos and definitely missing in the one from the El Paso morgue." She made eye contact with Perry. "Your Emily Santiago appears to be an imposter."

The cop stared defiantly. "You can't be sure she didn't have the mole removed. Or that *your* Emily isn't the imposter."

"No, I can't, but even if she did, there would be some telltale scarring on her lip. It was that big." She paused to let that sink in before adding, "Do you have a copy of her autopsy from your morgue?"

Ross flipped through the pages of the file in front of him and produced the form, scanning it quickly before handing it to her.

After reading it all the way through, Kate turned her attention to Winters. "No mention of any mole or scarring of any kind on her face. I personally sewed up a two inch gash on her left cheek that would have also left a visible scar. That's not there, either. In my opinion, this woman was not the Emily Ruiz Santiago you represent, Mr. Winters."

"What made you think she was your client's daughter in the first place?" Benny asked, finally finding his voice.

Winters shifted uncomfortably in the chair. "Six months ago Emily reappeared in the system's radar. Credit check for apartment rental, job at the local grocery store, application for a Target credit card in El Paso, along with a request to begin drawing on her inheritance. We thought she'd kicked the habit and was trying to get her life back. When I sent an investigator to check it out, he followed her for a few days and reported back that she had cleaned up her act and was trying to lead a normal life there. Needless to say, I was elated that she'd finally gotten herself back on track, since one of the provisions of Horatio Santiago's will was that his daughter would not receive a penny if she remained on drugs. I knew how strung out she'd been when I saw her in Vineyard, and I needed assurances that the money would not go toward feeding a drug habit—a clear violation of the conditions of her father's will."

"And you were able to verify that?" Benny asked.

"As best I could. The investigator explained to her that if she wanted the sizeable monthly stipend she'd requested, she'd have to pass a weekly drug test. Our man said she'd been a bit confused at first, but she'd quickly agreed. That worked fine the first four and a half months, but when the lab called to report that she'd missed two scheduled drug tests, I sent the investigator back. That's when he discovered that she'd been killed."

"So you're saying the woman killed in El Paso was not Emily Santiago?" Ross Perry asked, leaning forward now.

"After looking at these autopsy photos where there's no mention of either a scar from the removal of the mole or one from the injury to her cheek, I'm inclined to lean that way. But before I say for sure, I need more evidence. I've filled out the necessary paperwork with the Vineyard police to have the body exhumed, which will give us definitive proof. In the meantime, since one of these women has to be Emily Ruiz Santiago, I'd like to go ahead with the reading of her will, although any transfer of monies will have to wait until we have official confirmation of my client's identity." He looked toward the El Paso cop. "There's really no further need for you here, Detective Perry. Thank you for coming by, but the reading of the will is a private matter."

A flash of anger at being dismissed crossed the cop's face before he gathered his papers together, stood up, and headed for the door. "I'm going to swing by the Vineyard Police

Station to see if we can put this case to bed. If I'm one-hundred percent convinced that my dead body isn't who we think it is, I'll head back to El Paso to try to find out her real identity."

He glanced at Kate one last time and then left, but not before she was able to lean over and check out his boots, mentally high-fiving herself for being right. They were definitely not your run-of-the-mill leather, probably either crocodile or alligator skin. She remembered reading somewhere that handmade boots like his could cost as much as thirty grand a pair.

So how did a cop from El Paso afford something like that?

"Anyone need another drink before we get started?" Winters asked. When everyone responded negatively, he reached into his attaché case and retrieved a legal looking folder. He opened it and began to read. "I, Emily Ruiz Santiago, hereby bequeath all my assets, real and personal, to be divided equally between Benjamin Yates and Kathryn Garcia, with the stipulation that they use at least fifty percent each toward continuing services for the homeless community in Vineyard, Texas."

Kate was only half listening as the lawyer read the rest of it, her mind unable to move past the notion that a woman she'd only seen a few times would leave half her fortune to her. And then there was the mystery of the other Emily. Could the El Paso woman have known Emily at some point in her life? Was it possible she'd known about Emily's wealth and saw this as the perfect opportunity to score some easy money? Especially if she knew that Emily was using her mother's maiden name and wasn't drawing on the account herself.

Maybe she'd been the one who'd killed her in the first place.

But wait. She was getting ahead of herself. According to the ME, Emily had died from an accidental overdose. As quickly as that thought formed in her mind, a more cynical one replaced it. What if Emily's death hadn't been accidental? She watched all the cop shows on TV. People used drugs all the time to kill someone.

Kate was jarred from her thoughts when the door opened and Colt Winslow walked in with his young detective behind them. She couldn't help herself and waved to Danny Landers, who grinned when he saw her, then frowned when Colt shot him a look.

"Sheriff, what can we do for you? We're right in the middle of an important legal matter here," Charlie Prescott said.

Colt ignored the man and looked past him to where Benny sat. "I'll need you to come down to the station with me, Benny. There are some things we need to clear up."

"Can't it wait, Sheriff?" the Houston lawyer asked, unable to hide his annoyance at being interrupted. "We're almost finished here, and I have a long drive back to Houston."

"Sorry for the inconvenience," Colt responded. "But no, this can't wait. Hopefully, it won't take long, and you can be on your way before dinner. You can even bring Charlie with you if you want."

"I could come down to the station as soon as we're finished here," Benny offered, his face now scrunched with worry. "What's this about, Colt? And why would I need Charlie?"

Colt inhaled deeply and hesitated before speaking, as if measuring his words carefully. "I just got a look at Ernie Jackson's life insurance policy. He's—"

"Who's Ernie Jackson?" Charlie interrupted.

"Not that you need to know, Charlie, but Ernie was the homeless man who died yesterday at the Mission."

"Why do you need to talk to me about that? Kate and I have already told your officers that Ernie had a seizure and died before the paramedics got there. I don't know what else I can say about that. And I sure as hell don't know anything about his life insurance policy."

"That's one of the things we need to discuss at the station."

"I don't understand," Benny said, his voice beginning to sound angry. "Discuss what?"

"For starters, why two people who frequented your establishment and who died within three months of each other both named you as their beneficiaries."

Benny's face turned as white as the linen curtains covering the windows in the conference room. "What are you talking about? I don't know anything about the man except that he was homeless."

Colt's face hardened. "Then how do you explain the fact that Ernie took out a one-hundred thousand dollar life insurance policy six weeks ago and named you as the beneficiary?" When Benny stared blankly, Colt continued, "Or the fact that we've been able to trace the first six-months premiums back to your checking account."

Chapter Six

Benny opened his mouth to protest further, but when he looked up, the sheriff was already waiting at the door. "Am I under arrest?"

Colt shook his head. "We just need to ask you a few questions to clear things up. Like I said, Charlie can come with you if want."

When Benny stood, he made eye contact with Kate, noticing the look of concern on her face. "I don't have a problem answering your questions, Sheriff, and I won't be needing a lawyer since I have nothing to hide." After mouthing *Don't worry,* to Kate, he turned and followed Colt to the front of the building.

He decided to wait until they arrived at the police station to try to explain the insurance premiums. He knew how it must look, and even though he considered Colt a friend, he was pretty sure he wouldn't get special treatment at the station.

When they got to the squad car, Danny Landers opened the door, and Benny slid into the back seat reluctantly. It was a tense ten minute drive uptown, and no one spoke until Colt pulled the cruiser into his space in front of the station.

"Hopefully, this won't take long," Danny said as he opened the back door and waited for Benny to exit the vehicle. Then he made a sweeping motion with his arm as an indication for Benny to follow Colt.

This wasn't the first time Benny had been marched into this building, but on all the previous times, he'd been in handcuffs and so high he hadn't realized he was under arrest until six or seven hours later. He was grateful they hadn't felt the need to cuff him now.

Once inside the building Colt picked up a folder on his desk before leading the way down the hall to a room where he instructed Benny to be seated at the small table in the center. After nodding to a woman standing in the doorway, he turned to Benny. "Can Jeannie get you something to drink?"

"No thanks, Sheriff. I just want to get this over with." Benny leaned back in the chair and kept his eyes on Colt.

Colt dismissed the secretary with a wave of his hand, waiting until the door closed before opening the file. After scanning the papers inside, he pulled one out and slid it across the table to Benny. "This is a copy of Ernie Jackson's life insurance policy taken out four months ago. As you can see, your name is very clearly listed as sole beneficiary."

Benny stared at the page, then took a deep breath and blew it out. "This is the first I'm hearing this, Colt. You have to believe me."

Colt held his stare. "I want to, Benny. You and I go back a long way. But it's just a little too coincidental that two homeless people died in or around your place of business within the past three months, and both of them left you a sizable amount of money. Wouldn't you agree?"

Benny swallowed hard. "I know how it looks, Colt, but I had no idea the man had named me on the policy. I swear."

"Was he your friend?"

"If you knew Ernie, you'd know how ridiculous that question was," Benny said, sitting up straighter in the chair. "The man was mentally ill and ran off anyone who tried to get close to him. He had a mean streak that even scared me at times. Given the fact that everyone hated him, he was lucky he didn't get knifed while he slept."

Colt reached into the file again and this time pulled out what looked like a bank statement. "So you can explain why you made out a check to the Kepner Life Insurance Company for $146.22?" Colt shoved the paper toward Benny. "According to the policy, that money was for Ernie's first six months' premium."

Benny shook his head, wondering if he should lie right now. He decided to come clean. "Hear me out before you rush to make judgments. I write checks for several of the Mission regulars. I —"

"Why would you do that, Benny? You have something going on with them where they pay you a fee?" Colt interrupted.

It was obvious neither Colt nor the young officer believed a word he was saying. He leaned across the table. "No fees. Most of them don't have bank accounts, so when they need a check written or something charged, I do it for them, but only after they give me the cash." He stopped talking long enough to swallow the lump in the back of his throat. This wasn't going like he'd hoped. "Ernie came to me awhile back and asked if I would write this check for him. Apparently, one of the men who lived under the bridge with him died recently, and his body wasn't buried. Ernie could never find out what had become of it and said he didn't want that to happen to him. So he took out a life insurance policy on himself to pay for a funeral."

"A hundred grand would pay for one helluva burial," Colt said. "From all reports, Ernie ate his meals out of the garbage bins behind the restaurants on the Square." He paused long enough to make Benny squirm. "Where'd he get the money to pay for the policy?"

"I have no idea," Benny said. "All I know is that he had a wad of cash on him the day he asked me to write the check. I didn't think it was any of my business to question where he got it. Some of these people get monthly Social Security checks, you know."

"He didn't," Colt fired back. He glanced up at the clock before he turned back to Benny. "So it's your statement today that you had no idea he'd put your name on the policy?"

Bennie's eyes lit up, hoping this meant Colt might be considering that he was telling the truth. "Honestly, I didn't." He cleared his throat. "I don't understand why any of this matters, though. Everyone at the Mission witnessed Ernie dying after he convulsed in the food line. Even if I had known about the insurance money—which I didn't—how could I be responsible for that?"

Colt looked at his young detective standing near the entrance before turning back to Benny. "You couldn't, if that's what really happened." He went into the file again for another sheet of paper. "Unfortunately, I'm looking at Doc Lowell's preliminary autopsy report. He seems to think Ernie Jackson may have been poisoned."

Benny shot out of the chair, and both of the officers were beside him immediately. "This is bullshit, Colt. Are you suggesting I poisoned the man for insurance money?"

"People have been murdered for far less than what you'll be getting, Benny." Colt pointed to the chair. "Now sit your ass back down before I put you in cuffs."

Benny did as ordered, then scrubbed his hands over his face. He assumed he'd come down to the station, answer a few questions, and be on his merry way. But the facts were stacking up against him, and he wondered if he'd made a mistake by not having an attorney with him. Unable to meet Colt's stare, he trained his eyes on the wall behind the sheriff. He was about to deny once again that he had anything to do with poisoning the homeless man when a sudden thought popped into his brain—one that gave him renewed hope that he might be able to convince them of his innocence.

"How could I have poisoned him when he hadn't even gone through the food line yet?"

Colt shook his head. "I don't know, but you can bet I'm going to dig deeper, and if you had anything to do with it, I'll find out. My officers are at your house as well as the Mission right now with warrants to search both places. If we find anything that even remotely suggests you did it, you'll be charged with Ernie's murder."

Benny's shoulders relaxed slightly, and he tried to smile. "I can guarantee they won't find anything. Now, do you mind if I head home? My wife must be frantic."

After Colt nodded, Benny stood and made his way to the front door. He knew they wouldn't find any damning evidence at either place, but that's not what worried him. With Colt looking closely at him now, he wondered how long it would take for the police to connect him to Emily Ruiz Santiago's death?

*****

Kate couldn't wait to get to her car to call her older sister. If anyone knew what had gone down at the police station, it would be Maddy.

After saying goodbye to Charlie Prescott and the lawyer from Houston who said he would call her when he had more information to share, she exited the building, struggling to keep from jogging to her car. Glancing at her watch, she picked up speed. Maddy got off work at five, and she didn't want to miss her.

As soon as she was inside the car, she dug in her purse for her phone, but before she could dial her sister's number, it quacked. She had no idea why she'd chosen that particular ringtone, but it made her smile every time—and today was no different.

"Hello," she said without glancing at caller ID.

"Kate, I'm glad I caught you. I tried your office, but they said you were out for the afternoon," the unfamiliar voice said.

She hesitated for a minute, trying to put a face to that voice. When she couldn't, she asked, "Who is this?"

The caller laughed, and immediately an image of greenish-blue eyes and light brown hair popped into her brain.

"Okay, now you've bruised my ego," he said. "I thought you'd remember me."

Ryan Kowalski! Oh, she remembered him, all right. When she'd met him at the Mission yesterday, warning bells had gone off in her head. A man that good-looking always meant trouble. She smiled to herself, recalling something her dead sister had said that really underscored that point. Tessa had remarked one day that anything with tires or testicles was bound to give you trouble. Ryan Kowalski didn't have tires, but he definitely had the others.

"How did you get this number?"

After an irate patient had bombarded Joe Solano with over a hundred calls one weekend asking about his wife's test results, he'd instituted a strict policy that no personal information could be released to anyone. She knew the receptionist would never give out her number, even to the hot dentist she'd met the day before.

Ryan laughed again. "You can relax. I'm not a stalker, you know. You mentioned having a sister who was a police officer yesterday, so I called the station."

Kate made a mental note to have a little chat with her sister. "What do you need, Ryan?"

"I had a really busy day today and didn't have time to stop for lunch. I wondered if maybe you'd like to meet up for a quick bite." When she hesitated, he added, "I have a few questions to ask about the Mission, and you really should indulge me, if for no other reason than for bruising my ego."

"I can't tonight, but thanks for the invite," she said, glancing down at her watch impatiently. In five minutes Maddy would leave the station, and if she didn't already know the details of Colt's interrogation of Benny, she wouldn't have access to the files. Kate didn't want to wait another day to find out in case there was something she could do to help her friend.

"Come on. You gotta eat," Ryan teased. "It will be a quick dinner, maybe one glass of wine. And did I mention I'm starving, fairly new in town, and hate to eat alone?"

She couldn't help herself and grinned. He was right. She did have to eat, and she'd skipped lunch herself. Tomorrow would be soon enough to find out about Benny.

"What did you have in mind?"

"You're the local. Surely you must know a place where we can get decent food and a nice glass of vino to take the edge off a horrendous day."

She thought for a minute before responding. "What about Emilio's? It's a really nice Italian restaurant in the Square, and although the menu is limited, everything Emilio serves is fantastic."

"I love Italian," he said quickly. "I'm about ten minutes from finishing up and leaving the office. If you get there before me, order a nice bottle of wine."

"Thought you said we'd only have one glass."

"Never trust a starving dentist," he quipped. "See you in fifteen."

As she hung up the phone, a mental picture of a Dustbuster popped into her head. What was up with her? In less than a week she'd imagined having sex with not one, but two different men.

*****

She parked the rental car close to the building. It was a little after five and most of the employees had already gone home. When she'd spoken to the medical examiner earlier that day, he'd agreed to meet her after hours when she told him she was Ernest Jackson's sister and would like one last look at her brother.

In truth, she'd never met Jackson, but if she could walk away with a copy of the death certificate, she'd be able to return to New York knowing her life was about to change big time.

As she walked up the steps, she was already planning a visit to the company lawyer as soon as the plane touched down at LaGuardia in the morning. The faster she got this little chore out of the way, the better. For the first time since the reading of her father's will, she'd finally be able to get on with her life. Alexander Pharmaceuticals would be hers—and hers alone.

A flash of anger rippled through her when she thought about her dad. Jonathan K. Alexander had never been loving or warm when she was growing up, but he'd been even less affectionate and more demanding after she'd graduated from MIT's Sloane School of Business with a Master's in finance. He'd always find a way to let her know how disappointed he was that she hadn't been a boy. When she'd joined the family business, he'd insisted she start from the bottom, and although she'd busted her ass every single day on the job, he'd kept her in that lowly position for ten years. Her boss, a young man with far less credentials than she held, had lorded his power over her at every turn, knowing her father wouldn't intercede on her behalf.

In her heart she'd always known how he'd felt about women on the company payroll. The proverbial glass ceiling was solid steel in his eyes. Women should be secretaries and office managers and leave the high pressure jobs to the men-folk. Had there been testosterone flowing through her body instead of estrogen, she would've never been subjected to the humiliation of working under such conditions.

But she'd been smart and had waited patiently for her chance. It had come one day when a huge shipment of pharmaceuticals from China ended up at the wrong port. After a loud, shouting match with the man responsible for the screw-up, her father had sent him packing. She'd stayed at the office after the old man had gone home and had spent hours on the phone smoothing things over. In the end, she'd managed to reroute the drugs before the heat could ruin them.

When her father had found out that she was the one to literally save his ass, he'd given her a few backhanded compliments before saying he would "try" her in the position vacated by the man he'd fired the day before. She'd taken full advantage, learning as much as she could about the inner workings of the multi-billion dollar company. But that had come with a price, and she'd had to give up any resemblance of a social life in the process.

After her father's stroke several years later, she'd finally been rewarded for all her hard work. Over the objections of two of her father's old cronies who sat on the Board of Directors, she was handed the reins of the company until they could seat a permanent person at the job—AKA someone with balls. But that had only made her more determined to show her father and the entire Board that she was just as capable—if not more so—to run Alexander Pharmaceuticals as any man out there.

And she had. In a little over two years, she'd computerized the entire operation which freed up several million dollars in payroll. She'd also gotten contracts with three of the largest pharmaceutical distributors in the country.

Needless to say, the Board had been thoroughly impressed and had made her position permanent. When her father died two weeks ago, she'd forced herself to pretend she was grieving. In reality, she'd been elated, seeing it as her chance to prove to everyone she was more than qualified to run the company. Her first order of business when she got back to New York would be to eliminate the men on the Board who had tried to bring in someone from the outside.

She'd show them just how powerful a woman could be as CEO.

But that had all blown up in her face at the reading of her father's will a week ago.

"May I help you?" the older woman at the desk asked, finally looking up from the crossword puzzle she was working on.

"I'm Rachel Alexander. I have an appointment with the medical examiner."

The woman shuffled a few pages before picking up a clipboard with a pen attached by a piece of string. "You'll need to fill this out first." She placed it on top the counter with a clatter.

Rachel squinted as she tried to decide what her next move should be. Her plan had been to swoop in there, identify the man she had never seen before in her life, and walk out with a copy of the death certificate that would give her full ownership of Alexander pharmaceuticals. "You must have misunderstood me on the phone earlier. I'm not here to pick up the body. I only need the certificate."

The older woman didn't even bother to look up from the puzzle. "Doesn't matter. Still need your information, or you don't get past this desk."

Grabbing the clipboard, Rachel began filling out the necessary paperwork. She decided to list her address as the Vineyard Gardens, figuring the less people knew about her, the better.

When she finished, she slid it across the countertop to the receptionist who allowed almost a minute to go by before she put down the newspaper and picked up the phone to announce her. "He said for you to go on back. It'll have to be brief because he has the sheriff's department breathing down his neck for the autopsy results."

Rachel glared. "And where am I going?" she asked, trying to keep the sarcasm of her voice.

Obviously, it hadn't worked, and the woman frowned, pointing with her left hand. "Down that hallway. It's the last door on the left." She grabbed a god-awful orange purse from under the counter and stood up. "You'll have to see yourself out. I don't get overtime."

Rachel stared at the receptionist for a moment, thinking it was women like her who gave all female employees a bad reputation. No wonder men thought they were incompetent.

She headed down the hallway, noticing immediately how cold it was. Despite the fact she'd always been hot-blooded, she shivered. She'd never been to a morgue before, but she was about to get her first look at a dead body.

After pushing the buzzer next to the door, she waited several minutes until a middle-aged man in disposable blue gear opened the door.

"You must be Ms. Alexander. Like I mentioned on the phone, I have a tight schedule, so this will have to be brief." He walked to a wall lined with drawers and slid one out.

Rachel inhaled and held her breath as he pulled the sheet off the top half of the body, and she got her first look at Ernie Jackson.

"Is this Ernest Jackson?" the doctor asked, glancing impatiently at his watch.

Finally releasing the breath she'd been holding, Rachel nodded, unable to take her eyes off the dead man's face. There was definitely a noticeable resemblance to her father. "Yes, this is my brother."

"You're sure?"

She lowered her head and nodded, hoping it would be interpreted as grief. She wasn't about to confess that not only had she never laid eyes on Ernest Jackson, but also that she'd never even known he'd existed until a few days ago.

The ME looked up from a folder on the desk in the corner of the room. "Unfortunately, I won't be able to give you the death certificate just yet until I run a few more tests. Leave your name and address with Adele out front, and I'll personally mail the official one when I can."

When she didn't move, he repeated, "Ms. Alexander, like I said, I won't know what killed your brother without further testing."

"What kind of testing? I thought he collapsed and died at the soup kitchen?" *Shit!* She'd hoped to get out of there before traffic picked up, order the biggest filet on the menu from room service, and celebrate with a nice bottle of wine.

"I'm not at liberty to say at the moment."

Something about his tone unleashed her suspicions. What was he hiding? "How long before you'll know what my brother died of?"

"Hard to say, but I'll get that certificate to you as soon as I can." He nudged her toward the door. "Now, I'll need to get back to work so that can happen. Leave your information with Adele."

There was nothing else to do but leave. The celebratory dinner would have to wait one more day. She let out an exasperated breath, praying that it wouldn't take any longer than that for the test results to come back. She was determined not to leave Texas without proof that Ernie Jackson was one hundred percent dead.

She turned and walked to the door, not bothering to tell him that Adele and her ugly orange purse were long gone. But it didn't matter. She'd accomplished what she'd set out to do when she'd dropped everything and flown to Texas three days ago. A few more days wouldn't make that much difference. From this point on, her father's lawyer would be able to take care of the necessary details. Ernie Jackson would no longer be a threat to her or to Alexander Pharmaceuticals.

Satisfied there would be no more problems, she thanked the medical examiner and walked out the door. Now all she had to do was wait, something that was not easy for her to do.

Tonight, she'd have that steak and wine anyway. It was just a matter of time before she could sit at her father's desk and know that no man would ever tell her what to do again.

Chapter Seven

Friday night at Emilio's was always a zoo, and tonight was no different. After driving around the parking lot twice waiting for someone to come out and free up a space, Kate finally drove two doors down and parked in the empty bank lot.

As she weaved her way through the overflow of people waiting outside the small Italian restaurant, she scolded herself for not calling ahead for a reservation. Another look at the mass of people waiting to be seated told her that even if she had called on her way over there, it probably wouldn't have helped. Hopefully, there would be two open seats at the bar.

The minute she walked in, the smell of marinara and garlic hit her, making her stomach growl in anticipation of what was to come. She'd planned on stopping for lunch—had even microwaved a Lean Cuisine—but she'd been called to the hospital the minute she'd sat down in the break room. The Navarro twins had decided it was time to say hello to the world and couldn't have cared less that she'd miss lunch.

Pushing past the mob of hungry people, she made her way to the hostess, only to discover the wait on a table for two would be forty-five minutes. After inquiring about seating at the bar, as luck would have it, she was led to two empty seats at the far end, away from the crowd and the noise.

Terrific! She wasn't ready to spend all night with a man she barely knew, even if he looked like he should be modeling Calvin Klein underwear.

Stop it! her subconscious screamed. *You're not some horny kid trying to get laid. Ryan is just a colleague looking for information.*

God! I love Emilio's, Tessa said, plopping down on the empty stool beside her. When Kate looked up, Tessa grinned. **What's up, Katie? It's not like you to drink alone.**

After recovering from the initial surprise of seeing her dead sister at the restaurant, Kate glanced around the room to see if anyone was looking at her as if she had three heads. Assured no one was, she leaned in. "I'm meeting Ryan Kowalski for a quickie."

Tessa threw her head back and laughed. **Obviously, your idea of a quickie vastly differs from mine, unless you have a naughty exhibitionist habit I don't know about.**

"A quick dinner," Kate corrected, then leaned closer. "Why are you here?"

Probably just to have fun, Tessa said, staring at the breadsticks the bartender had just placed in front of Kate. **And remind me again who this Ryan dude is.**

"The dentist we met at the Mission."

Oh, the one with the dreamy eyes and the smile that must have every girl in Vineyard hoping he's carrying a supply of condoms in his wallet?

Kate nodded. Tessa must have read her mind. "Yeah, that's the one." She glanced quickly around the bar to see if he'd arrived. When there was no sign of him, she lowered her head and tried to talk without moving her lips. "Colt took Benny to the station to question him about Ernie Jackson's death."

Thought he had epilepsy and died during a seizure. Tessa scrunched her face. **Maybe I was sent back to help Benny and not you. He is part of our family, you know.**

Kate hadn't thought about that, and for a nanosecond a gush of relief pulsed through her body. If that were true, it meant that she and her sisters were in the clear. But the elation was quick lived when she realized Tessa was right— Benny was part of the family. And she was closer to him than any of her siblings were since she'd been volunteering at the Mission from the beginning. But close family friend or not, until now the ghost had only appeared when a sister was in trouble

What happened down at the police station? Tessa asked.

"I don't know. I was hoping to talk to Maddy to find out, but then Ryan called." She stopped talking when she noticed the hot dentist walking toward her with that killer smile in full force.

Yowsa! Tessa whispered as she scrambled to get off the bar stool before Ryan slid on top of her.

"Traffic was a bear," he said. "I thought I left all that in Austin when I was in college."

Kate laughed. "Not much to do in Vineyard after five but eat downtown." She motioned to the bartender. "I was going to order a glass of Chardonnay, but I wasn't sure what you preferred."

"Chardonnay sounds great." He scanned the crowded restaurant. "Do we have a long wait?"

"At least forty-five minutes, and I'm bushed. Hope you don't mind, but I told the hostess we'd eat at the bar."

"Perfect," he said, reaching for a menu. "What do you recommend?"

Anything that ends with you flossing in her bathroom tomorrow morning, Tessa blurted, causing Kate to pink up.

I couldn't have said it any better.

"I'm a creature of habit and always get the Chicken Parmesan. Lucky me, it's tonight's special."

"I knew you couldn't pass up your favorite meal at a discount," a familiar voice said from behind her.

She swiveled on the stool and nearly bumped into Danny Landers's shirt. Leaning back, she tried to pretend that her face hadn't just made contact with his upper anatomy, but she wasn't quick enough to stop the musky smell of his wonderfully refreshing cologne to hit her nostrils.

She raised her eyes to meet his and gave him a skeptical look. "You're one to talk, Danny. How quickly you've forgotten that on the ride to the spa the other day, you mentioned how you hit all the restaurants on the nights they have specials."

"I'm a cop, remember? We don't make big bucks like you doctors." The twinkle in his eyes nearly melted her on the spot before he turned to the bartender and ordered a rum and coke.

She recovered quickly, then remembered that Ryan was sitting next to her. She turned to him. "Do you two know each other?"

"I don't think so." He offered his hand. "Ryan Kowalski."

Danny eyed him suspiciously before shaking his outstretched hand. "Danny Landers. Kate and I go way back," he said before turning and waving to someone at the front of the restaurant.

When Kate's eyes followed in that direction, she was a little disappointed to see Danny motioning for a woman to join them. As the newcomer headed their way, Kate was even more dismayed to discover it was Vineyard's newest assistant district attorney.

Dressed in a blue jersey knit dress that showed off a fantastic figure, Miranda Walters could have stepped out of a fashion magazine. Her strawberry blond hair was coiffed in a stylish bob that brought out her gray-blue eyes, and her plumped up red lips were definitely sporting some silicone. As much as Kate hated to admit it, Miranda Walters was even prettier than she remembered.

Kate stood to greet her. "Hey, Miranda, I heard you were back from Laredo. You look great."

Miranda leaned over to give Kate a hug.

"Miranda, this is Ryan Kowalski," Kate said, suddenly remembering her manners.

The ADA's eyes darkened. "We've met," she said curtly.

Ryan nodded without smiling. "Miranda was the first person to welcome me when I set up shop in Vineyard."

Kate mentally slapped her forehead. How could she have forgotten one of her sisters mentioning that the new dentist in town and the returning district attorney had once been an item?

"Are you waiting on your table?" Danny asked. His hand was on the back of Kate's stool and occasionally made contact with her neck, sending a slight shiver down her spine.

"Forgot to make a reservation," Kate said, not willing to divulge the fact that her date had been spur of the moment. "We're just going to grab a quick dinner right here."

"No way," Danny said. "We were supposed to meet Flanagan and his new girlfriend tonight, but she had last-minute babysitting problems. No use wasting those two extra places at our table."

Kate glanced toward Ryan, and the look on his face said it all. Neither one of them wanted to spend the night with Danny Landers and Ryan's ex.

She turned her stool back to the bar and picked up a breadstick. "We're fine, Danny. We're not planning to stay long and —"

"Bullshit!" He waved to the bartender just as the pager vibrated in his shirt pocket. "Can you put their drinks on my tab, Luca, and have them sent to my table?"

When the bartender nodded, Danny twirled the stool around, but this time Kate was prepared and already leaning back. Once was enough to have her face level with the shirt and the chest hairs that peeked from the opening.

Putting out his hand, he assisted her from the bar stool. "It will be like old times."

Kate glanced up, noticing the way Miranda had latched onto the young cop's arm like a steel rod to a magnet. Without warning, the green monster danced in her head before she mentally clubbed it to death. She and Danny were just friends, but right now, friends with benefits was very tempting. Seeing him here tonight with Miranda would never make her top ten list of things she wanted to remember.

"We've both had a long day. Hope you don't mind if we eat and run," she said, seeing that as a valid excuse for not having to witness the hot assistant district attorney pawing Danny all night.

"Welcome to my world," Danny said before turning and leading the way to the front.

The hostess was waiting and directed them to a quiet, romantic table in the back.

When they were seated, Miranda reached across the table and grabbed Kate's hand. "Who would have guessed that Lainey's little sister would end up a doctor? Although I have to admit it shouldn't come as that much of a surprise. I knew you would either have MD after your name or end up on the New York Times bestselling list with your vivid imagination." She paused long enough to take a sip of her Cosmo. "I remember one time when you lined all your stuffed animals on the couch in your living room and splashed ketchup all over them. Then you made up this elaborate story about how you'd all been in a plane crash, and somehow you'd survived to save them." She laughed. "There was ketchup all over the couch."

I remember that, too, Tessa said, now standing behind Miranda and holding up two fingers behind her head like she used to do when they were younger. **Mom was ready to kill you.**

Despite herself, Kate smiled. "I was grounded for three weeks over that, but I didn't care. I healed every single one of them."

"I always knew you'd be a doctor," Danny said, holding her eyes captive with his own. "I just never dreamt you'd be an obstetrician. I would've sworn you'd go into trauma, knowing how much you liked pretending that everyone was bleeding."

Kate was about to come back with some smartass remark about how she hadn't had to imagine when she was with him because he was so klutzy, but the waiter appeared at that moment.

Everyone ordered dinner, and then Danny held up his drink. "To old and new friends."

After the group toast, Kate was about to ask Miranda why she'd left Laredo when the woman's phone rang. After checking caller ID, the lady lawyer turned to Danny. "It's Colt. I have to take it." She stood and hurried to the front of the restaurant.

When Miranda was out of hearing range, Kate focused on Danny, hoping the drink had loosened his lips a little. "Why do you think Colt is calling her?"

He smirked. "You know I can't tell you that, Katie, not even if you wear those sexy clothes again. That trick will only work once."

She couldn't help it and grinned. "Never say never, Danny boy. You men can be easily distracted by a little T & A."

"Sounds like I need in on this conversation," Ryan said, leaning forward. "Kate in sexy clothes has me intrigued."

Just then Miranda reappeared but didn't sit down. "Sorry, Danny, I have to run. Doc Lowell's pretty sure he knows what poisoned Ernie Jackson, and I'm meeting Colt at the morgue in fifteen minutes."

"Poisoned?" Kate's voice rose an octave. She glanced around to see the people at the next table staring at her. Almost in a whisper, she asked, "What makes him think that?"

Miranda hesitated momentarily before speaking. "It will be all over the news by tomorrow, anyway, so I guess it won't hurt to tell you. Doc found several things during the autopsy that led him to that diagnosis, but we won't know for sure until we get the toxicology back."

"Does he think Ernie might have come in contact with something that killed him? Like ptomaine from bad mayonnaise?" Kate asked, hoping even as she spoke that this wasn't the reason Benny was taken down to the station earlier. "Ernie eats out of a dumpster, you know."

"We do know," Miranda said. "But the ME says it looks like he's ingested ricin, and you don't swallow that by accident."

"Ricin? Isn't that what terrorists use as a weapon of mass destruction?" Ryan asked.

"It can be," Danny said before his forehead wrinkled in deep thought. "The only time you hear about it is when some idiot tries to send a letter laced with ricin powder to someone high up in the government. Maybe Jackson got his hands on a tainted envelope in the dumpster."

Kate searched her brain to remember what she'd learned in med school toxicology classes, but only bits and pieces came back. "Ricin is derived from castor beans, but if I'm remembering correctly, it takes about thirty-six to forty-eight hours to kill." Her eyes widened, and she looked at Danny as if he could help her. "Ricin poisoning causes diarrhea along with seizures which result in multi-organ failure." She swallowed hard and lowered her head. "Ernie had all those symptoms."

"Where could he have gotten his hands on ricin?" Ryan asked, finally speaking up. "It sounds kind of far-fetched to me."

Miranda shrugged. "Who knows? Could be someone has a grudge against the homeless. Or maybe he did find it in a dumpster and unwittingly ingested it. Right now I have to get down to the morgue to try to find out if any of those scenarios are true." She grabbed her purse, then bent down to kiss Danny on the lips. "I'll make it up to you, honey. I promise."

When she was gone, Kate decided to work on Danny one more time. "Is that why Colt interrupted the meeting with the

Houston lawyer and hauled Benny down to the station today?"

He opened his mouth to say something then thought better of it. "You'd better ask your brother-in-law about that, Kate. All I know is that right now, Benny is a person of interest."

"A person of interest? You gotta be kidding me. Benny wouldn't hurt a flea. He's devoted his entire life to first, the military, and now the homeless community here in Vineyard. The man even sunk most of his savings into the Mission where …" Her hand flew up to her mouth. "Oh my God!"

Danny slid his chair closer and stared into her eyes. "What is it?"

Kate took a deep breath. She hoped she wasn't about to throw Benny under the proverbial bus—hoped what she was remembering was only coincidental. But insignificant or not, the police needed to know, since the last time she and her sisters had gone behind Colt's back and then withheld information about a crime, Deena and Maddy had nearly gotten themselves killed. She reasoned that the cops would get a search warrant anyway if they hadn't already and discover what she was about to reveal.

Taking a big gulp of her wine for courage, she faced Danny. "Castor beans are also called rosary beads and are used to make jewelry in several foreign countries."

"What's so important about that?" Danny asked, leaning so close to her now, she could smell the rum on his breath.

She hesitated only a moment before she continued, "There's a really pretty red necklace hanging on the wall at the Mission. When I asked Benny about it, he said it had been a gift to him from Emily Ruiz. Apparently, she got it in India and was worried that someone would steal it on the street. She called it her rosary bead necklace."

Danny reached for her hand. "You have to repeat what you just told me to Colt right now, Kate." Turning to Ryan, he shrugged. "Sorry, but I have to steal your date, Kowalski. Enjoy the Chicken Parmesan." He reached for his wallet and threw two twenties on the table to cover the drinks, then pulled Kate's chair back so she could stand.

Then he turned and led the way to the front but not before Kate saw the beginnings of a smile tip the corners of his mouth.

Tessa, who had been unusually quiet up to this point, followed close behind. **It's Benny who needs me, not you,** she whispered in Kate's ear.

Kate didn't bother to turn around, unable to meet her sister's stare. If Tessa knew that she and Benny shared a secret about the dead woman, she might not be so quick to assume that he was the one she was sent to help.

Chapter Eight

"You don't really think Benny had anything to do with Ernie's death, do you Danny?" Sitting in the front seat of the police car, Kate stole a quick glance his way, noticing the twitch in his jaw. A telltale sign he was in deep concentration mode.

"I don't know what to think, except that it's hard to argue with physical evidence. Guess we'll just have to bring Benny back to an interrogation room and see what he has to say about it."

As he turned into the morgue parking lot, Kate was sure there was a pinball tournament going on in her stomach. She hated that what she was about to tell Colt might very well be the damning evidence that would bring a world of trouble on her friend.

Maybe it was just a weird coincidence that Benny had an Indian castor bead necklace on the wall at the Mission. Or that Dr. Lowell suspected ricin poisoning, and that ricin is derived from those very beans. But what if the medical examiner was wrong about his initial examination of the body? Only toxicology tests would prove definitively that it was indeed ricin that had killed the homeless man, and those results wouldn't be available for days. Surely, they couldn't arrest Benny based on the fact that he had a rosary bead necklace belonging to Emily Ruiz.

As soon as Danny turned off the ignition, he walked around to open her door. Attempting a smile, he waited while she got out of the car. "I know you, Kate. Right now you're feeling really guilty because you think you're getting your friend in trouble." He put his arm around her shoulder and guided her to the entrance. "If Benny is innocent, I promise we'll find out soon enough."

She nodded, amazed that after all these years he could still read her so well. Allowing him to lead her, she followed him through the door and over to the reception area where a very annoyed Adele Masters sat behind the desk, looking like she was ready to wage war with the first person who opened their mouth.

"Hey, Adele," Danny said. "I'm surprised to see you here. Thought tonight was the softball tournament at the park."

She sulked. "It is. I was there when Doc summoned me back. Said he needed me to type up his preliminary findings before morning." She tsked. "Larry was on a roll, too. When I left, nobody had gotten a hit off him."

Danny patted her hand. "I'll see if I can hurry things up so you can get back over there." He pointed down the hallway. "Is Colt in there?"

Adele nodded. "Along with Doctor Lowell and the ADA. Heard the two of you were getting pretty friendly these days."

He ignored the remark and pointed to Kate. "She's got something really important to tell Colt. Something that could break this investigation wide open."

"Doc was pretty adamant about no interruptions."

"Don't worry. When they hear what Kate has to say, they'll thank you for letting us go back." He winked at the woman, who tried unsuccessfully not to grin back at him. "If he throws a fit, I'll take the blame. I'll even ask him if I can stay out front and man the desk so you can get out of here and watch Larry pitch that no-hitter. No reason why you can't come back before the cock crows tomorrow and fire off that report he wants."

Kate stood behind Danny, observing as he worked his magic on the angry receptionist.

"You always were my favorite cop," she said, motioning for them to go back. "It won't be the first time I'm in hot water with him."

"And probably not the last." Danny gave her a thumbs up before leading Kate down the hallway.

All three people in the room turned when he pushed the morgue door open and followed Kate into the room.

"Hey, Colt," Kate said before the sheriff had a chance to react. "Can I talk to you alone?"

He tried to hide the annoyed look that crossed his face. "We're right in the middle of something here. Can it wait until tomorrow?"

"No. I thought of something that might help your investigation. I'll just stand back here out of the way until you can get a free minute."

She allowed her eyes to venture to the metal table where Ernie Jackson lay. The first thing that crossed her mind was that she'd never seen him this clean before. She took a step closer, staring at the Y incision down the homeless man's torso, wondering what the medical examiner had found inside the zipper of stitches.

"Kate, if you'll just wait out in the lobby, I'll cut loose in a minute and come talk to you." Colt shot Danny a I'll-deal-with-you-later look.

"I really think you need to hear her out," Danny said, standing his ground under the brutal stare that should have had him quaking at the knees.

Colt's eyes skewered first Danny, then Kate before he turned back to Mark Lowell. "You and Miranda work on the details for a minute while I see what these two think is important enough to barge in here and interrupt me." He moved to a far corner, out of earshot of the other two, and motioned for Danny and Kate to follow suit.

There was an awkward moment of silence while he continued to glare. "Okay. Let's hear it—and it better be good."

"Kate remembers seeing a castor bead necklace hanging on the wall at the Mission. Said Benny told her that Emily Ruiz asked him to keep it for her," Danny blurted. "That could be the source of the ricin."

Colt's eyes narrowed. "Who told you it might be ricin that killed Ernie?"

Danny sucked in a deep breath, and Kate knew he was trying to figure out an answer that wouldn't get his girlfriend in trouble.

"I was having dinner with Miranda and Danny when you called," she explained before Danny could speak. "Being a medical professional myself, I picked up on the ricin aspect from listing to her end of the conversation with you." She glanced Danny's way and had to bite her lower lip to keep from returning his gratitude smile.

Colt harrumphed. "Well, it's probably not ricin, after all. Mark said that's usually only lethal when it's either injected or inhaled. Since Ernie's lungs didn't show any damage, and there are no track marks anywhere on his body, his death is more likely to be from some sort of food or other poisoning, possibly mushrooms or arsenic. Mark's sending tissue and hair samples off to the CDC in the morning. We'll put a rush on it and hopefully, get some answers soon."

"Ricin poisoning is no longer a front runner?" Danny asked.

"Like I said, Ernie showed no symptoms of injecting or inhaling it. Most people who accidentally ingest ricin eventually recover. So no, Mark is leaning more toward one of the other poisons."

"That makes sense since the castor bean can be swallowed whole without causing any problems," Kate said. "A person would have to chew it to make it lethal. Of course, Ernie Jackson was just crazy enough to do that, especially if he saw the necklace on the wall and decided it looked like cherries or something he could eat for dessert."

"That didn't happen," Colt fired back. "When Mark first mentioned ricin poisoning, I called Benny and asked if he had access to any castor beans. When he told us about the necklace at the Mission, I had Flanagan ride over there with him to take a look. No missing beans."

Kate blew out a sigh of relief. "So Benny's no longer a suspect?"

"I didn't say that. Ernie's liver and kidney enzymes were off the chart, and there was blood in his urine. Those are classic drug toxicity symptoms, leading Mark to believe he was definitely poisoned, but with what chemical remains the question. In the meantime, until we can rule out Benny's involvement, he'll remain a person of interest." He pointed to the door. "Take Kate back to that restaurant while we finish up here. Not sure how much longer I'll need Miranda."

Danny nodded, before walking toward the medical examiner and the district attorney. "Hey, Doc, any objections to me sitting out front so Adele can get back to the softball field? Larry's pitching a no-hitter so far, and she should be there to see it."

Mark looked surprised by the question and was about to respond when Danny held up a hand to stop him. "She said she'd come back tomorrow morning to type anything you need."

After a minute, the ME shrugged. "There's really no need for you to stay, either, Danny. Tell Adele to go have fun. I can't send those reports out until Monday, anyway, although that's going to piss off Ernie Jackson's sister."

Colt whirled around to face him. "Ernie had a sister?"

The doctor nodded and stepped closer. "Surprised me, too. She came all the way from New York for the death certificate. Beats the hell out of me why she's in such a big hurry to get the official document. A few more days won't kill her. I'm not ready to sign off on a cause of death just yet."

"Remind me to get her information before I leave." Colt turned back to Danny. "I'll see you at the station in the morning. We can pow-wow about all this then."

Danny nodded, then walked over to Miranda. "I'll take Kate home and then come back to wait on you."

The ADA shook her head. "We have a lot of work to do before I can leave, plus I'm bushed. Call me tomorrow, and we can finish our dinner date."

"Sounds good." He turned and directed Kate toward the door.

When they got to the receptionist's desk at the end of the hall, Adele was already waiting by the door with purse in hand. "Did he say I could leave?"

"Yep, but I promised him you'd come back in the morning to type up those reports. I know it's your day off, but—"

She squealed and quickly closed the gap between them. After giving him a big hug, she waved goodbye. "You should come with me and see for yourself how good my Larry is."

"Maybe I'll ride over there after I take Kate home. Now go, before you miss the whole game."

As she pushed open the door, Kate ran over to her. "Adele, what was Ernie sister's name?"

The receptionist scrunched her eyes in concentration." I can't remember exactly, but I know it wasn't the same as Ernie's. Anderson, Adams, some A name. Sorry. I was in such a hurry to get to Larry's game that I really didn't pay much attention." She paused before continuing, "I do recall that she was staying at the Vineyard Gardens, though. Why do you ask?"

Kate shrugged. "No reason. Doc just mentioned that Ernie had a sister. Guess I'm just a little curious since the man was such a loner and seemed to have a knack for pushing people away." She waved goodbye. "Get to the game. Danny and I will lock up and be right behind you."

As she walked to the cruiser, Kate was already deciding which of her sisters she'd take with her in the morning to Vineyard Gardens.

*****

"Got any more of these? Something about peanut butter and chocolate together gets me every time." Lainey grabbed the last cookie and popped it into her mouth. "And I was doing so well on my diet."

"I wanted that one," Maddy scolded. "You've clearly scarfed down more than your share, Lainey."

"Quit squabbling," Deena reprimanded. "There's more." She took the empty plate over to the counter and refilled it from the cookie jar in the cupboard. When she set it back down, all three sisters dove in.

Geez! You'd think they were hundred dollar bills instead of cookies. Tessa appeared out of nowhere and stood behind Kate, eyeing the goodies in the middle of the table. **These were always my favorite, too.**

"Tessa's here," Kate announced. "So now we can officially get started on why I called this family meeting."

"You're not in trouble, are you?" Deena gave her a worried look.

"No. Nothing like that," Kate hastily explained. "But Benny still may be, and I can't help thinking if it was one of us facing a murder investigation, he'd be the first one to do whatever he could to help." She turned her attention to Maddy. "I never did find out what went on down at the station after Colt interrupted the meeting with the Houston lawyer and took Benny downtown."

"You know if Colt finds out I'm telling you guys this, he'll put me on desk duty—or worse." Maddy lifted her arms in the air. "What the hell! It won't be the first time he's mad at me. Anyway, Ernie Jackson took out a life insurance policy for a hundred grand and named Benny as the beneficiary."

"Oh no! That can't be good," Deena said. "Poor Benny."

"That's not the half of it," Maddy continued. "Benny paid the first six months premiums." When the sisters gasped in unison, she held up her hand. "There's more. When Colt asked about it, he said he sometimes does this for the homeless people when they need it. Said they give him the cash, and he writes the check."

"Did Colt believe him?"

"You know Colt. He never believes anyone at first. That's what makes him a good cop. He sent Flanagan and Rogers down to the Bell Street Bridge to ask around to see if anyone else has ever asked Benny to do that for them."

"Hope Benny's telling the truth, or it's really going to get ugly for him." Kate sighed.

"But I'm not talking about that."

"What's going on now?" Deena asked, her apprehension getting more pronounced.

Kate gave Maddy a raised eyebrow. "Do you want to tell us what you know about Ernie being poisoned?"

"Ernie Jackson was poisoned?" both Lainey and Deena asked in unison.

Maddy met her youngest sister's gaze. "Yeah, I heard, but that's old news, Kate. Because of Ernie's symptoms, poison has always been the suspected culprit."

"And did you know they thought it might be ricin and that Benny has a caster bead necklace hanging on the wall at the Mission?" Kate asked.

"Heard that, too, but Landers told me the ME had pretty much ruled out ricin."

Kate's eyes lit up. "You talked to Danny today?"

"Yeah, why?"

Why? Because our little sister is trying to figure out how to get Miranda Walker's hooks out of him.

Kate gave the ghost the evil eye. "That is so not true, Tessa."

"What'd she say?" Deena asked as the others leaned closer to hear the explanation.

"Nothing worth repeating," Kate replied.

"Then tell us."

"Okay. Last night I met Ryan Kowalski for dinner at Emilio's, and while we were there, Danny and his latest squeeze—AKA Vineyard's newest assistant district attorney—walked in. Danny insisted that we join them, but before we could even order, Miranda got a call from Colt. He was down at the morgue and said that the ME was leaning toward ricin poisoning as the cause of Ernie's death. That's when I remembered about the necklace at the Mission and told Danny about it. He insisted we leave immediately to tell Colt."

You must really be falling for the guy if you won't even tell your sisters about him. Tessa moved around the table to face Kate. **Remember me? I was there and saw the way you got all nervous and giggly when Danny showed up. Either you were drunk or you were excited to see him. Which one was it, little sis?**

Kate considered that for a minute before figuring what the hell. "Okay, maybe I am just a little curious to see if there's anything between Danny and me, but Tessa's blowing it way out of proportion and chastising me for not confiding in you guys."

"If you're interested in that boy, then go for it," Deena said. "We all know he's had a thing for you for years."

"Used to," Kate was quick to add. "Now that Miranda Walters has her hooks in him—your ghostly sister's words, not mine—I can't seem to get his attention."

"The classic love story—I'm only interested if you aren't." Maddy nodded and laughed. "Gotta hand it to that boy. He sure knows how to play you."

You got that right, Tessa said, unable to hide the mischief in her eyes. **Which is why you need to dangle Ryan whatever-his-name-is in front of Danny boy. That only-interested-when-you-aren't thing works both ways, you know.**

Kate mused over that for a minute, finally deciding that Tessa was probably right. She made a note to flirt more with Ryan when Danny was around.

"Okay, enough about me. I found out last night that Ernie Jackson has a sister from New York. Apparently, she's in town and really pushing the ME to produce an official certificate of death. We need to find out why that's so urgent." Kate reached in for another cookie and took a bite before continuing. "So, who's up for a trip to her hotel for a little talk with the woman? We need to find out why getting that document is so important to her."

"I can't believe Ernie had a sister," Maddy said, shaking her head. "But since this is still an active police investigation, I should probably stay in the wings. I can be way more useful sneaking out information if Colt doesn't suspect I'm involved. We all know how mad he'll be if he finds out the Garcia sisters are on the hunt again. Remember, the man came close to firing me not too long ago for almost screwing up his investigation."

"Someone needs to remind our brother-in-law that without our amateur sleuthing, he might never have solved that case." Deena chuckled. "Although I have to admit, you and I did almost bite the dust on that one."

"Does that mean you're going with me?" Kate asked.

Deena glanced down at her watch. "Dammit! I can't. I have an appointment with Joyce Chambers today. She's talking about totally redoing her fifty-five hundred square foot home." She made an imaginary dollar sign with her pointer finger. "Cha-ching!"

"Okay. Guess that leaves you and me," Lainey said, popping out of the chair. "When do you want to go?"

"Now would be good," Kate said. "Just in case the woman finds out the document she's waiting on won't be finalized for a while and hops on the next flight back to the Big Apple. I need to stop by Ryan's office to apologize for leaving him high and dry last night. It's on the way and should only take a minute." She stood and kissed Deena on the cheek. "Thanks for the cookies, Sis. We'd all starve if it wasn't for you."

After setting up another meeting for the next day at Starbucks to update everyone on their visit to the hotel, Kate waved goodbye to Maddy, promising to call if they found out anything juicy from the New Yorker that couldn't wait until the next day.

Before she and Lainey made it to the door, Tessa ran up. **Oh no you don't. What's Colt gonna do if he finds out I'm helping you? Kill me?** She chuckled. **No way I'm missing out on this one. Can you even imagine a female version of Ernie Jackson?** She scrunched her face to resemble the Grumpy Cat look. **I can't wait to see if she's as mean and ugly as he was.**

*****

Benny sat in his car several rows across from where two men were digging. He'd been there about an hour, mesmerized by the activity, wanting to leave, but unable to make himself turn on the ignition and head back down the hill. He straightened up as the crane lifted the wooden box from the ground—the same wooden box, he'd watched them lower into the earth three months earlier.

Noticing the police car approaching the two men, he scooted down in the front seat. He'd purposely picked this spot since he had a good view but was too far away to be noticed. Then he slid up just enough to peek out the window with the binoculars and saw Colt Winslow park the cruiser, before directing the county ambulance following to pull in behind him. Watching them drive further up the hill, his breath quickened. By the time they stopped alongside the road next to the crane, he was on his way to full-panic mode. Even though he knew why they were here—his heart still kicked up a notch when the sheriff walked closer to the grave site for a better look. An audible gasp escaped his lips when the crane lifted the coffin into the air and then laid it on the ground in front of the newly unearthed grave.

Emily was inside that wooden box. Sweet, shy Emily, who was as beautiful inside as she was on the outside. Didn't seem right that her body was about to be violated all over again, especially now that she was finally at peace. Why couldn't they let her stay that way? No drugs, no johns, no more having her face used as a punching bag.

He blew out a breath, wondering what they'd find when they did the autopsy. But he already knew the answer to that question—and that's what had his stomach swirling like a grade five Texas tornado.

With a heavy heart, he saw them load Emily into the back of the ambulance, but even after the driver climbed into the vehicle and started down the hill, followed by the sheriff, he couldn't find the energy to move.

After a few more minutes spent watching the gravediggers finish up, he turned on the ignition and headed back to the Mission to wait. The ambulance doors were open when he passed the county morgue, and he figured Emily was probably already on the metal slab, awaiting the final assault on her body.

He wondered how long it would take for Colt to come after him once the ME found his DNA on the clothes she'd been buried in.

Chapter Nine

Kate pulled into the last available empty space in the parking lot at the Vineyard Dental Depot and turned to her sister. "Do you wanna run in with me, or are you okay waiting out here?"

"I'll wait. I have a couple of phone calls to make while you go see the good looking dentist." Lainey pulled the cell phone from her purse. "No rush."

Kate opened the car door and slid out. "I'll leave the car running so you don't melt in this heat."

She walked to the front door of the dental office, a little apprehensive about facing Ryan again. On one hand, she really did need to apologize for running off and leaving him the night before, but on the other, if Danny Landers wasn't interested in her, maybe it was time to start looking for a substitute. And although her flirting skills were in serious need of an overhaul, she could do worse than a nice guy like Ryan Kowalski.

The first thing she noticed when she entered the waiting area was that the place was packed. No wonder they were open on a Saturday morning. It looked like half of Vineyard was there, waiting to see the two dentists. There was a gigantic beverage area across the room, and judging by the number of people with cups in their hands, it was a big hit. Glancing around, she spotted a huge aquarium with lots of colorful fish in one corner and a decked-out play area with enough children's books to fill a library in the other.

Another reason for the crowd. They could bring their kids, get free coffee, and hang out.

She crinkled her nose at the thought. Elaborate or not, it was a dentist office, and it still topped her list of things she absolutely hated to do.

Just as she approached the front desk, she caught a glimpse of Jerome Woodson at the end of the hallway talking with a petite woman who could only be described as stunning. Long dark hair framed a delicate olive face and piercing black eyes. Just as Kate was about to look away to ask the receptionist if Ryan was available, the woman looked up at her. When Jerome followed the woman's gaze to Kate, he waved.

"I'm looking for Ryan," she said through the window.

Jerome walked over and opened the door to the examining area. "He's in the middle of a root canal, but if you need to talk to him right now, I can check to see if he's at a stopping point. Or maybe I can help you." He entwined his arm with the pretty woman who had followed him down the hall and was still smiling at Kate.

Kate shook her head. "Oh, no. It's nothing that can't wait." She turned to go, then swung back around. "Actually, I'd really appreciate it if you'd tell him I stopped by with a mea culpa for abandoning him last night."

Jerome's eyes widened. "Funny! He never mentioned he was with you last night."

Before she had a chance to explain, the small woman stepped forward. "Jerome, who is this, please?" she asked with a thick Hispanic accent.

Woodson stepped closer to the woman, almost in a protective stance. "Excuse my manners. I'd forgotten you two hadn't met." He nodded toward the woman. "This is my wife, Ana Maria. Honey, this is Dr. Kate Garcia. She works with Ryan and me in the pro bono program for the Vineyard homeless."

Kate reached out and shook her hand. "It's nice to finally meet you," she said, wondering why in the world she said that. If it hadn't been for the ring on Woodson's finger she would never have known he even had a wife.

A young dental assistant in purple scrubs appeared out of nowhere. "Dr. Woodson, your next patient is ready."

Before he could respond, Kate held up her hand. "My sister's waiting for me in the car. If you'd give Ryan the message, I'd be grateful." She focused back on Ana Maria. "It was so nice meeting you. I'm sure our paths will cross again."

"It would be my pleasure." The woman flashed another of her gorgeous smiles before Kate turned and headed for the door.

Back in the waiting area she was aware of the glares in her direction from some of the people who obviously weren't pleased that she'd been seen before them. But her mind wasn't on that. She was already thinking about her and Lainey's next stop at Vineyard Gardens.

"So, did you make nice with the hottie?" Lainey asked after Kate was again behind the wheel of her Honda Accord.

"He was in the middle of a root canal. I had to have one of those a few years back, and trust me when I say, I would have killed anyone who took the doctor away and made me wait with my mouth held open by some sort of vice grip. So, the answer is no, I didn't see Ryan, but I did give the message to his partner." She started the car. "And by the way, I got to meet Woodson's wife. Let me tell you, the boy must have some hidden money to snag a woman like that."

"What do you mean?"

"She's freakin' gorgeous. No wonder he let it be known right from the get-go that he was off limits."

"You noticed that, too?" Lainey said with a laugh.

"Who didn't? He practically waved that ring under our noses." Kate drove out of the parking lot and headed down the road, already forgetting about meeting Woodson's wife. The next stop was going to be a bit tricky trying to convince Ernie Jackson's sister that they were legit and not just two nosy sisters trying to help out a friend.

"So, not to change the subject, but Colt tells me you've been giving Danny Landers the come-on look," Lainey said as Kate merged onto the freeway toward the airport.

"What?" Kate tried to look indignant. "Oh dear God! Am I that obvious that even Colt noticed?"

Lainey laughed. "Yep, and you know how much it takes for that man to pick up on stuff like that. I remember when I first came to Vineyard after Tessa's death. I tried so hard to get him to notice me—even got liquored up one night and kissed him."

Kate twisted in her seat to face her older sister. "You're telling me that my big, important, news anchor sister made the first move on the good sheriff of Vineyard? Mr. play-it-by-the-book Colton Winslow?"

Lainey's laugh turned into a giggle. "What was even funnier was that the man turned me down cold."

"Ouch! They say a girl needs love and romance to have sex, but all a guy needs is a naked woman. That rejection must've killed you." Kate swerved to avoid hitting an SUV that had just cut her off. After laying on the horn, she turned back to Lainey. "I'm so glad you and Tessa cleared the air about Colt and are friends again."

"I wouldn't go that far," Lainey said. "Tessa and I have been at each other's throats since we were kids. Doesn't mean we don't love each other. And yes, we did work out our differences, but we were never the kind of friends that you and she were. We're too much like water and oil. It took her dying to get me to come back to Vineyard and face Colt after all those years."

See. I knew that hidden among all the crappy consequences caused by my death, there was probably one good thing that came out of it, Tessa said, settling in the backseat and leaning forward.

"Hey, Tessa. Lainey and I were just saying how nice it is that we're all together like a real family again. I hated it when you two weren't talking to each other."

"Where is she?" Lainey asked. When Kate pointed to the backseat, Lainey swiveled around. "I'm glad, too, Tessa. I always thought everything came so easy to you, and it threw me to find out you were just as insecure as I was."

Tell her not to get too carried away with all that BS. Tessa leaned back into the seats. **On second thought, it's nice to hear her say that, even though she thought I was a shit at the time. I never dreamed she'd forgive me.**

Kate had to bite her lower lip to keep from saying she agreed with Lainey. Tessa had played dirty when it came to her younger sister, but she decided it would be wiser not to stir that pot again. Tessa and Lainey had come to terms back when Lainey was the only one Tessa graced with her appearance after her death.

So what are you going to say to Ernie's sister when she asks why we're there? Tessa asked.

Kate repeated the question for Lainey before replying, "We haven't quite figured that out yet. You got any good ideas?" When Tessa shook her head, Kate glanced toward Lainey. "She's got nothing. How about you?"

"Hmm." Lainey narrowed her eyes in concentration. "What about if we tell her we heard she was in town and wanted to stop by to express our condolences. We can say we were with Ernie when he took his last breath and wanted her to know he didn't suffer."

That's pretty damn lame, Tessa interjected. **I say we lie and tell her we're from the police department there to investigate her brother's death.**

"Are you kidding me? Colt would throw our butts in jail so fast our heads would spin if he found out we were impersonating cops. Not to mention that Lainey has to sleep with the guy. That might make for some really cold nights for her." Kate exclaimed.

"Impersonating cops?" Lainey shuddered. "Don't bother with whatever Tessa suggested. If we did that, I might as well sign the divorce papers right now. I say we use the condolence-call thing. You're a doctor, Kate. You can wow her with big medical words."

Kate thought about that for a minute. "It just might work. While I'm giving her the detailed medical breakdown, maybe you can slip in a question or two about her brother. Try to find out where he got the money to pay Benny for his life insurance premium."

I see where that strategy might work better than the one I suggested, Tessa said with a smirk on her face. **I always said, you two got all the brains in the family.**

"Ha!" Kate said. "I know for a fact that both of us would have given up those good grades in a New York minute for just a fraction of your looks."

Yeah, well, that did get me two husbands and a helluva lot of money. Tessa frowned. **A lotta good that does me now.**

"It got you Gracie," Kate said, reminding of her daughter. "That's priceless."

I can't argue with that. Now, let's go have a talk with Ernie's sister.

Kate turned into Vineyard Gardens parking lot and blew out a noisy breath. "Are we ready to do this?"

Both Tessa and Lainey nodded, although neither looked convinced as they all got out of the car and headed for the entrance.

Vineyard Gardens was a four-star hotel nestled off the interstate on the outskirts of town. Completely renovated several years earlier, it had quickly become one of the favorite sites for Dallas/Fort Worth conferences because of its close proximity to the airport. So it wasn't surprising to find it bustling with masses of people, all wearing conference badges.

Kate and Lainey weaved their way through the crowd to the concierge desk where there was already a long line waiting.

"Guess everybody is trying to snag tickets for one of the Dallas West End tours. Heard they were fantastic," Lainey said, glancing over at the reservation desk where the lines were even longer.

"Either that or the Fort Worth Stock show is this weekend," Kate said, moving to stand beside her sister.

To their surprise, the line moved quickly, and soon, they were face-to-face with the hotel concierge, who looked like she should be in the bathing suit edition of Sports Illustrated instead of manning a desk at the fancy hotel. Tall, blonde, and with a smile that probably got her anything she wanted from the opposite sex, the woman looked up as they approached.

"Can I help you?"

Lainey gently pushed Kate aside and moved in front of her, a covert signal that she'd do the talking. "I'm Lainey Winslow of Good Morning Dallas, and this is my assistant, Kate Garcia. We're here to do an interview with one of your guests, but in our haste to get here, we left the woman's information in the taxi." She stopped talking and waited to see if Renee Cullum, according to her name tag, would take the bait.

"I knew I recognized you," the woman said, excitedly, before turning to her computer screen. "Finding her won't be a problem. What did you say her name was?"

Lainey turned slightly to give Kate a very obvious "watch and learn, little sis" look. Turning back to Renee, she scrunched her forehead. "That's going to be a problem since the I've already mentioned that information is in the cab, and for the life of me, I can't remember much about her that would help." She lowered her eyes. "Oh dear. This woman had a very tight schedule. My producer will be so disappointed, especially since we were going to do a clip on how Vineyard Gardens has become quite the convention center since it was renovated."

I can almost see the wheels turning in Renee's pretty blond head right now. She's probably trying to figure out how to get a piece of that action herself. Tessa inched her way in front of Lainey.

"I would be glad to personally show you around and help out any way I can," the concierge said softly.

Bingo, Tessa said with a smirk. **I knew she wouldn't miss an opportunity to be in the spotlight. This girl thinks exactly like me.**

Kate motioned with her head for Tessa to go around and peek over Renee's shoulder as she brought up a screen on the computer. Tessa nodded her understanding and moved behind the concierge.

"With you showing my camera guys around when they come back later this afternoon, it should be perfect," Lainey said. "The ratings always go way up when someone as gorgeous as you is in the picture."

Laying it on a little thick, aren't we, Lainey? Standing behind the concierge, Tessie opened her mouth and shoved her fingers into it, simulating the gag reflex and causing Kate to giggle.

When both Renee and Lainey turned to see why she was laughing, she held up her hand. "Sorry. I was just watching a woman over there who can't weigh more than a hundred pounds with clothes on, going off on some two-hundred-pound-plus guy who tried to cut in front of her in that long line."

With her back to the desk, Lainey mouthed *Tessa?* After seeing Kate nod, she shook her head and turned back to Renee. "About that interview. All I can remember is that the woman's name started with an A and she was from New York."

"Well, that's a start," the blonde said, as she brought up the guest list on the computer.

Tessa was hanging so far over Renee's shoulder that Kate thought there was a real possibility that the ghost would end up in her lap. She had to turn away to hide the smile that resulted as that visual flashed into her head. Poor Renee would have to have some serious therapy if that happened.

"Ah, here we go. I have a Rachel Alexander from New York City in Room 1438." Renee frowned. "Did you say she was here for the Mary Kay conference? Because if she is, this probably isn't who you're looking for. This woman checked in three days ago, and most of the Mary Kay ladies are just showing up today for the week-long conference that starts tomorrow." She pointed to the line at the registration desk, which seemed to have doubled since the last time Kate looked that way.

"I'm pretty sure she's not with that group," Lainey said. "I have an idea. Why don't I take my assistant up to the room and see if this Alexander woman is waiting on us? If she's not, it's no harm, no foul. In the meantime, I'd appreciate it if you kept this quiet. We'd like to catch everyone going about business as usual when the film crew arrives later today. It will make the piece appear more natural." She grabbed Kate's arm. "Of course, you'll have plenty of time to freshen your makeup."

She nudged Kate toward the elevator before both of them cracked up.

Some blondes are just lightheaded detours off the information superhighway, Tessa said, joining them with a giggle. **And Lainey, I am so impressed with you. Guess you did learn something from me after all.**

"Seriously, Tessa. You're proud because you taught Lainey how to lie?" Kate said, unable to maintain a stern face.

"She's taking credit for what I just did back there?" Lainey scowled. "Tell her I learned that in my journalism classes. Sometimes, you have to get really creative to get people to open up. Especially when privacy laws forbid them to reveal the room number of a hotel guest."

"As much as I love how you played this, Lainey, do you really think it's fair to let Renee believe she's going to be on your show?" Kate asked.

Lainey raised her eyebrows. "See, that's one of the perks of being an anchor, my dear. I think the good people of Dallas would love hearing about how it only took renovating an older hotel to draw in the kind of crowd we're seeing today. On the way out, I'll schedule a real interview with her for a later date."

Okay, smart stuff, you think you have all the answers. Now, show me how you're going to work that magic on the New Yorker, Tessa said as they exited the elevator on the fourteenth floor and headed down the hallway.

The door to Room 1438 opened on the second knock, and the Garcia sisters got their first look at Ernie Jackson's sister. Towering over five eight with mousy brown hair that was cut close to her face, the woman could have doubled as his twin.

"What do you want?" she asked in a gruff voice that had Kate falling behind Lainey once again to let her do the talking.

"Are you Ernie Jackson's sister?" Lainey asked.

Lame start, Lainey. That's like asking Marie Osmond if Donny is her brother, Tessa said, sarcastically. **Look at her. Of course she's his sister.**

"Did you bring the death certificate?"

Kate studied the woman. She looked to be in her late thirties, and despite the lack of makeup, her skin shimmered in the artificial lighting. Lainey had done her part downstairs by finding the room and now stepped aside to let Kate go in front of her, slapping her palm in a kind of tag team maneuver.

She held out her hand. "I'm Doctor Kate Garcia, and this is my sister, Lainey Winslow. We were with your brother the day he died and thought we'd come by to pay our condolences since he didn't have many friends. I was actually part of the team that tried to revive him and even went with him in the ambulance. Unfortunately, the EMT technicians and I, along with the hospital ER personnel, did everything we could for him to no avail." She paused to see how the woman reacted to that explanation.

To her surprise, the New Yorker shook her hand. "I'm Rachel Alexander. I appreciate the gesture, but my brother and I weren't close."

That's weird. According to Renee, this woman came to town a few days before her brother's death. Try to find out why, Kate. Tessa stepped forward to stand beside her younger sister.

"Do you mind if we sit?" Kate asked. "There's something we'd like to discuss with you."

Clearly, the woman would have loved to say no to that, but apparently her manners trumped her preferences. She pointed to the couch in the corner. "Yes, but I have an important conference call this morning, so we'll have to be brief."

She sat down on the edge of the bed as the sisters took the couch. "What is it you wanted?"

Tessa had wandered over to the desk where there were papers scattered by an open laptop. Kate tried to delay her response, hoping the ghost would find something useful that she could use to get the conversation started.

Wow! This chick's the CEO of Alexander Pharmaceuticals. Who would have guessed a guy who ate his meals out of a dumpster had a brainiac sister.

Kate decided to put the woman on edge right off the bat. "Since you run an international pharmaceutical company, you'll understand the medical details." She saw the look of surprise on Rachel's face, but before she could ask how they knew that, Kate continued. "Ernie had a violent seizure right before he died and displayed other symptoms commonly seen in poison cases. For that reason, the ME has delayed issuing the death certificate, and they—"

"They can't possibly think I had anything to do with that," Rachel interrupted. "I thought he had a stroke or something."

Oh boy! Her mind jumped way too quickly to denying any involvement. Something's fishy here. Tessa shifted her attention to the open laptop, read further down the page, and her eyes widening. **Oh my God! This is from Rachel's**

attorney about her dad's will. In order to get Ernie's share, she needs his death certificate ASAP. No wonder she's in such a big ass hurry. The sooner she gets it, the sooner she controls his share of the company.

"Why would you think anyone suspected you, Ms. Alexander?" Kate probed, unsure how to use the information Tess had just provided. Even though she wasn't a cop, she knew that if Colt found out about the will, he would definitely put Rachel Alexander on his "person of interest" list.

Rachel realized her mistake almost immediately and tried to explain. "Until two weeks ago I had no idea I even had a brother."

"That's odd," Kate said, leaning forward. "You arrived in town three days before your brother's death. One might conclude that according to your father's will, you'd enjoy a serious financial gain with Ernie out of the way. His share of a multi-billion dollar company reverting back to you must have been quite a motivator."

If she was looking for a reaction with that disclosure, she got it. The woman's eyes flashed anger. "I have no idea how you know all this, but Ernie was my father's illegitimate son. The first I heard about him was when the old man died and the will was read. Seems my father met Ernie's mother during a business trip to Dallas. For decades he'd supported her. They lived in an exclusive luxury high rise. After she died five years ago, Ernie, who was diagnosed with schizophrenia as a child, went missing. Apparently my father hired an investigator who found him on the streets in Vineyard." She nailed Kate with a glare. "He tried setting Ernie up in a more secure environment so he could make sure his useless son was properly cared for, but he ran off too many times to count."

"I thought you said you didn't know about your brother until two weeks ago," Kate said, beginning to suspect the woman was playing them.

"I didn't. After the will was read, one of the company execs filled me in on the story. He said Dad had instructed him to open a bank account in Ernie's name so he could use the ATM card and withdraw money to live on. But he never touched it until about six weeks ago."

Kate's eye lit up. "Six weeks ago? How much did he take out then?"

"I don't know—under a hundred dollars, I believe. Why?"

"No reason," Kate lied. It would serve no purpose for Rachel to know that it was probably the money Ernie gave Benny when he asked him to write a check for the first six months of his life insurance premiums. The same money that had the cops looking seriously at Benny as the killer.

"So did you come to Vineyard looking for a way to make Ernie disappear?" Lainey asked.

Kate remembered her sister once saying that angry people blurted out things they wouldn't ordinarily confess to, and she realized Lainey was working hard to get Rachel to do that now.

"Look here. I've already told you I had nothing to do with that man's death. Yes, I did hope I could buy him out, since he was obviously not capable of taking care of himself, let alone running a company the size of Alexander Pharmaceuticals."

The corner of Lainey's lips tipped in a smile when she got the results she was looking for, and Kate had to bite back her own glee.

Lainey plays the bad cop well, Kate. Now, it's time for your good cop imitation, Tessa said, moving from behind the desk to sit between her sisters.

"Please excuse my sister," Kate began. "It's just that we had become close to your brother. His death came as such a shock to both of us."

Oh hell! You lie better than Lainey does, Tessa exclaimed.

Kate shot her older sister a look designed to shut her up and focused back on the New Yorker. "Right now the police are looking at accidental poisoning, which isn't a big stretch since the man ate out of garbage bins." She stood. "So, you never spoke to your brother the entire time you were here?"

"No. I followed him for a day or so, waiting for the perfect time to approach him with an offer to buy him out. I was in my car outside the soup kitchen, but like I told that other cop this morning, I never got a chance to—"

Other cop? Something wasn't right. Why hadn't Maddy called to tell them Colt was going to be at the motel to talk to the woman. Their older sister knew she and Lainey were planning to visit her, and she should have realized they might get caught snooping around in the investigation. "Do you remember the policeman's name?" she asked, thinking that maybe Colt had sent one of his deputies instead of coming himself. Even so, it still would have been a disaster if whoever had questioned Rachel Alexander had casually mentioned to Colt later that they'd seen his wife at the hotel. Maddy should have warned them.

"I don't think he gave me his name, although he had a very southern accent."

Oh great! Tessa said. **More than half the population in Texas has a southern accent**. **She might as well have said he was driving a pickup.**

"Oh, and I remember thinking his cowboy boots were really unique," Rachel added. "I almost asked him where he got them. My company sometimes has corporate parties at a dude ranch north of New York City. I thought it would be cool to go home with a pair for the next big hoedown."

The light bulb went off in Kate's head, as a visual of Ross Perry in Charles Prescott's office the week before flashed in her head. The El Paso police officer had been wearing very expensive-looking boots that were definitely unique.

"Was he tall with a dimple in his chin?"

Rachel smiled. "Some things you just don't forget. I remember thinking he must get a lot of female attention with that dimple alone."

"For sure." Kate agreed before shaking Rachel's hand. "Thanks so much for talking with us today. Hopefully, the ME will get this all figured out and you can be on your way back to your life in New York."

She motioned for Lainey to stand, then led her to the door. Once they got to the elevator, she turned to her sister. "That wasn't a Vineyard cop she was talking about. It was

Ross Perry, a cop from El Paso who's in town to investigate that other Emily person who died in the bank robbery. You know, the one who named me and Benny in her will."

Lainey looked confused. "Why would a cop from El Paso be interested in Ernie Jackson's long-lost sister?"

"That's what we're going to ask the dimple-chinned cop ourselves, just as soon as we grab a burger and fries. I'm starving."

"Me too," Lainey said. "I'll call Maddy and get her working on where we can find this guy. Truth be told, I can't wait to see those boots. Maybe I'll find out where he gets them as well. I'm always trying to one-up the mayor's wife at the wine festival pre-party."

"Hope Colt got a raise recently. If I'm right, those were alligator boots and must have cost a fortune." She pulled out onto the highway. "No matter. That dude's got a lot of explaining to do."

Chapter Ten

Ross Perry looked through the peephole. Despite the hoodie the man was wearing, there was no question who was standing outside his door. *Damn!* He didn't feel like having a discussion about Emily Ruiz Santiago. Not now. He needed to pack his suitcase and be on the next flight to El Paso. Another knock—this time louder—startled him, and he cracked the door open just enough to look out.

"Whatever you want, make it quick. I'm booked on a two-thirty flight out of here." He stepped back as the door was pushed open from the outside, and the man walked in.

"Leaving without even saying goodbye?"

Ross shrugged. "Nothing more to discuss. Things blew up in my face back in the lawyer's office when that lady doctor convinced everyone that our girl wasn't the heiress from Houston. I told you what I wanted. Unless you're here to tell me some good news, we have nothing more to discuss. If not, you've got forty-eight hours before I make a call to the Vineyard Police Department."

The man pushed the hoodie back and walked over to the minibar. "Want one?" When Ross nodded, he pulled out two small bottles of Jack Daniel's and then turned away from

Ross to pour the liquor into the tumblers on the dresser. "Guess we'll have to live without rocks this time, unless you want to run down the hall to the ice machine. I know I'm not going."

The man came back to Ross and gave him one of the drinks, then sat down on the edge of the unmade bed with the other one in his hand. "How in the hell did this get so fucked up?"

"I have no idea."

Ross took a big swig of the whiskey, knowing he would need more than one drink to deal with this problem. He sat down in the chair behind the small desk and took another small sip before answering the question. "All I know is that you said she was clean."

"Thought she was," the man said. "How was I supposed to know you and your girl would get greedy? How'd she find out about Emily's inheritance in the first place?"

Ross shrugged. "It was me. After she got drunk one night, she told me who she really was. I decided to run a check on her and the woman whose name she was using. That's when we decided to cash in on some of that inheritance money. What I want to know is how it all came crashing down."

"We'll probably never know, so there's no sense wasting time on it. We've got bigger problems. We have to figure out a way to deal with my boss, get him on board with our new arrangement with you. And what about your colleagues in El Paso? Do any of them know the situation? The last thing we need is to have more cops snooping around."

"I know. I know." Ross blew out a frustrated breath. "No, I never told anyone about our deal. And you should know I'm working on a solution. I'm trying to figure out a way to connect the homeless guy who just died to the real Emily's death."

"What good would that do? When they find out what we did, I don't have to tell you what they'll do to you—to all of us."

"They won't find out. I promise." Ross lifted his glass and drained it before walking to the minibar and retrieving a bottle of tequila. "Sorry. No more whiskey. Want vodka or something?" When there was no response, he poured the tequila into his glass and sat back down at the desk. "I went to see the dead guy's sister today to find out if there was any way I could put ideas into her head about her brother and the ex-addict who runs the soup kitchen in town. The sheriff is already leaning toward the guy being involved since he benefited from her brother's death, as well as Emily's."

"That still won't help, and my boss's reaction will be nothing compared to Gustavo's. When that man hears about our fuck-up—and I guarantee he will—he'll send his henchmen across the border to find out how it all went wrong so quickly. If he connects her to you, it won't be pretty."

Ross stood, reaching for the end of the desk as a wave of dizziness hit him like a ninety-mile-an-hour fastball. "I would never implicate you." The room was spinning now, and his mouth felt like a West Texas dust storm had just blown through it.

The man smiled. "I know. I made sure of that."

Ross's vision was so blurry now, he was barely able to see the other man grab his phone from the desk, then take the glass out of his hand and wipe it with a handkerchief.

After doing the same with the other glass, the man pulled the hoodie over his head and walked to the door.

Fireworks exploded throughout the room in so many different colors, Ross didn't see him leaving. A kaleidoscope of images bursting with much the same colors filled the entire space in front of him. With each new vision, his breathing became more shallow until he was gasping for air. His eyes were now so heavy he could hardly keep them open, but the eruptions continued in his brain until he finally could no longer hold his head up.

Son of a—was the last thought he had before the door closed and his head hit the desk with a thud.

*****

"Let's go to Ruby's for lunch," Kate suggested. "All that lying has me starving."

"I know. Me too, but I haven't eaten there in a while. Those delicious calories are tempting, but—"

"Oh, come on. It will be nice to see Ruby, plus we can split a serving of bread pudding," Kate pleaded.

"Yeah, but what about the chicken fried steak and mashed potatoes with all that white gravy? If I'm going to Ruby's, no way I'll be sharing that." Lainey turned to her sister. "Oh, hell! I'm sick of my diet anyway. Lead the way."

"That's the spirit." Kate slapped the steering wheel and squealed. "With that attitude, maybe we should each get our own bread pudding."

"My thoughts exactly. Calories be damned."

The parking lot at Ruby's was nearly full when Kate pulled in. Luckily, they found a spot at the very end of the lot.

"No worries," she said to Lainey. "We're going to burn enough calories walking to and from my car to splurge on an extra biscuit or two."

Nestled in the heart of downtown in a building that had been renovated several times and proudly sported a placard honoring it as a historical site, Ruby's Diner had been a Vineyard favorite for over three decades. Kate pushed the door open and made a sweeping motion with her arm to allow Lainey to enter. She followed, wondering how many of the lunch bunch crowd, now jam-packed into the large dining area, worried about calories as much as she and Lainey did.

"Well, if it isn't the Garcia girls," Ruby said, running up to them. "It's been ages since I saw either one of you in here. I was about to get my feelings hurt."

Kate laughed out loud and hugged the restaurant owner. Standing a little over five feet—and nearly just as wide—Ruby McDonald had always been a friend of the Garcia family.

Bet she wouldn't say that if she knew I was with you, Tessa said. **She hates my guts.**

"With good reason, don't you think?" When Kate realized she'd spoken out loud, she glanced toward Ruby who was now staring at her with a questioning look. "I said we had a good reason to stay away, Ruby," she said, reacting quickly. "When you find a way to make a low fat version of your chicken fried steak, I'll be here every day."

Good save, Katie, but totally wasted on her. Look at the woman. No way she's gonna pull the fat out of anything here. Tessa walked behind the rotund woman and pointed to her backside. **This is one big booty back here. When they coined the phrase 'pull up your big girl panties,' they were definitely talking about Ruby McDonald.**

"Can't do that, Kate," Ruby replied. "Do you see all these cowboys in here? Not a one would come near the place if I tried to sneak something healthy onto the menu."

A woman can never be equal to a man until every female on the planet can walk down the street with a bald head and a beer gut and still think she's sexy. Tessa tsked. **And for the record, the only reason she hates me is because she and my ex were buddy-buddy. From the minute I divorced him, she's treated me like a second class citizen. Not that I care.**

Kate ignored Tessa as Ruby linked arms with her and Lainey and nudged them forward. "Come on. I have a table waiting for you in the back."

As they moved through the restaurant, Kate heard someone calling her name. When she scanned the restaurant to see who, her eyes immediately zoned in on Danny Landers and Colt Winslow sitting at a corner table, both waving their arms.

"Oh, crap," she muttered under her breath. She pasted on her best smile and waved back.

"I forgot the good sheriff was here, Lainey. I'm sure you'll want to sit with him." Ruby changed directions and led them over to where the two cops were sitting.

Kate tried to act nonchalant, but the truth was, seeing Danny here had caught her off guard. Quickly, she ran her fingers through her hair and prayed she still had on a bit of lipstick. She knew she had to play it cool, though. After all, he was no longer interested in any relationship with her other than friendship because these days Miranda Walters was rocking his world. Her head whispered that maybe that was for the best since there was so much history between them, but her libido was shouting something entirely different.

When he stood and pulled out the empty chair next to his, she couldn't stop from returning his smile.

So much for staying cool. "Hey, Danny," she said, trying to recover quickly. "What brings you guys here today?" She nearly slapped herself. Neither Danny nor Colt needed to watch their weight and probably ate at Ruby's several times a week—just like all the other guys down at the station. Tessa was right. It was only girls who were obsessed with eating healthier.

"I was about to ask you the same thing," Colt said after she and Lainey were settled at the table. "Thought you were at Deena's planning a party or something, Lainey." He looked first at his wife, then at Kate, and she had the sinking feeling that he was on to them.

Lainey stole a quick glance Kate's way before reaching for a menu to buy more time to come up with a good answer. "We were, honey, but Deena had to leave for an appointment. So, Kate and I decided to indulge ourselves."

"Thought you told me just the other day that this place was off limits to you." Colt was still staring at his wife, as if he was able to read her mind and knew exactly what she had planned for the rest of the day.

"I talked her into it," Kate said, feeling the heat skittle up her cheeks when Danny reached for the sugar and accidentally brushed her hand. "Besides, it's a girl's prerogative to change her mind, isn't it Colt?"

After a minute, his face finally relaxed into a semi-smile. "Absolutely. I never could figure out why Lainey worried about her figure in the first place." He leaned over and kissed his wife's forehead. "I'll love you even if you do get chunky." He ducked when Lainey tried to slap his arm.

They all say that, but it's a big-ass lie, Tessa said, now standing behind Danny. **This boy's looking better every time I see him. Find a way to jump his bones before I do, Katie,** she said before frowning. **Oh God! For a minute there, I forgot I was dead.**

Kate bit back a smile. Although she and Lainey had always been and still were best friends, after Lainey left Vineyard and was gone for so long, Kate and Tessa had grown closer. Even before she ended up as a ghost, Tessa had always been able to make her laugh.

She was jolted back into the present when Danny touched her arm. "Kate, she's ready to take your order."

She snapped out of it, noticing how everyone at the table was looking at her. The waitress standing over her was not too happy with her, either. "Sorry. I was thinking about one of my patients. I'll have the lunch portion of the chicken fried steak, please," she said, proud of herself for resisting the bigger serving.

While they waited for their order, they made small talk with Ruby who had reappeared and was her usual chatty self. Maddy had mentioned earlier that Colt had given the order to have Emily's body exhumed that morning. Kate was dying to find out about that, but there was no way she could ask. Colt was like a bloodhound and would sniff out her intentions before the words ever left her mouth. Then she and Lainey would have to sit through another of his stay-out-of-police-business lectures.

No, she decided to pass on bringing up that subject and couldn't believe her ears when Ruby did it for her. She wanted to jump up and kiss the woman right there.

"Hey, Colt, I heard they dug up that homeless girl's body this morning. What are y'all looking for?"

If looks could kill, Ruby would have been joining Tessa in the afterworld. But being the gracious man that Colt was, he merely smiled at the curious owner. "Now, you know I can't discuss an ongoing investigation, Ruby."

Apparently not everyone in the room was afraid of Colt. Unfazed by his words and the scowl covering his face, Ruby continued, "Let's get real, Colt. We all know that girl died of a drug overdose. So what was so important that you'd mess with her grave?"

After an uncomfortable pause with Danny and Colt exchanging glances, Danny said, "There's a chance we could find the dealer who sold her the cheese heroin with a few more blood tests. The thinking is that maybe they can find something specific that'll lead us to the drug's origin and narrow down the search for the scumbag who sold it to her."

Ruby nodded her approval "That would be great. Rumor has it the stuff is coming in from Dallas."

"That's probably true." Colt looked at Danny and gave him a head bob to show his appreciation for the quick thinking. "But if we can walk away with even one more clue to help us save more addicts from dying, we felt exhuming Emily Ruiz Santiago's body was worth it."

"Bet you'll be checking her DNA to see if she's really the rich girl from Houston."

Colt's face colored first pink, then scarlet, before he took a deep breath and blew it out slowly. Kate would have bet a month's salary that he was counting to ten in his head. He hated it when important things about his investigation were leaked to the public, but he shouldn't be too surprised. Vineyard was a small town, and gossiping was the number one pastime. No doubt Ruby knew about the Emily dilemma before the lawyer hit the interstate on his way back to Houston.

"That's one of the things we'll check, Ruby." Again, Danny came to his rescue before glancing down at his watch. "Colt and I need to be at Vineyard Gardens in forty-five minutes. Could you check on our order, please?"

Ruby started to say more, then nodded instead. "Did you all get the chicken fried steak today?" After a resounding 'yes' from everyone, she turned to Colt. "I'm real curious about that. DNA. You will let me know, right?"

Colt chewed on his lower lip before answering. "I don't think that will be necessary, Ruby. My guess is you'll know the results before I do," he said, unable to hide the sarcasm.

The restaurant owner chuckled. "Gotta love the Vineyard grapevine, don't you, Colt?" She started for the kitchen and said over her shoulder, "I'll have your order right out."

Both Kate and Lainey giggled, despite the look Colt shot their way. "What's so damn funny?"

"You are, honey," Lainey said. "You spend all day at the station dealing with criminals, and you can't even intimidate a little woman like Ruby. It's kind of fun to watch." When he glared at her, she pointed. "That's payback for the chunky remark, by the way."

After a moment, his narrowed eyes relaxed. "I probably deserved it. And for the record, Ruby could never be called a little woman. Now forget that and tell me about the party you two planned at Deena's."

A flash of panic stopped Kate in midair as she brought the ice tea glass to her lips. *Now's when he gets us to confess what we're up to*, she thought.

"It's going to be an open house at Deena's to introduce Vineyard to her new interior decorating business. She's decided to call it Designs by Deena," Lainey said, without even breaking a sweat.

Damn, she's good! Tessa said. **Maybe I should've taken lessons from *her* way back when.**

Kate took another sip of her tea, thoroughly impressed with her older sister's ability to think on her feet. Now all they had to do was tell Deena she was having an open house— and that her business finally had a name. She stole a quick glance at her sister and nodded her approval.

"So, Miranda's getting back into town on Friday. I was wondering if you and Ryan would like to go over to Emilio's with us on Saturday—you know, since we got interrupted the other night."

Kate was so busy watching Tessa's juvenile attempt to get her to laugh by making faces behind Colt's back, that it took all of a minute to realize Danny was talking to her. Remembering her dead sister's words that sometimes a man was only interested when a woman wasn't, she decided to try to dangle Ryan Kowalski in front of him, just like Tessa had advised.

"Can't," she said with a shrug. "Ryan and I are having dinner with Cindy and Greg on Saturday."

She watched a frown cross his face. That was just the reaction she wanted when he learned she was taking Ryan as her plus one to her co-worker's house. Glancing up at Tessa, who was giving her the thumbs up, she turned away to let Danny stew over that—at least she hoped that's what he was doing. Before he could say anything else, the chicken fried steak arrived, and all talk was forgotten while they devoured it.

When they were finished, Colt shoved his plate away. "I couldn't eat another bite if you paid me."

"No bread pudding, sweetie?" Lainey asked. "Are you afraid of getting too chunky?"

"All right, already," he said with a half-scowl. "I've been properly chastised and will never mention that word again." He drained the last of his sweet tea. "Sorry, Danny wasn't lying about us having to leave for an interview. What are you two doing the rest of the day?"

Again, Lainey rose to the challenge. "Macys is having a big sale we want to check out."

He groaned. "There goes our retirement."

"No retirement money, dear, but this is probably the last time we'll be able to eat out for a while. Sorry, it will be you, me, and my cooking for the next couple of weeks. Since I only know how to make a few things—none that could qualify as good—we'll be eating a lot of salads. That might be beneficial, considering—"

"No more!" Colt held up his hand then bent down to kiss her forehead. "We're outta here. I'll stop and pick up a pizza on my way home tonight."

On the way to Kate's car with two takeout boxes of bread pudding, Lainey turned to her. "You never mentioned your date with Ryan on Saturday."

Kate stopped in her tracks and faced her sister. "Because there is no date. I was just using one of Tessa's tricks and throwing Ryan in Danny's face to see what would happen."

"It was obvious he didn't like it. For the life of me I don't understand what he sees in Miranda Walters, anyway, unless things have changed drastically since we were teenagers. Back then, one hour in the same room with her was all I could stomach," Lainey said when they continued walking to the car.

"Yeah, I remember that, too, but while she was away from Vineyard, her chest got a little bigger. Guys have a way of looking past the annoying stuff just to stare at the boobs."

When they got to the car, Kate opened the door and slid in, then blew out a breath. "Whew! For a minute back there. I thought we were going to get caught. Then you came through with your A game. Good job, Lainey." She high-fived her sister.

"Hope I'm as good with the El Paso cop as I was with Colt. Tessa should be proud."

"**I am**, Tessa said, appearing out of nowhere. **Now, get the lead out of your ass, Kate. We've already wasted too much time, and I'm dying to see those boots.**

Kate was no longer listening to either sister. Her mind was on her brother-in-law. He'd said he and Danny were on their way to an interview. She was pretty sure they were talking about Rachel Alexander and prayed the New York exec wouldn't mention her and Lainey's earlier visit. There would be hell to pay if she did.

Chapter Eleven

The Rosemont Inn was conveniently located on Airway Boulevard right outside DFW Airport and attracted travelers who needed to pop in and out of the Dallas/Fort Worth area in a hurry. Kate had assumed Ross Perry had fallen into that category. You'd think he would have hopped on the next plane to El Paso right after he discovered that the dead woman he'd originally thought to be Emily Ruiz Santana was in fact, not her at all.

So why had he hung around Vineyard for an extra few days just to pay a visit to Rachel Alexander in her hotel room? Her brother's death had nothing to do with the Emily thing. What could he have possibly wanted to discuss with the New York businesswoman before he headed home?

"Tell me again why we're making a special trip to see this cop, Kate," Lainey said, clutching the take-out boxes like they housed gold bricks instead of Ruby's bread pudding.

Kate shrugged. "I don't really know how he's connected to Ernie Jackson's death or why he's still snooping around in Vineyard where he has no jurisdiction. I just have a gut feeling that it's all connected somehow."

"Hmm. That's weird." Lainey turned slightly to face her younger sister. "Are you sure the Alexander woman was talking about him when she mentioned her earlier chat with a cop? Is it inconceivable to think that Colt may have sent Flanagan or Rogers over there this morning to question her about her brother's death?"

"Anything's possible, I guess, but I'm thinking it wasn't Colt or anyone on his staff who stopped by this morning. Didn't you hear him mention that he and Danny had an appointment at Vineyard Gardens after lunch? Why else would they be going to that hotel except to talk to Ernie's sister? It doesn't make sense that they would keep that appointment, knowing one of their fellow officers had already been there."

"I see your point. So, maybe Alexander met with someone from the ME's office. Or the DA's office."

"Doubtful. Not too many people in either office—or all of Vineyard, for that matter—have a killer chin dimple and wear custom-made, alligator-skin boots," Kate wise-cracked. "No, I'd bet that bread pudding in your lap that it was indeed our Lieutenant Perry who paid Rachel Alexander a visit this morning. What I can't figure out is why."

"Hey, you can take chances with your dessert, Kate, but don't screw around with my sugar fix for the day." She lifted one of the boxes and sniffed. "Ohmygod! This smells so good. As soon as we finish with Perry, we're going to Starbucks for a Carmel Macchiato to go with it—my treat."

After a short drive from downtown to the airport, they found the hotel and parked close to the entrance. Once inside the lobby Kate immediately noticed that this place was nowhere near as nice as the Vineyard Gardens just a few blocks down the road. Ornate, dark drapes covered the windows, and although the tile was nice, it didn't compare to the marble flooring in Rachel Alexander's hotel. Kate decided that Ross Perry's choice of sleeping quarters probably had more to do with the El Paso Police Department's budget than his personal choice, especially since he'd obviously chosen to extend his stay on the company dime.

Both she and Lainey avoided eye contact with the desk clerk and walked directly across the lobby to the elevators. Thanks to Maddy, they knew that Perry was staying in Room 803 and that he was scheduled to check out this morning. Kate hoped they weren't too late.

The eighth floor looked deserted when they got off the elevator, which was a blessing in itself. The fewer people who saw them, the better, in case Colt got wind of their visit somehow. Without witnesses it would be harder to prove they'd been there.

Kate stopped in front of Room 803 and glanced over at her sister. "Perry might take our little visit the wrong way and think we're checking up on him. It could get ugly in there, you know. Now's the time to turn around and get out of Dodge if you're nervous about all this."

Since when did you become such a wuss, Katie?

Kate whirled around to find Tessa standing in Lainey's shadow. "Oh yeah! Talk it up, Tessa. I notice you're hiding behind Lainey."

"She's here again?"

Kate nodded and pointed to where Tessa was still frowning over her remark. "And already giving me grief. Lucky for her we need her special talents to sneak around in there and find clues about Ross Perry like she did with Rachel Alexander. Without the info Tessa found about her father's death and the will, we wouldn't have had any leverage with her." She touched her forehead and gave her sister's ghost a salute. "Good job, by the way." Turning back to the door, she hesitated momentarily, then knocked. "It's now or never." When there was no response, she knocked again, this time with more force.

"You think he's already gone?" Lainey asked from behind her.

"Hope not. I'm really curious to find out why he went to see Rachel Alexander today." She knocked one last time before spotting a woman pushing a housekeeping cart round the corner and heading their way.

Before she could say anything, Lainey stepped closer and whispered in her ear. "Is getting into this room for a quick look important enough for me to get devious?" When Kate nodded, she added, "Even if it might mean we could be charged with breaking and entering?"

What's up with Lainey? It's not like she doesn't sleep with the sheriff. Does she really think he'd put her behind bars? Tessa huffed. **Grow some balls, girls.**

Kate gave Tessa a disapproving look. "Your ghostly sister is harassing us again. Her mantra has always been 'No guts, no glory' yet she's still hiding behind you." She gave Lainey a nod. "Now show me how it's done, Sis."

Lainey rooted around in her purse as the housekeeper closed in on them. Just as she was about to pass by them, Lainey stopped her. "Can you help us? My husband and I checked out of this room earlier, and when I got to the ticket counter, I realized I'd left my camera behind. Dumb me left the room key on the dresser when we left."

The small woman gave Lainey the onceover with squinted eyes. "What is your name, please?" she asked with a heavy accent that Kate guessed was South American. Then she reached for a clipboard from the bottom shelf of the cart.

"Perry," Lainey blurted. "My husband's a cop. What's your name so he can tell your boss how helpful you were?"

Your husband's a cop all right, but I'm pretty sure he won't be happy about you coercing this poor woman into helping you commit a crime, Tessa said, finally coming out from behind Lainey.

"Christiella," the woman said before checking the clipboard. After glancing up at them one last time, she opened the door. "Close it when you leave," she added, before she resumed the trek down the hallway with the cart.

And just like that they had access to Ross Perry's room where, if they were lucky, they'd find something he'd left behind that might prove useful in determining why he was so interested in Ernie Jackson's death.

A few feet into the room, Kate gasped and pointed to the desk in the corner of the room where the El Paso cop was slumped, a half-empty glass of clear fluid in front of him.

When Lainey saw him, she put her finger to her mouth. "Shh. Back out of here slowly before he wakes up and catches us."

Before the sisters could do that, Tessa sauntered over to the desk and bent down next to Perry's face. **This dude is dead to the world,** she said. **And I mean that literally.**

Kate's medical instincts kicked in, and she closed the distance between where she stood frozen to where the cop's head was resting on the desk. She didn't need to check his pulse to know that Tessa was right, but she felt for the carotid anyway.

"He's definitely dead," she said to Lainey, who was staring at her like she was crazy.

"Dead? Ohmygod! From what?"

Kate shrugged. "I have no idea, but the temperature of his body suggests it hasn't been too long since he took his last breath." She bent down to smell the half-empty glass, then pointed to a small envelope beside it. "Looks like Perry was mixing some kind of illegal drugs with his liquor," She blew out a long noisy breath as she pulled the cellphone from her purse "We have to call Colt, although I don't think I need to remind you that the man is going to blow a gasket when he finds out we're the ones who found him."

"Oh, holy Mother of God!" Lainey said. "There'll be no living with him when he realizes I lied about Macys." She rolled her eyes. "Not to mention how he'll react to our snooping into another one of his investigations. He nearly divorced me when we tried to help Maddy last year."

Kate thought for a moment. "Why does he have to know? We can use Perry's cellphone to call mine. That way we can say he called and asked me to stop by his hotel room so he could discuss the Emily woman who died in El Paso one last time before he left to go back home."

Lainey's eyes lit up. "That's genius, Kate, and it just might work." She glanced around the room. "Do you see his phone anywhere?"

Kate did a quick search of the room. There was no phone in sight. "Maybe it's in his pocket. Check it out, Lainey."

"Me? No way! I'm not about to put my hand in a dead man's pocket. You do it. You're the doctor."

Tessa walked around both sides of Perry's body. **No need to. It's not there.**

After Kate did another quick scan of the room and the bathroom without finding the phone, she blew out a frustrated breath. "So much for that great plan, although now that I think about it, Colt would have figured out the call was made after the guy died. So, unless one of you has another idea, guess we'll have to make that call to the friendly sheriff and take the heat."

Just as she was about to do that, she decided she wasn't ready just yet to face the wrath of her brother-in-law. Hoping her sister could somehow put a spin on the fact that her two younger sisters were at the Rosemont Hotel in a room with a dead guy, she called Maddy.

But as she hit *Talk*, she knew even St. Jude couldn't help her out with this one.

*****

Danny Landers stared out the window, tuning out his boss, who was rambling on about some new police regulation that had him all riled up. Normally, he hung on Colt's every word, seeing him as the older brother he never had. But today, he couldn't stay focused. His mind kept flashing back to lunch at Ruby's and sitting across the table from Kate Garcia.

God! She got prettier every time he saw her. And when her hand brushed his, he thought an electrical charge had rippled through him. It took him back to that day many years ago when he first realized he wanted more than a friendship with her. And just like then, he found himself longing to grab her and pull her into his arms and find out what he'd been missing all these years.

Of course, that would have been a major disaster. Number one, Colt would have freaked out because he was on the job and in uniform, which was definitely grounds for suspension—or worse—and because Kate was family. And number two, Kate probably would have punched him, just like when they were kids and he'd done something stupid. That thought made him smile until he noticed that Colt had stopped talking. Turning toward him, he frowned when he saw the perplexed look on his boss's face.

"Something funny about the governor heaping more regulations on our already-difficult job, Danny?" Colt asked.

Although Colt had turned back to concentrate on driving, Danny felt his displeasure and knew that if he could see his mentor's face, his eyebrows would be drawn into a V between his eyes, like they always were when he was halfway pissed off.

"Sorry, boss. I was just thinking about how you let Ruby get under your skin back at the diner," he lied.

Colt puffed out a breath. "That woman's going to be the death of me yet. How in God's name does she get her information faster than we do?"

"Sooner or later you're going to have to give up trying to act like a big city cop. This is Vineyard. Everybody knows everybody else's business. Hell, Ruby has probably already been alerted that we're on our way to talk to Ernie Jackson's long-lost sister. My guess is, before we even get back to the house, she'll know exactly what we discussed."

Colt shook his head, but despite his attempt to show displeasure, Danny could see the corners of his lips tipping into the beginning of a smile. "Gotta love small towns, I guess. But sometimes they can be a pain in the ass."

Pulling the cruiser into the parking lot at Vineyard Gardens Hotel, Colt found a spot close to the entrance. Before he shut off the engine, he turned, his face now revealing a more playful side. "Are you going sweet on my sister-in-law, Danny?"

There was another reason Danny loved his boss. He could read minds. Right now, he wished that wasn't so.

"Why do you ask?" He hoped he sounded nonchalant, unsure how Colt would react if he knew that "going sweet" came with fantasies involving her and a bed. But the truth was, he wasn't sure himself if he really was beginning to have feelings for his childhood best friend or if his testosterone was simply playing games with him whenever she was around.

Colt harrumphed. "I thought you had a better opinion of my investigative skills, Landers." He reached for the notebook on the dashboard. "Hell, you practically drool every time you see her, not that I can blame you. Kate has always been a looker."

Danny shrugged. "It's that obvious, huh?"

"Yeah." Colt turned off the engine and turned to face Danny. "If it's any consolation, though, I've known Kate for a lot of years, and I think she's a little smitten herself."

"Smitten? What the hell does that mean?" Danny asked as he exited the cruiser and followed his boss into the hotel lobby.

"You know—smitten. Kate worked hard to get where she is today, and she gave up a social life to do it. I can see her eyes light up when she looks at you, and I wonder if she's ready to make up for lost time."

"We were best friends nearly all our lives. She still sees me as the kid from across the street who made her laugh." Danny stopped in front of the desk.

Before Colt could respond, a well-dressed forty-something gentleman approached them. "Can I help you?"

Colt pulled out his badge and shoved it his way. "Sheriff Winslow and Officer Landers from the Vineyard Police Department. We're here to see Ms. Rachel Alexander. Could you ring the room to let her know we're on our way up?"

"Absolutely, Sheriff." He picked up the phone. "Anything I should be concerned about?"

"Not really. We just need to talk to her about an ongoing investigation." Colt thanked him and started toward the elevator. Halfway there, his phone rang. "Winslow," he said at the same time he hit the Up button on the elevator. After listening for a moment, his face turned serious. "And what did you find that was important enough for a personal call, Doc?"

When the elevator arrived, Colt stepped away to continue the conversation. Danny listened patiently, figuring he was talking to the ME about the autopsy for either Ernie Jackson or Emily Ruiz. He didn't have to wait long for the boss to disconnect and turn his way.

"That was Mark Lowell. He's finishing up with Emily Ruiz Santiago's autopsy. Although the toxicology samples won't be back for a few days, we might have just caught ourselves a break. He said—"

"What kind of break?" Danny interrupted.

Colt grinned at him. "Be patient, lad. I'm getting to that. If you remember, Emily was buried in her old tattered clothes because she had nothing else. By the time Flanagan got to her pad under the bridge, everything was gone. Guess word travels fast in that community. Anyway, Doc acted on a hunch and was able to lift a sample off the edge of her blouse."

"A sample?"

"Sperm."

Danny was confused. "How's that going to help us, Colt? Everyone knows the woman hustled for drug money. The DNA could be from any one of a long list of johns."

"That's true," Colt replied. "Or it might be our first good lead toward finding whoever is selling cheese heroin in Vineyard, assuming the dealer took his fee out in trade. That's pretty much how most of the female junkies get their dope." He sighed. "It's a longshot, I know, but right now it's all we have. Last night, a kid overdosed on the stuff in Denton County. That tells me that someone in the vicinity is still selling it, and the sooner we find him and send his sorry ass to jail, the safer our kids will be."

Danny nodded, then grinned. "Ten bucks says Ruby already knows all this."

This brought a huge scowl to Colt's face. "No sucker alive would take that bet. I swear, that woman is psychic. Come on. We've got an interview to do, and we're already late." He punched the button on the elevator once again. "Maybe this Alexander lady can shed a little light on her brother's death, which is beginning to look more and more like a freak accident rather than a homicide."

"When will his autopsy results be ready?"

"Soon, I hope," Colt said just as his phone blared again. "What's up today? I told Jeannie not to bother me unless it was an absolute emergency." He looked at caller ID. "It's Maddy," he said before answering and putting his newest female officer on speakerphone.

"Colt, there's been another death," she began.

Colt shot Danny a look. "Where?"

"At the Rosemont Inn." Maddy hesitated before continuing. "It's Ross Perry, the cop from El Paso who came to Vineyard investigating the other Emily who was killed—"

"I know who he is, Maddy. What's he still doing in Vineyard? I thought he said he had no further business here after Kate proved that the woman who died in El Paso was an imposter and not the real Emily Santiago."

"I don't know, Colt. I only took the call that he was dead."

"Weren't you supposed to go home early to take Abby to a soccer game?"

There was a long pause. "I did." Maddy stammered.

"So, why'd the hotel call you on your cell?"

There was an even longer pause. "The hotel didn't call."

Colt blew out a frustrated breath. "Maddy, I don't have time for games. What the hell is going on?"

"It was Lainey who called. She and Kate found the body."

Chapter Twelve

"Is it done?" the voice on the other end of the phone asked.

He put down the slice of pizza and took a quick swig of the beer before answering. "Yeah. I told you not to worry."

"You also told me that Perry wouldn't be a problem, but that was before he rode into town and demanded money. So pardon me if I'm a little nervous about taking you at your word."

"Okay, already. I said I'd deal with the cop, and I did. Now, can we move on?" He took a quick bite of the meat lover's pizza. He didn't know why, but killing the cop had made him ravenous.

"How are you going to handle the homeless guy?"

"What do you mean?"

"I'm talking about the autopsy. It's my understanding the results will be released in a few days."

He huffed. What did they think he was? A buffoon? "What part of not to worry don't you get? I told you there's no way anyone will be able to trace Jackson's death back to me."

"You'd better damn well hope that's true, my friend. I have to answer to a man who doesn't believe in second

chances. My ass is on the line right along with yours. He'll
—"

"I said I got this. All you need to worry about is making sure that twenty grand finds its way into my bank account."

"You're joking, right?" There was a long pause. "You seriously don't expect him to throw twenty big ones your way just because you fixed something *you* screwed up in the first place, do you?"

"There was no way I could have known Perry would react the way he did. I told you from the beginning that I thought it was a bad idea to get him involved."

"That may be true, but I wouldn't hold my breath waiting on the money. Nor would I press the issue. That would only remind the boss you didn't vet Perry the way you should've."

He thought about that for a minute, deciding that pursuing the subject might be pushing his luck. Up to this point, things had been running smoothly, and he had a nice fat chuck of change in the Cayman Islands to show for it. He needed to take a step back and wait till this all blew over and they could get back to making serious money again.

"Gotta run. Just stay focused, and we should all be okay." The phone disconnected before he had a chance to respond.

He grabbed the beer and drained it, slamming the empty bottle on the desk in front of him. All his life people had been second-guessing him, and he hated it just as much now as he had when he was a kid. You'd think after two perfect murders, he would finally get the respect he deserved.

*****

The door opened and all three sisters glanced at each other as Colt walked into the room, followed by Danny Landers. One look at his face said it all as he zoned in on his wife with a disapproving glare. Making sure she was out of Colt's line of vision, Kate reached over and grabbed Lainey's hand, hoping to send some strength her way. But even as she squeezed it, she knew that no show of solidarity among the sisters would balance out the anger on her brother-in-law's face.

Without a word, he sauntered past them and walked to the desk. Pulling latex gloves from his pocket, he slapped them on and then felt the dead man's neck.

"I'm a doctor, Colt. Don't you think I would know if a person is dead or not?" Kate asked, before she could stop herself. Now was not the time for sarcasm. The man was already close to exploding and didn't need more fuel added to that fire.

Other than an icy glare her way, Colt didn't react, and she breathed a sigh of relief. The next few minutes were spent in silence as the sheriff examined the body, picked up the drink and sniffed it—much like Kate had done minutes before— then reached for the envelope beside the glass.

"Looks like he was mixing street drugs with his alcohol," Kate said, hoping to get him to respond. She decided his silence was way worse than his lecture would be. The sooner he reprimanded them about finding the dead guy, the better. But again, Colt only shot her a look. She stepped closer to Lainey, hoping her sister might be better equipped to try to calm her husband down.

This whole scene was worse than she'd imagined. Even Danny, who always had a smile on his face, wouldn't make eye contact with her. Instead, he walked over to the desk and picked up the small envelope with gloved hands.

"If I were guessing, I'd say this was special K, Colt," he said after examining it, careful not to let any of the powder spill out.

"What's special K?" Lainey asked, before receiving a third killer glare from her husband.

"Ketamine," Danny responded.

Kate racked her brain, trying to figure out how Perry could have gotten his hands on ketamine. It was a drug used to anesthetize animals at veterinary hospitals and occasionally in minor surgeries for humans, and because the ketamine she'd seen had only come in vials, she'd assumed the powder was crack or cocaine.

"Ketamine's a liquid," she blurted. "Why makes you think that's what this is?"

Danny looked up at his boss, who still hadn't spoken. When Colt nodded, he explained, "Last month the emergency veterinary hospital over on Clemens was robbed, and all that was missing was their supply of ketamine. We knew it was just a matter of time before it showed up on the streets. For the past three weeks, we've been finding these envelopes in the homeless communities under the bridge. Analysis showed it was ketamine, or Special K as the kids call it. We've stepped up our efforts to find the scumbag who's selling it."

"How do they change it into a powder so they can sniff it?" Lainey asked, finally finding her voice.

"Microwave," Danny responded. "It evaporates until only a powder is left. Sometimes they mix it with a little extra something for a better high."

"Why would a junkie go to all that trouble just to go to sleep?" Kate asked. "Ketamine is an anesthetic drug."

"Maybe for dogs," Danny said. "The kids put it in a line and snort it at rave parties because of its hallucinogenic effects. There's also a liquid ketamine that can be put into a drink." He pointed to the glass. "Perry may have been double dipping to get the ultimate psychedelic trip."

"Do you think mixing it with alcohol killed him?"

Before Danny could answer, Colt walked over to the far corner of the room where the two sisters were standing.

Oh, shit! I know that look. Grab your tush with both hands because this boy is about to rip you both a new one. Tessa, who hadn't said a word up to this point, moved to stand behind Lainey.

"Lainey, what were you and your sister doing in Perry's room?" Colt's voice sounded calm, but his eyes told an entirely different story.

Lainey glanced at Kate for help.

"I wanted to talk with him one last time about his victim from the El Paso robbery and the Emily Ruiz that died here." Kate crossed her fingers behind her back, hoping the big Guy up above wasn't listening.

"How did you know he was still in town?" Colt fired back, obviously not impressed with the lie. "And who told you where he was staying?"

Be careful what you say, Kate, or you're liable to throw Maddy to the wolves on this one.

Kate bit her lip. Tessa was right. She'd have to be careful how she responded. If Colt knew that Maddy was the one who had given them the heads up about Ross Perry, her job could be on the line. Everyone knew how much he hated interference in his investigations, and if he found out the newest addition to his force had been the one to leak the information, the fact that she was his wife's older sister wouldn't protect her against his wrath.

"He called me," Kate lied again, knowing that would be easy for a cop to check out but unable to come up with anything else at the moment. "He wasn't convinced his victim was impersonating the real Emily and wanted to ask a few more questions."

Colt scanned the room. "So, where's his phone?"

Kate shrugged. "How would I know? I can only tell you that when we got here, he was already dead." She clamped her mouth shut before she blurted out that they couldn't find his phone, either.

"How'd you get into the room?"

Oh, crap! This boy already knows the answers to his questions before he even asks them. He's playing you. Tread cautiously.

Lainey stepped forward. "The housekeeper let us in."

Colt eyed her suspiciously. "And why would she do that, dear? She could get fired for giving you access to someone else's room. At the very least, you would've had to have shown her some form of identification." He raised his eyebrows, waiting for her answer when it was obvious he already knew she had none.

Lainey lowered her eyes. "We thought Perry had already left for the airport, and we wanted to get a look in the room in case he left anything behind that might help us find—"

"Help you find what, darling?" Colt moved closer to his wife just as Tessa took another step farther away.

"Okay, Colt," Kate began. "We went to see Ernie Jackson's sister earlier, and she mentioned that Perry had questioned her this morning about her brother." She paused to see if her brother-in-law was buying it but couldn't tell by his facial expression. His raised eyebrows did indicate he was definitely listening to the story, though, and she continued, "Anyway, we were just trying to find out why he was interested in the homeless man's death. And when we found out he had already checked out we thought there'd be no harm in getting a peek at his room."

"And what if you'd walked in on him while he was in the throes of his psychedelic trip?" Colt huffed. "Have you ever seen someone high on a hallucinogenic like PCP?" When neither responded, he threw up his hands. "I thought not. Let me tell you, they have the strength of an ox. Mix that with the paranoia that goes with it, and my guess is, he probably would have perceived you two as the enemy when you came crashing in uninvited to his one-man party. Neither one of you would've stood a chance in hell of getting out of here without serious bodily harm—or worse."

Just then the door opened and Mark Lowell walked in, followed by two CSI technicians. "Hey, Colt, what do we have here?" Then he noticed Kate and Lainey in the corner. "Oh, boy! Don't tell me the Garcia girls are playing Nancy Drew again."

Colt ignored the ME and looked first at Kate and then Lainey. "I'm not finished with you two. Meet me at the station in an hour, and we'll continue this *conversation*." The last word was said with more sarcasm than Kate had ever heard out of Colt's mouth.

"Do you need me to drive them, Colt?" Danny asked. "You can stay with Doc, and I'll come back to pick you up." He glanced toward Kate, and for a second she thought she saw the corners of his lips tip into the beginning of a smile before he reverted back to cop face.

"They got here on their own. They can find their way to the station by themselves."

Quickly, Lainey grabbed Kate's arm and led her to the door. Neither said a word until they were in the car on the way to the police station, each deep into their own thoughts.

Kate was the first to break the silence. "Hopefully, Maddy will be waiting and can coach us about what to say and what not to say." She blew out a long breath. "I can't remember when I've ever seen Colt this mad."

"We have nothing to worry about," Lainey said as she picked up the take-out boxes from the floor of the front seat. "Colt tries hard, but he doesn't scare me."

This brought a smirk to Kate's face. "Yeah, you have leverage. You give the man orgasms. I can't even offer him a free Pap smear."

Lainey's eyes lit up with amusement. "Yeah, you're right. You got nothing." She pointed ahead. "Okay, to be honest, I said I wasn't afraid, but the truth is, he's going to be a challenge. It wouldn't hurt to face him all caffeined up with Ruby's bread pudding in our bellies. Pull into the Starbucks's on the right, Kate. We've got a few minutes, and I promised you a Carmel Macchiato."

*****

Ryan Kowalski drove into the underground parking below his high-rise condo. After sliding the new Ferrari 458 Spider into his slot, he sat there for a few minutes, enjoying the smell of the new leather seats. All his life he'd been fascinated with sports cars, and now that he could afford one, he hadn't wasted any time indulging in his dream model.

Rubbing his hand over the dashboard, he chuckled to himself, remembering the look on the salesman's face when he'd whipped out his checkbook and paid cash for the car. It had almost made up for all those years when there was never enough money for anything but the basics. Growing up in Abilene after his mother had passed away from liver cancer, he'd always had to watch his friends going to school wearing the latest fashions while he'd had to be content with worn-out jeans and over-washed t-shirts. He remembered how embarrassed he'd been pulling into the school lot and parking his rusted-out Ford pickup next to all the new Jeeps and shiny Ford F-10s. He knew he should have been grateful to even have his own vehicle. His old man had taken the truck in trade for dental work done on the young daughter of the

Mexican janitor who cleaned his office at night. But it had been hard seeing the pity on the faces of his classmates when he'd walk across the lot.

His dad had tried hard to raise him by himself, but he'd always been the king of frugality. Although he'd owned the strip mall that housed his dental practice, there never seemed to be enough money for anything fun, even though there was always an abundance of occupants paying rent. Fighting his mom's cancer had taken a financial toll on the family and had left little for anything but necessities. For as long as Ryan could remember, his father had made them live as cheaply as they could until the medical bills were finally paid off. But even after they were debt-free, his dad continued hoarding money. The irony of all this was that all that time he'd been "saving for a rainy day," a lung cancer diagnosis two years ago had wiped out any chance of his father ever enjoying his small stash.

Ryan sighed, thinking that was never going to happen to him. He'd left that life behind him and now had a thriving dental practice here in Vineyard with his college roommate and best friend. Money may not make you happy, but it sure made life easier and more fun, especially now that his bank account allowed him to do all the things he'd dreamed of but could never do as a kid.

He got out of the car, glancing back once more to admire his latest toy on his way to the elevator. He'd known the minute he'd walked into the Ferrari dealership and spied the cherry red Spider that it definitely was coming home with him. He hadn't even tried to talk the salesman down. The red

Ferrari was a far cry from his old pickup and was definitely a chick magnet. He'd realized that as he watched the transition in the attractive receptionist's attitude toward him after he'd signed the contract. She'd even slipped him her phone number on his way out.

Oh yeah! He was about to enjoy life to its fullest.

He smiled to himself, thinking that the adorable Kate Garcia wouldn't be able to resist him when he showed her his new car. He'd been attracted to her the second he'd laid eyes on her at the Mission and thought it might be the start of a beautiful relationship when she accepted his offer of dinner. But he'd seen the way she'd looked at Danny Landers that night at Emilio's, and although the cop had brought Miranda Walters with him, it was obvious his attention had been focused on Kate. Hopefully, the new car would make her forget her cop friend in a hurry.

Thinking about Miranda, he frowned. The two of them had been an item when he'd first moved to Vineyard and was settling into his condo. Her condo was several floors up from his, and he'd run into her at the elevator one afternoon. Up to that point, he'd been concentrating so hard on building a career that he hadn't had much time for a social life and was painfully rusty in his dealings with women. So it surprised him when she'd flirted outrageously with him. Sharing a drink later that night had led to breakfast in bed, and he'd gone back to his condo, positive he was going to love Vineyard.

His affair with the city's newest assistant district attorney had lasted about three weeks before she abruptly ended it without explanation. Truth be told, although he missed the wild sex, he was glad to be out of that relationship. The woman was just as aggressive in real life as she was in bed, and most of the time, he resented her for it. He'd spent his entire life not being in charge, and he didn't like that she'd brought out every buried feeling of inadequacy he'd thought he'd left behind in Abilene. But things always worked out the way they should, and it hadn't taken Miranda long to hook up with the good-looking cop who had to be six or seven years her junior like he was. She was a cougar in all aspects of her life, and although he was relieved to be out of her clutches, he pitied the poor felons who were unlucky enough to face her in a courtroom. He even felt a twinge of empathy for the young inexperienced cop who was probably so enchanted by her prowess under the sheets that he had no idea he was sleeping with a bonafide man-eater.

He stepped off the elevator on the seventh floor and walked to his condo at the end of the hall. He'd chosen this unit even before he had the money to afford it because of the great view of Lake Vineyard.

After walking in, he grabbed a beer and settled down in front of the TV to watch the Rangers game. How pathetic was it that a guy with a brand-new, three-hundred thousand dollar Ferrari parked in the garage was about to spend a Saturday night by his lonesome. Before he was able to get too caught up in his pity party, the phone rang.

He snatched it up without even bothering to check caller ID. "Hello."

"Ryan, this is Kate Garcia."

He couldn't help himself and instantly cheered-up. "Hey, Kate. What's up? I was just thinking about you."

"Hope they were good thoughts." There was a slight pause. "I know this is short notice, but my colleague has invited me to his house for dinner tonight, and I wondered if you'd like to come. Greg and his wife are great people."

"It just so happens that my plans tonight didn't pan out," he lied, hoping she didn't hear the desperation in his voice. "I'd love to meet your friends."

"Terrific. Dinner's at seven-thirty. Can you pick me up a little early so we can swing by the liquor store for a nice bottle of wine?"

"Sounds great. What's your address?" After jotting it down, he said goodbye and disconnected. Leaning back into the sofa, he was already planning how the night would end. It was a given that after one look at his new red toy, the lady doctor would definitely want to come back to his house to see the view of the lake from his bedroom window.

Chapter Thirteen

Kate hung up the phone and shoved it back into her purse. "It's official. I have an honest-to-God plus one for tonight."

Lainey turned her way. "Just like that?"

"Yep. I thought it was only fair to invite Ryan Kowalski since I left him stranded at the restaurant the first time I agreed to have dinner with him."

"He's pretty hot," Lainey remarked. "And I remember him being rather smooth."

"Oh, he's smooth, alright," Kate said. "I pegged him as trouble the minute I laid eyes on him last week at the Mission."

"So did you walk into the police station right now, suddenly get horny, and decide to give him a call? You knew about this dinner over a week ago. Why now?"

Kate glanced around and grinned. "If you remember, I mentioned to Danny that I had already invited Ryan to Greg and Cindy's when he asked if I wanted to have dinner with him and Miranda tonight. I felt like I had to just in case Danny checked."

"Hey, guys, I got here as quickly as I could. Had to leave Abby's soccer game with the score tied. You owe me."

Both Lainey and Kate turned as Maddy walked into the waiting area and motioned for them to follow her back to her desk.

"Kate asked Ryan Kowalski to be her plus one tonight for dinner," Lainey said, taking a seat in the chair directly across from Maddy's desk.

"Who?"

"Ryan Kowalski. He's the new dentist in town, and Kate's trying to make Danny Landers jealous."

"I am not," Kate fired back indignantly, before she bit her lip. "Okay, maybe a little, but I think it's a losing battle. That boy is no longer interested in me."

"I wouldn't be so sure if I were you." Lainey reached across the desk for the bottle of water Maddy offered. "He'd be blind not to have noticed the way you look at him."

They say love is blind, Tessa said, appearing out of nowhere and plopping down on the edge of the desk. **Lingerie sales generate over thirty-two billion dollars a year worldwide. Obviously, whoever said that has never been to Victoria's Secret the week before Valentine's Day.** She waved at Kate.

"Tessa's here," Kate said before looking impatiently at the clock at the wall. "Now, can we get to the part where you help us come up with a story to tell Colt, Maddy?"

The oldest Garcia sister rubbed her chin. "I thought about it all the way over here. Sometimes, it's best to tell the truth so you don't get caught up in the lie. Remember, Colt's a trained police officer and knows how to trip you up."

"Boy, that's for sure," Lainey said. "We both may need a lawyer before this is all over."

Don't use Prescott. The man's so crooked he'd spit out a corkscrew if he ever swallowed a nail.

Kate held back a grin. "Tessa wants to remind you not to use Charlie Prescott if it comes to that, Lainey. She's still mad because he tried to screw her over after she died."

Damn straight. He's part of the ninety-nine percent of lawyers who give the rest of them a bad name.

This time Kate couldn't help it and grinned. "Enough about lawyers. We're wasting time here." She glanced again at the clock.

Maddy took a sip of the water before handing it to Kate. "Okay, what have you already admitted to?"

Kate glanced toward Lainey before answering. "We may have let it slip that we were there to nose around and see if Perry had left anything behind that we might be able to use."

"Oh, God! It's worse than I thought." Maddy took a deep breath and blew it out. "You didn't tell him I gave you information, did you?"

"Of course not. We're not stupid, you know," Lainey said.

Maddy sent a disapproving look her way. "You're not? How smart was it to break into Ross Perry's room and find him dead, Lainey? And how did you get in there in the first place?"

"Don't go getting all judgmental on us, Maddy," Kate said, feeling like she was twelve again and had just been caught using her older sister's makeup. Maddy still had a way of seeing right through a lie. "Some of the things we all did to keep you out of jail might not have been smart, either."

"Sorry. You're right," Maddy said. "It's just that I worry about you two doing stupid things when I'm not with you." She raised her arms in defeat. "So how *did* you get into his room?"

"We told the housekeeper I was Perry's wife," Lainey said. "After we realized he was dead, there was no other choice but to call and report it." She paused and waited for Maddy's reaction, but her older sister only shook her head. "We looked for his phone so that we could call Kate's and then say the cop had asked her to come over to discuss something."

Maddy's shook her head. "Probably wouldn't have worked since it would have been so close to when you discovered the body—not to mention the ME might have pegged the time of death before the call was made which would only have you in trouble for tampering with evidence and interfering in a police investigation." She shrugged. "But it would have taken a day or so for the ME to pinpoint the time of death so that Colt could compare it to Perry's phone records."

"Yeah, I thought about that. But we were desperate and even a few days would have helped calm him down." Kate leaned closer to the desk and lowered her voice. "Perry was high on drugs and alcohol. Isn't it possible that I noticed something was wrong? Then when he didn't answer the door, we convinced the maid to let us in."

Yeah. That would work if you hadn't already told Colt you were there because you'd questioned that homeless guy's sister earlier and found out Perry had paid her a visit that morning. Tessa lifted herself from the edge of the desk and walked around to stand behind Maddy.

"Oh crap!"

"What?" Maddy asked.

"Tessa just reminded me that I've already admitted the real reason we were there. Colt might—"

"Colt might what?"

They all jumped as the sheriff suddenly appeared behind them. Kate cringed even though his angry eyes were focused on Maddy. "So, I guess your sisters called you to help them get out of this mess. Is that right?"

Maddy shrugged. "Wouldn't you call me if you were in trouble, Colt?"

He slammed his hand on the desk, spilling what was left of the bottle of water. "That's not the point here, Maddy. What matters is that your two younger sisters could've walked in on a drug-crazed man with a gun."

"Three younger sisters," Kate blurted, unable to look up at what she knew was probably a glare meant to kill.

"Deena was there, too?"

She shook her head and waited for this to sink in.

"Oh dear God! Are you telling me Tessa is back? When is that woman going to stay dead?" He threw his hands in the air in a gesture of surrender.

"Sheriff, I have the district attorney on the line. Says he needs to speak to you about a man he sent to prison last month," Jeannie called from her desk.

He acknowledged his secretary before making a sweep of the sisters with menacing eyes. "Don't any of you move. I'll be right back."

As soon as he was in his office, Kate turned to Maddy. "That went well," she said sarcastically.

"What went well?" Much like his boss had done only moments before, Danny Landers appeared out of nowhere.

"My sisters were just trying to explain to Colt why they were in Ross Perry's room," Maddy explained.

"Good luck with that. The man is majorly pissed because you girls are interfering in another one of his investigations." He did an eye roll. "I don't think I've ever seen him this angry. I'd back off if I were you."

"We can't just let Benny take the heat without trying to help," Kate said. "Seems like both Colt and your friend Miranda are hell-bent on sending him to jail for a crime he didn't commit."

"No one's railroading him, Kate. Even you have to admit that the evidence is pretty compelling for at least checking him out as a person of interest." Danny paused and glanced toward Colt's office before leaning down to whisper in Kate's ear. "Miranda gets back from Laredo in the morning. I'll try to get a feel for how determined she is about pressing charges against Benny."

"In the morning? I thought you said Miranda was coming home tonight," Kate said, thinking she may have jumped the gun and asked Ryan Kowalski out for nothing. Having him as her plus one didn't seem to matter as much now that Danny wouldn't be on a date with the assistant district attorney.

"She was, but she wanted to spend an extra day with her friends." He straightened up. "So that means I'm available for dinner, and tonight's special at Emilio's is chicken scampi, your second favorite Italian dish."

Kate tried hard not to smile, but the absurd look on his face was too much. It was like they were kids again and he was trying to convince her to catch frogs with him in the mud down by the lake—something she only had to do once to know that she never wanted to do it again.

"Well, what do you say?"

How she wished she could rewind the day and delete the call she had just made to Ryan. Taking Danny to Greg's house—not as a plus one but as a friend—would be way more fun, even if there was no romance involved. She knew Greg and Danny would hit it off immediately since they both had the same screwed-up sense of humor.

"Can't," she finally said after her good manners overruled her calling Ryan and canceling. "I've got that dinner at Greg and Cyndi's. Remember?"

His face registered disappointment, and for a minute, Kate was tempted to change her mind.

"Forgot about that," he said softly. "Maybe next time." He looked up just as Colt walked out of his office and headed their way.

"Come on, Danny. We've got to get a search warrant." He pointed his finger at Lainey and Kate. "Go home, you two. I'll deal with you later."

Behind Colt's back, Danny gave the sisters a half grin and a finger salute before following his boss out the door.

"I wonder what that's about," Lainey commented, her eyes still focused on the door as if the answer would somehow materialize.

Maddy was already on her feet. "Let me ask Jeannie. She'll know who Colt was taking to a minute ago."

She made her way over to the secretary's desk and bent down. She was too far away for Kate to hear what was being said, but there was no doubt that whatever Jeannie told her had not made her happy. They watched her walk back to her desk, anxious about what she had learned.

"Colt and Danny are on their way over to the courthouse to get a search warrant for both the Mission and Benny's house again. Then they're bringing him back in for more questions about the possible murder of Emily Ruiz Santiago."

"Murder? The woman died of a cheese heroin overdose," Kate said, squinting her eyes in confusion.

"That's true, but there's new evidence that suggests Benny might have been there when she overdosed. If they can prove he was the one who gave her the drugs, then he's responsible for her death."

"What new evidence?"

"Colt was talking to Doc Lowell on the phone. They found Benny's DNA on the edge of Emily's blouse."

"What? Benny was Emily's friend—probably her best friend. It stands to reason his DNA might have rubbed off on her blouse when he dealt with her. If she was high on heroine, he may have had to restrain her," Kate said. "And how do they even know it was Benny's?"

"His DNA is on file from when he was in jail after he got back from Afghanistan," Maddy said. "You can't argue with lab results, Kate. You should know that."

"There are a lot of reasons why his DNA might be on her clothes. Maybe she—"

"The DNA came from a sperm sample." Maddy's eyes turned empathetic. "I'm sorry, honey. I know you love the man like a brother, but now you have to let Colt do his job. If Benny is innocent, he'll be cleared. Jeannie said Colt's asked her to get the security tapes from all the businesses in the Square. Hopefully, they'll show Emily walking into the woods alone or better yet, injecting the lethal heroin herself.

"The sooner the better," Lainey said. "No way Benny was carrying on with that homeless woman. He loves his wife and daughters."

Kate blocked out the conversation between her sisters as soon as Maddy mentioned the security tapes Colt had requested. She was sure at least one of them would show Benny supporting the upper half of Emily's body into the wooded area behind the Square.

She wondered how long it would take after that for her brother-in-law to figure out that she was the one holding up the other end of the body.

Chapter Fourteen

Kate glanced one last time in the mirror before she walked to the door, making a decision that when she found some time, she'd look into a shorter, easier to manage hairdo. The current below-the-shoulders style was getting boring, although it was nice to be able to pull it back into a ponytail and throw on a Cowboys ball cap. Fortunately, she and her sisters had all inherited Sylvia Garcia's thick, dark hair with just enough curl to be manageable. But it was time for a change. She made a mental note to squeeze in a trip to her favorite hairstylist on her next Thursday off.

Fluffing the back of her hair one last time, she opened the door and was surprised to see Ryan Kowalski standing there with a dozen yellow roses in one hand and a bottle of wine in the other. As his eyes moved up and down her body, she wondered what had possessed her to choose the same red silk blouse she'd worn the day she'd tricked Danny Landers into divulging important information concerning Maddy's murder charge a year ago. After Lainey had mentioned that Danny was still crushing on her after all those years, she'd been chosen to distract him long enough for them to gather the information they needed to keep their oldest sister out of jail.

Danny pretty much had the same reaction to seeing her out of her usual scrubs and loose fitting sweaters that Ryan was having right now.

No one could argue that the man standing there with roses in his hand wasn't smooth, and that alone sent all kinds of red flags waving in her brain. She wasn't ready to dive into another relationship just yet. She still needed time to find out if her growing feelings for Danny Landers were more than friendship or just jealousy because she couldn't have him now. And Miranda Walters did.

So why was she wearing something she knew showed off her assets?

When he finished surveying her body, he said, "You should never wear scrubs again."

Dressed in khaki colored slacks and a light blue shirt that brought out the color in his eyes, Ryan looked absolutely adorable, and Kate had to remind herself again to proceed with caution.

"Are you going to ask me in, or do I stand out here all night?"

"Oh, sorry." She opened the door wider and made a sweeping motion with her arm. "Forgot my manners for a minute."

He walked past, then turned to hand her the roses. "A little birdie told me these were your favorite."

She took the roses from him, wondering who that little birdie was. "You didn't have to do that, Ryan, but they're gorgeous. Thank you. And yes, I do love yellow roses." She pointed to the sofa. "Is that wine for Greg and Cyndi, or do you want to open it now?"

"It's for dinner tonight. I did a little digging and found out this is a specialty of Spirits of Texas."

Kate reached for the bottle and read the label. "Voignier. This was my sister Tessa's legacy. She imported grapes from Southern California and wowed the Texas wine drinkers with it. Lainey runs the winery now and makes a handsome profit on this brand." She paused and narrowed her eyes. "First the roses, now the wine. You're scoring major first impression points here, Kowalski. Should I be getting nervous?"

His eyes turned mischievous. "I'm glad to hear that my efforts are working, and yes, you should be a little cautious. After seeing you in that outfit, my intentions might not be as honorable as when I first knocked on the door." He sat down without taking his eyes off her. "You really are gorgeous, you know."

She made a face. She was beginning to feel like a school girl on her first date and decided to use humor to keep from blushing. "You probably say that to all the girls. Bet you'll be checking out my teeth next."

He grinned up at her. "Already have. You passed with flying colors."

She sat down on the sofa beside him. "I've had the same dentist since I was a teenager. He'll be glad to know you approve."

She decided to maneuver the conversation away from her since she was sure her face was a little flushed after all the compliments. Her last relationship had ended several months before, and she hadn't gone on a real date since, unless you counted all the bozos that were setups from well-meaning friends and family. And her semi-serious relationship with the neurosurgeon hadn't prepared her for all this attention since he was more interested in himself and how wonderful he was than anything else.

"Since we don't have to stop at the liquor store for a bottle of wine now, do you want me to fix you a drink before we go?"

He shook his head, then stood. "I have a new toy outside and can't wait for you to see it."

She jumped up and grabbed her purse from the table. "Lead the way. I love surprises."

The minute she saw his "new toy," her eyes widened. "Oh my God! Is that a Ferrari?"

He tried to act nonchalant, but she could see he was as excited as a sixteen-year old getting the keys to his first car. Not that a teenager could afford a car like this, though. At least not any teenager she knew.

"I've wanted one of these since before I could drive," he explained, opening the door for her. When he was in the driver seat, he said, "We have about thirty minutes before we have to be at your friend's house. How about you show me what you love about Vineyard?"

She glanced up at the roof. "Does the top come down?"

"You're not worried about your hair?"

"Are you kidding me? I've never been in a Ferrari before. And this one is red. To hell with my hair."

His chest puffed out like a proud papa as he lowered the top and started the ignition. "What could be better than driving around town in my new car with the prettiest girl in Vineyard?" He pulled onto the main road. "Now show me why this city is going to turn out to be the best move I ever made."

Showing Ryan Vineyard Lake up close and some of the other fun things the city had to offer turned out to be more enjoyable than she'd anticipated. She couldn't remember when she'd laughed so much. By the time they pulled up in her coworker's driveway, it felt like she'd known him a lot longer than two weeks.

"That was fun," he said as he opened the door and waited for her to exit.

"Ah! Chivalry is not dead, I see," she said, playfully. After swinging her legs out, she found herself close enough to him to smell his citrusy aftershave, and she took a step backwards. "Seriously, I enjoyed giving you the tour of Vineyard, especially with everyone gawking at us in this fabulous car."

He reached behind her and shut the door. "They say money doesn't buy happiness, but I, for one, can tell you, it sure beats the heck out of riding around in an old Honda." When her face fell, he laughed out loud. "Just kidding. I couldn't resist. Your Honda is great." He led her up the steps to the porch. "So, how will you introduce me to your friends?"

"As my chauffeur," she kidded, playfully punching his upper arm. "That was for the Honda remark."

"Touché!"

Once inside and introductions made, Greg and Ryan hit it off immediately as both of them were huge baseball fans. Time seemed to fly by, and before she knew it, they were through eating and settling down in the living room for an after dinner cocktail.

Before sitting down himself, Greg refilled their glasses. "Well, I gotta say, Kowalski, you're definitely a step up from most of the guys Kate brings around."

"Shut up!" Kate said. "For all you know, he might be a serial killer."

"Or a bank robber," Greg deadpanned. "That's some kind of car you drove up in. One of these days you'll have to take me for a ride."

Ryan tried hard not to show how excited he was but couldn't resist. "I was lucky enough to come into some money recently, and I decided 'what the heck?' You can't take it with you."

"Boy, that's a fact," Greg said. "Look at that homeless woman who died with all that money."

Ryan took a sip of his drink before he turned to face Kate. "Yes, that same little birdie who told me you liked yellow roses also said you were about to come into money yourself, thanks to that woman. Maybe we can have matching Ferraris."

"Then you wouldn't be able to rag on me about my beat-up Honda," she teased before getting serious. "Most of Emily's money will go back into the Mission and the homeless community."

"What?" Greg leaned forward. "From what I hear, that woman had a boatload of cash. Surely, you'll be able to enjoy some of it."

The conversation was making Kate a little uncomfortable, and she tried to change the subject. "We'll see. Hey, Cindy, you outdid yourself with the Mexican lasagna tonight."

"Do you want the recipe?"

Greg nearly doubled over in laughter. "You're talking to Kate Garcia here, honey. Her idea of a home-cooked meal is going into a home and eating food that someone else cooked. She wouldn't have a clue what poblano peppers are."

"Speak for yourself, dip wad. Of course I know what poblano peppers are. I'm Hispanic. Remember?" She bit her lip to hide a grin. "Unfortunately, I have no idea how to cook them."

Everyone laughed as Cindy refilled their drinks once again. Kate watched her interact with Ryan and decided it was fun letting her hair down once in a while. But she was getting a little tipsy, and if she wasn't careful, she might be tempted to find out what Ryan's less-than-honorable intentions were.

When the doorbell rang, everyone turned that way and waited silently until Greg led Danny Landers into the living room. Kate couldn't help herself and smiled at him, but his steeled expression never changed.

"I'm sorry to barge in like this, folks, but I need to talk to Kate." He made eye contact with her before glancing at Ryan. "How's it going?"

"What do you need to speak to me about, Danny?" Kate asked, but she really didn't want to hear his response. She could tell by the look on his face that whatever it was, it would no doubt ruin what so far had been a perfectly good evening.

He held her gaze for a moment before speaking. "Colt needs to talk to you."

"Now? Danny, I'm on a date."

"I know, but this can't wait." He focused his attention back on Ryan. "Sorry, man. I always seem to interrupt you two."

"What's this about?" Ryan asked.

Danny took a deep breath. "I'm not at liberty to say right now. I can tell you that maybe with a little luck, this won't take long, and I can bring her back for a late night drink."

"Is this about the surveillance tapes?" Kate implored him with her eyes to say no, but she knew even before he nodded that he was not going to tell her what she wanted to hear.

Her stomach twisted as she realized she was about to face her brother-in-law and would have to come clean. Colt was a by-the-book cop and wouldn't cut her any slack because she was family. She respected him for that. Leaning over, she kissed Ryan on the cheek. "I'll make it up to you. I promise."

He nodded as she stood and said her goodbyes to her hosts, then she headed out the door with Danny. Turning back, she waved one last time, knowing that she wouldn't be coming back there for any late night drinks. As the door closed behind her, she tried to prepare herself for Colt's questions and wondered if Benny was already down at the station.

Climbing into the police cruiser, she looked around for her sister Tessa, but she was nowhere to be found. For the first time, she understood why her sister had been sent back and talked to only her. She was the one in trouble.

Chapter Fifteen

Neither one said a word until they were almost to the police station and Danny turned to her. "You know Colt's going to come at you with some pretty tough questions, Kate. If I were you, I'd be honest with him because eventually, he'll find out the truth, anyway."

She nodded without looking his way. "Is Benny already there?"

"Flanagan and Rogers picked him up about an hour ago," he replied. "Colt's got him in an interview room now."

"Will I be allowed to be in there with him?"

"You know that's not the way it works." He pulled the cruiser into a parking slot up close to the front door of the station, and then faced her. "I shouldn't be telling you this, but if you get uncomfortable with the questions, say you want a lawyer. There's one in Colleyville who's as arrogant as they come. Although Colt hates it when this guy is defending one of our suspects, the main reason he dreads seeing him in the courtroom is that the man is good and usually gets his clients off on one technicality or another."

"You think I need a lawyer?" He saw her close her eyes for a second as if she was finally beginning to realize how much trouble she was in. "I didn't do anything wrong, Danny."

He cut the engine and stepped out of the car before walking around to her side to let her out. Watching her face, now twisted with worry as she slid out, nearly killed him. It was all he could do not to take her into his arms and promise her that everything would be okay, just like he used to do when things didn't go right for her.

But he knew he couldn't. She was in over her head now, and there wasn't a damn thing he could do about it.

He opened the door and followed her into the station, stopping to check in with Jeannie. Then he guided her to the chair next to his desk and motioned for her to sit down. With a heavy heart, he pulled out the preliminary paperwork required on all incoming police suspects.

Kate—an incoming police suspect? *God!* He hated his job sometimes.

Halfway through the paperwork, Colt appeared and nailed his sister-in-law with a killer glare. "Have you Mirandized her yet?" he asked, still looking at Kate.

"Is that really necessary?" Danny asked, wrinkling his brow. "She's just here to answer a few questions."

Colt shot him a look before focusing back on her. "I think she's a little more than a suspect at this time, Danny. So yes, read Kate her rights." He started to leave, then turned around. "When you're finished with all that, come back to the interrogation room to sit in with me when I interview Benny. Jeannie can keep her eye on this one." Then with a softer voice, he said, "Kate, do you want something to drink? Coke? Water?"

She shook her head. Danny had never seen her this scared before, and he had to bite his lower lip to keep from grabbing her and taking her far away from all this. But he was a cop with a job to do. And right now, she had to be treated like any other person of interest being questioned about an ongoing case.

Her expression never changed the entire time he recited the Miranda spiel. When he was finished, he opened his desk drawer and pulled out a form. "You'll need to sign this, Kate. It's stating that I read you your rights." He shoved it toward her, then got up and walked over to Jeannie's desk. Before returning to Kate, he retrieved a bottle of water from the breakroom and gave it to her, along with the slip of paper with the name and number of the defense lawyer from Colleyville. "Your mouth will get really dry in there," he said before leaning down to whisper in her ear. "Don't get freaked out by all this. Colt does that Miranda thing with everyone. Thinks it intimidates them."

It took every bit of willpower to walk away from her, but he did. On the way to the interview room, he called Maddy to let her know Kate was at the station. Out of the corner of his eye, he could see Jeannie on her way over to keep Kate company until Maddy could get to the station to be there for her sister, just as he'd asked her to do.

He walked into the interrogation room in time to hear Colt read Benny his rights. Both of them looked up.

Benny Yates, who stood about six-three tall and weighed well over two hundred and fifty pounds, was sitting across the table from Colt. Beads of sweat were visible on his forehead, and he was tapping nervously on the desk with two fingers. Despite his size he looked less like the former marine he was and more like a man who knew his life was about to change big time.

"So, Benny, let's get right to the point and not waste time with small talk," Colt began. "Why were you carrying Emily Ruiz Santiago's body into the woods the night she died?"

Benny shifted uncomfortably in the chair. "Who said I was, Sheriff?"

Colt opened the folder in front of him and pulled out a photo. "Security cameras from two of the restaurants on the Square." He slid the picture across the desk.

Benny stared at it before meeting Colt's glare. "It's not what it looks like."

"Oh really! How about you telling me what other explanation there could be for you and my sister-in-law to be carrying either a dead or comatose woman into the woods and dumping her there."

"Leave Kate out of this. She only came to help after I called her."

"Help with what, Benny? Help you hide the body after you assisted Emily in getting high on a little too much heroin?"

Benny shot up from the chair, and both Colt and Danny lurched forward. Danny reached him first and shoved him back into the chair. "Behavior like this will get you leg chains and cuffs, Mr. Yates. I'd suggest you sit back and relax and answer the questions truthfully. Otherwise, it's going to be a long night."

Benny took a deep breath. "Do I need a lawyer, Colt?"

"That's up to you, Benny, but right now, we're only trying to get the facts. Once you call a lawyer, we can't help you." Colt put his hands behind his head and leaned back in the chair. "Your call."

Benny lowered his head into his hands for a moment before he straightened up and made eye contact with Colt. "I've always known you to be a decent man. I know I didn't do anything wrong. So, for now, no lawyer." He took a sip of the water in front of him. "I'm sorry. Normally, I'm not a violent man, but that last remark was too much. I cared for Emily and was working to get her off drugs. There's no way I would ever help her get high."

"Were you having an affair with her?" Colt asked.

"Hell no! She was like a sister to me. I was only trying to talk her into giving up her life on the street and getting some help."

"Did that include having sex with her?" Danny asked.

Benny glanced quickly at Colt before focusing back on Danny. "I never had sex with her."

Colt opened the folder in front of him again, pulled out a piece of paper, and slid it across the table in one swift movement. "This lab report says differently."

Benny leaned forward, picked it up, and read it, then slumped back into the chair. "Again, it's not what you think, Colt." His voice was pleading with them to believe him.

"I've known you a long time, Benny. I don't want to believe the worst, but I only know what the evidence shows. It would go a long way with the DA's office if you'd quit lying and tell us the truth here. Maybe then I can help you."

Benny lowered his head and nodded. "Emily came to the Mission late that night when she saw the light on. I'd had a big blow-up with Wendy about spending my own money on the place, and I went down there to unpack the supplies that had arrived earlier that day—and to calm down a little." He paused to take a sip from the bottle of water in front of him. "Anyway, she was crying because her last john had robbed her at gunpoint and made off with all her money after she'd serviced him. This was so soon after the beating she'd taken the week before, and she was frantic. I tried to comfort her, and the next thing I knew, she was all over me with her hands and her mouth." He choked back a sob. "God help me! I wanted to stop her, but it felt so good, and before I knew it, it was over. Afterward, I pushed her away, and she ran into the bathroom. All I could think about was how I was going to explain this to my wife."

"Does Wendy know?"

He shook his head. "I waited for Emily to come out so I could go home and try to make it right. After about thirty minutes, I got a little worried and went into the bathroom to see if she was okay." He looked up again. "I swear to God, Colt. She was lying against the commode with a needle still in her arm and a whitish foam coming out of her mouth. It was the most grotesque thing I've ever seen."

"Why didn't you call 911?" Colt asked.

Benny shook his head. "I don't know. When I felt no pulse I figured she was already dead, and I guess I was still feeling guilty because of the oral sex. So, I called Kate instead."

"What did you think Kate could do for a dead woman?" Danny asked, unable to keep the anger out of his voice. If this man hadn't involved her, she wouldn't be sitting out there right now waiting to be interrogated herself.

"Emily trusted Kate. I thought if there was the slightest chance she could somehow help her, I had to try." He swiped at a tear that had escaped the corner of his eye and was making a slow path down his cheek. "But Kate only confirmed what I already knew."

"Why didn't you just call the station and let us deal with the body?" Colt's tone had softened a little.

Benny took another drink of the water. "That was purely selfish, Sheriff. The Chamber of Commerce has been trying to find a reason to close down the Mission ever since I opened. I knew if they found out someone had overdosed on the premises, it would be just what they needed to shut me down. I figured Emily was already dead. What was the harm in moving her someplace away from the Mission? I chose the woods behind the Square because I knew it wouldn't take long for someone to find the body."

"And Kate agreed to that?" Danny asked, still angry at the man for asking Kate to break the law with him.

Benny nodded. "Not at first. She wanted to call you, Sheriff. Said you'd know how to fix it so that nothing bad resulted from it. But I was sure we'd be forced to close our doors to the homeless and talked her into helping me with the body. It took a lot of persuading, but I finally convinced her that my plan was the best way. There was nothing more we could do for Emily, and I figured we weren't doing anything that horrible."

"Horrible, no, but moving a dead body is a felony, not to mention the much more serious charge of obstruction of justice."

Bennie's eyes widened. "This is all on me, Sheriff. Tell me what I have to do to keep Kate from being charged."

Colt stood up. "I'm afraid that's not possible, Benny. When you picked up the phone and got her involved and she agreed to help you move Emily's body into the woods, she left herself wide open to the same charges as you."

Benny's eyes filled with tears. "I think I want that lawyer now."

*****

Wish there was something I could do to make this all go away for you, Katie, Tessa said, suddenly appearing out of nowhere.

Kate stole a glance at Jeannie to see if she was reacting to the ghost, but the receptionist's expression never changed. She gave her sister a nod to acknowledge her presence.

They all looked up when Benny walked out of the interrogation room, followed by Danny and Colt. Shoulders slumped, Benny looked beaten. Despite his attempt to smile at her, he wasn't able to pull it off.

Before Colt could stop him, he rushed to her side. "I'm so sorry, Kate. I told them this is all on me."

"Benny!" Colt shouted. "Right now, I haven't booked you on anything, but that may change if you say another word to her. I can't have you conversing with Kate until I can get her statement and compare it to yours." He motioned for Flanagan to take Benny to another interrogation room.

Wow! Colt's really playing the bad cop here. This is more serious than I thought, Tessa said. **It's all becoming very clear to me now. Although Benny could use his own personal guardian angel right about now, you're the one in trouble, Kate. We may have to call for a sister get-together and regroup.**

Just then the front door swung open and Maddy rushed into the station. "I came as soon as I heard." She was breathing as if she'd just run a marathon. "What's going on, Colt? Why is Kate here?"

"Calm down, Maddy. We're only going to ask your sister a few questions to see—"

"Is she in trouble?"

"Depends on how she answers the questions."

"Does she need a lawyer?" Maddy walked behind Kate and put her hands on her shoulders protectively. "Because I can have that guy from Colleyville over here in thirty minutes." She bent down and kissed Kate on the top of the head. "Just say the word, honey."

Kate reached up and patted her sister's hand. "I'm good for now, Maddy, but I'll let you know when to make that call."

At the mention of the lawyer whose name and number were on the slip of paper in her pocket, Colt's face went from annoyed to irritated in a nanosecond. Maybe Danny was right. Maybe she shouldn't go into the interrogation room without legal help in case she said something that might incriminate her.

Colt inhaled and blew out the breath slowly. Then his expression softened. "That's not necessary. We just need to hear her version of the story to see if it corresponds with what Benny said."

"What story?"

Again, annoyance danced across his face, but to his credit, he kept his cool. "Flanagan can fill you in. Right now, Danny and I need to take Kate back and ask her a few questions."

"I'm going with her," Maddy said, defiantly.

Colt shook his head. "You know that's not going to happen. Because she's your sister, you're officially off this investigation."

"You're her brother-in-law. Shouldn't you be removed from the investigation, too?"

"Would you rather have the state police grilling her?" He looked away as if he was searching for exactly the right words. Then his facial expression softened. "I promise we'll take good care of her. We just need to get our facts straight." He pointed to his office. "You can watch the whole interview on my computer in there."

"Okay, but the minute I think your questions are leaning toward tricking her into saying something she shouldn't, I'm calling that lawyer."

"I wouldn't have it any other way, Maddy." Colt turned to Kate. "Ready?"

Kate stood and followed him back to the interrogation room. She'd been in this room many times when she'd come to the station and needed to talk to Maddy privately, but it was not the same as she remembered. Housing only a table with two chairs on both sides, it now looked stark and bare— and for some reason, desperate. And when had they painted the walls a dusty gray?

She took a few calming breaths to squelch the "fight or flight" reflex invading her body. Quickly, she glanced behind her and was relieved to see Tessa walking into the room beside Danny before he closed the door. Knowing that one of her siblings was with her, even if it was only the ghost of her dead sister, was comforting in an odd sort of way.

Settled in her chair, she took a sip of water. "What do you want to know, Colt?"

He leaned forward in his chair. "For starters, why don't you tell me about your relationship with Emily Ruiz Santiago."

"Emily was one of my pro bono patients. I only saw her occasionally and treated her a week before she died." She paused. "That's all on record from three months ago when I identified her body in the morgue."

"So you're saying that after that incident when she took a vicious beating from one of her customers, you never had further contact with her until the night Benny called you to help him move her body?"

Be careful how you answer him, Kate. He might be family, but right now he's looking to trip you up. Tessa said, now standing beside her sister.

"That's correct. She had a vaginal tear that required several stitches to repair, and I was worried about an infection. Nancy and I went down under the bridge on Bell Street one night to try to convince her to come back to the clinic for follow-up care, but we never found her. The next time I saw her was the night Benny called."

"Walk us through that," Danny said, softly. "Help us understand why you and Benny felt it was necessary to move the body in the first place."

Colt sent a glare his way. He was trying to prompt her on what to say, and she wanted to smile her gratitude but knew it would only get him in trouble with his boss. For the next twenty minutes, she recounted the events of that night, being careful not to say anything they could use against her in court if it came to that.

"Did Benny tell you he had sex with Emily before she died?" Colt asked when she was finished.

She suspected Colt had thrown that out to get a reaction from her, but she simply nodded, thankful that Maddy had already mentioned they had found Benny's semen on Emily's clothes.

"He told you?"

"I knew about it," she replied, careful not to divulge that the information had not come from Benny himself. She still couldn't believe that her friend had gone that far with Emily, but she had to trust that it had nothing to do with her death.

"And when you got to the Mission, Emily was already dead?"

She made eye contact with her brother-in-law. "Of course, she was, Colt. She was a junkie, and no matter how many times Benny and I tried to change that, she wasn't ready to give it up."

"Did Benny help her with the drugs?"

"Benny's a recovering addict himself. If he'd known that she'd gone to the bathroom to shoot up, he would've kicked her out right then and there, no matter how much he cared for her. He had a zero tolerance rule at the Mission."

"Are you aware that moving her body is a felony?"

She glanced first at Danny, then back to Colt. "Do I need that lawyer now?"

He shook his head. "Nobody's charging you with anything yet, Kate. I'm merely trying to let you know how serious this is."

"I know how serious it is," she fired back. "I also know how much the homeless people of Vineyard need the Mission. We were only trying—" She was interrupted when Jeannie walked in and hurried over to Colt.

"There's been a carjacking over at Save Right," the receptionist blurted. "Flanagan and Rogers are there now. Preliminary reports are that two men overpowered a woman loading groceries into the trunk, forced her into the back seat, then drove off with her car."

"Were you able to ID the vehicle?" Colt asked.

"It's registered to a Jerome Woodson, and we think the woman might be his wife, although we're can't be sure from the security tapes. Mr. Woodson is on his way over here now."

"Oh my God!" Kate said, before she could stop herself. She focused on Danny. "He's the dentist in practice with Ryan Kowalski over on Hamilton Avenue. I met the woman last week when I went there to talk to Ryan."

Colt ignored her and gathered up the file in front of him. "That's all for now, Kate. I don't think I have to tell you not to leave town. We may need to question you again."

She wanted to say something sarcastic like "just where do you think I'd go?" But all she could think about was the carjacking and the beautiful Hispanic woman she'd met at Ryan's office.

Silently she lowered her head and said a quick prayer for Ana Maria Woodson's safety.

Chapter Sixteen

Kate glanced up as Danny held the door open for her. His blue eyes staring into hers were mesmerizing, and she nearly tripped. "Am I really in trouble?"

"A little, but hopefully, nothing that will send you off in an orange jumpsuit." The worried look on his face said differently. "You're free to go, Kate. I'd give you a ride home or back to your dinner party, but I need to stay here and work on the carjacking."

"I'm bushed, and it's too late to go back to Greg's." She glanced up at him. "Maddy can take me home."

Maddy ran up as soon as she saw Kate emerge from the interrogation room. "You did good, kiddo." She pulled her close in a bear hug.

"Tessa thinks we need a sister meeting." She wiggled out of Maddy's embrace. "Can you get an hour or so off on Monday and meet up with us at Deena's house?"

"For sure. I'll bring subs, and Deena can make her awesome Margarita Swirls, even though I won't be able to drink with you guys," Maddy replied, guiding her over to her desk. "In the meantime I'll nose around and try to find out how far Colt is willing to go with this since I'm pretty sure your answers verified everything Benny told him."

"Do you think Benny's off the hook?"

"I never said that." Maddy did a quick scan of the police station, and when she was sure no one was close enough to overhear, she leaned in closer. "Guessing by the way Colt's demeanor changed toward the end of your interview, you must have said the same thing as Benny. Colt's missing means and motivation. I'd put money on him being convinced neither you nor Benny had anything to do with Emily's overdose."

Kate puffed out a breath. "That's a relief."

"But having said that, knowing Colt, there will be some sort of consequences for both of you to pay."

"What kind of consequences?"

Maddy shrugged. "Most likely, probation, community service, and maybe a fine. But that depends on whether the district attorney decides to come after you with the much more serious charge of obstructing justice. I've always known Colt to be a fair man, but you never know. Plus, we haven't seen Miranda Walters in action yet. Hope she hasn't noticed the way Danny looks at you, or you might be screwed."

"She wouldn't abuse her powers as the ADA, would she?" Kate wrinkled her nose and gave her sister a sideways glance. "You think Danny looks at me in a romantic way or just as an old friend?"

Maddy laughed. "You'd have to be blind to mistake that look for friendship. As for Colt, you never know. He's still pretty mad about finding you and Lainey in Ross Perry's room. He might press the issue just to teach you a lesson."

"I was hoping Lainey could smooth that over for us."

"Wouldn't it be nice if it were that easy? Colt doesn't—" Maddy paused as Jerome Woodson walked into the station.

Kate turned in that direction and met his gaze. When he got closer, she said, "It's horrible what happened to your wife, Jerome. Hopefully, the thugs will let her out somewhere unharmed and just make off with your car."

He glanced her way, and she noticed how calm he seemed to be. "That would be great," he said before scanning the station. "Where's the Sheriff?"

Maddy pointed to Colt's office where he and Danny were hunched over the computer, probably studying footage of the carjacking from the security tapes of the parking lot at the grocery store.

As Jerome walked away, Maddy turned to Kate. "Is it just me or did you think his response was weird? Most people would be frantic about now if someone they loved had been kidnapped."

"You think his wife was kidnapped?"

"Why else would they take her with them? All they had to do was grab her purse with the keys and make off with the car. Instead, they shoved her into the backseat, and one of the perps slid in beside her."

"Oh no! That does sound like it's more than just a carjacking." Kate glanced into Colt's office where Jerome Woodson had joined the two cops in front of the computer. Once again, she said a prayer for his wife's safe return.

*****

"Do you recognize either of these two men, Dr. Woodson?"

Jerome shook his head. "I've never seen them before in my life. Obviously, they saw an opportunity to steal a car and took it."

"Seems odd they'd pick a seven-year-old Camry when there was a brand new Lexus SUV sitting right next to it," Danny commented. "Looks like your wife was more of a target than her car."

Jerome leaned closer to the screen. "Why would anyone want to kidnap my wife?"

Colt turned to him. "That's what we're hoping to find out. Is there anyone who's been harassing her lately? Any threatening calls?"

"Not that I know of." Jerome kept his eyes on the computer. "She's only been in Texas for about six months and doesn't know many people."

"Where did she live before she moved to Texas?" Danny asked.

"Oklahoma."

"So, you've been married a short time." Danny was beginning to think that getting answers from this man was like pulling teeth. He bit his lip to keep from grinning when he realized his cliché was perfect for the dentist.

Jerome shifted from one foot to another, and if Danny was reading him right, seemed nervous. "I met her when she moved to Vineyard, and we were married two weeks later."

"And when was that?"

"I already told you. Six months ago yesterday."

Colt pulled up the video once again, and after watching it, turned to Jerome. "Your wife looks scared. Is there a possibility she knows her attackers?"

"It's possible, but like I said, Sheriff, we've only been married a short time. I really don't know all her friends."

Danny studied the man, who had moved around the desk and was no longer looking at the computer. Dressed in khaki slacks and a golf shirt with the dental clinic's logo on the pocket, Jerome Woodson stood about five-eight and looked to be a little underweight for his height. Wire-rimmed glasses magnified dark eyes that held no emotion. There was something about this guy that struck Danny as odd, but he couldn't say what. Maybe it was the fact that he sensed Woodson was holding something back.

Was it possible he was in some kind of trouble and his wife was snatched to persuade him to do something he'd refused to do? Or maybe he was just one of those guys who didn't display much emotion in public. "Is there something we should know about your wife that might give us some clue as to why someone would abduct her in the well-lit, parking lot of the grocery store?" he asked.

"Like what?"

Danny went right to the point. "Like maybe you and she are having problems with someone or with each other."

Woodson shook his head. "No problems. We're just ordinary newlyweds, Officer." He looked away from Danny and fixated on Colt. "I'm still not convinced this wasn't just a run-of-the-mill carjacking that Ana Maria was caught up in."

"That's certainly one of the theories, but we can't rule out the other," Colt said. "If it was just a routine carjacking, hopefully, they'll decide your wife's too much trouble and let her out on the side of the road somewhere."

"God, I hope so! If that's all, gentlemen, I'd like to go home in case she somehow finds her way to the house."

Colt glanced toward Danny before nodding. "We're done for now. One of my men will go with you in case you get a ransom call."

"I don't think that's necessary, Sheriff."

"Nonetheless, I'd feel better if one of my men was there with you." Colt picked up the phone and spoke to his secretary to arrange for Flanagan to escort Jerome to his home and to stay there in case a ransom call was made. After clicking off, he turned back to the dentist. "Rest assured, Dr. Woodson, we'll get to the bottom of this. I'm waiting now to hear back from the FBI to see what they can do to help us."

"The FBI? Why are they involved?"

"Kidnapping is a federal crime. Assuming whoever took your wife will transport her across state lines, the Bureau has access to data banks and investigative software that we aren't privy to." Colt waved Flanagan in and pointed to Woodson. "Take him into the interrogation room and have him take a look at the known gangbangers involved in car theft in Vineyard and the surrounding counties before following him home." Then he motioned to Danny. "Come with me."

When the door closed behind them, Colt turned to Danny. "Something's not right, and I want to have another look at the security tape before we let him leave. I have this gut feeling, but I don't know where it's coming from."

Danny nodded. They were definitely missing something, and until they found out what it was, a young woman's life was at stake.

*****

"Hello, Kate. Heard you might be in trouble."

Kate glanced up as Miranda Walters suddenly appeared at Maddy's desk. Dressed in a pair of jeans with holes in the knees and a halter top that definitely showed off her ample cleavage and flat stomach, the assistant district attorney looked like a college student just returning from a Saturday night sorority party.

"Hey, Miranda," Maddy said. "Glad you're here. Maybe you can shed some light on which way your office is leaning about Benny and my sister."

Miranda picked at her painted nail. "You know I can't discuss that with you, Maddy. But I will tell you this. Frank is getting ready to run for a new term and is looking for a case that will swing the votes his way."

Kate gasped. "He'd use me and Benny to get reelected?"

The assistant DA shrugged. "He's a politician, Kate. He'll use whatever he can to stay in office." She scanned the room. "Is Danny around?"

Maddy pointed to Colt's office. "He and Colt just finished talking to Jerome Woodson, and he went in there."

Her face dropped. "Woodson was here?"

"Still is. His wife's car was hijacked in the parking lot at Save Right. The thieves made off with the car and her. They're hoping Woodson recognizes the two men in the security footage."

"What do you need Danny for?" Kate asked before she could stop herself. She'd have to be careful and keep that inner green monster in check.

She had no claim over Danny Landers, and Miranda did. She'd have to find a way to be happy for him instead of trying to figure out how to get him to notice her. And right now she needed to remember that Danny's current love interest had the power to make her life miserable. Making a play for her beau could certainly have a detrimental effect on Miranda's decision to prosecute her and Benny.

"Nothing important," Miranda responded. "I got back into town earlier than I expected and wanted to see if he was available for a late night cocktail with me." She glanced toward Kate. "I'd also like to catch up with you over a drink. Are you available Monday night?"

"Isn't that a little unorthodox without her lawyer present?" Maddy asked, eyeing the ADA suspiciously.

"Relax," Miranda said with a grin. "This has nothing to do with her case. I just haven't had a chance to catch up with her since I moved back to Vineyard." She gave Maddy a playful punch in the arm. "I promise—no questions about Emily Ruiz Santiago." Turning back to Kate, she asked, "So, what about that drink on Monday?"

Kate nodded, thinking it might go a long way in getting a favorable outcome in her and Benny's felony charges. "I can get away as early as five-thirty."

"Perfect. I'll pick you up then."

Miranda walked toward Colt's office just as Jerome Woodson opened the door of the interrogation room and stepped out. For a second, his face registered surprise at seeing her before he reverted back to his old unemotional self. Kate knew Miranda had gone out with Ryan Kowalski a few months back. She couldn't possibly have had an affair with his partner as well. Could she?

*****

Rachel Alexander waited at the gate at DFW Airport, trying unsuccessfully to read the Wall Street Journal. Finally, after skimming over the same paragraph three times, she folded the newspaper and tucked it into her carry-on for later.

Hoping to convince her stepbrother to sign over his half of Alexander Pharmaceuticals to her in exchange for a generous payout, she'd come to Vineyard a little over a week ago. She chuckled to herself, thinking it hadn't taken long at all, and she hadn't even had to lay out one dime to gain control of the company her dad had left to both of them.

Ernie Jackson's untimely death had been the answer to her prayers. And even though she'd land at LaGuardia without a death certificate to finalize her total control of the company, the medical examiner had promised it would be forthcoming as soon as they could pinpoint a cause of death. The ME had mentioned the possibility of poison being the culprit the last time she'd spoken to him, and it was her understanding they were just waiting for toxicology results to come back to make it official.

But she didn't need a lab report to know what had killed her brother. The man climbed into dumpsters for his meals, for God's sake. Someone with a desire to see Ernie dead could have laced the thrown-out chicken fried rice with a little white powder. Wasn't that what the nut jobs of the world sent to high ranking politicians in envelopes? Anyone could find the stuff if they looked hard enough, even in a small town like Vineyard.

She smiled to herself. It had all been too easy, and now she was on her way back to New York to face the all-male Board of Directors. This time she wouldn't allow them to bully her or intimidate her. She refused to let them make her feel inferior because of her gender.

No, *this time*, they'd all find out who was in charge, and thanks to Ernie Jackson's death, she'd take no prisoners.

Chapter Seventeen

Gathered around Deena's dining room table on Monday morning, the Garcia girls took a break from formulating a plan to help Kate and Benny. Munching on the meatball subs Maddy had brought, along with the frozen margarita swirls from Deena's new margarita machine made thinking easier—and more fun.

Oh, how I wish I could have one of those swirls, Tessa said, plopping down in the chair across from Kate and staring at her sisters doing what they all did best—eating and drinking.

"I wish you could, too. And for the record, as much as I hate to say this, I really miss your sarcasm sometimes. I'm almost glad when one of us gets into trouble, and you show up to grace us with your potty mouth."

Tessa smiled. **That's the nicest thing I've heard you say about me in a while, Kate. Guess you'll just have to get into trouble more often.**

"What'd she say?" Lainey asked, before taking the last bite of her sub.

"She was touched that I called her a potty mouth," Kate wisecracked.

"Yeah, right!"

Kate gave a thumbs up to her sister's ghost before turning to her other siblings. "Okay, we've pretty much established that there's nothing else we can do except wait to see what the DA decides to charge Benny and me with. Maddy, can you tell me what I might be looking at?"

Maddy drained the last of her lemonade and held the glass out to Deena. After her sister refilled it, she took a quick sip. "Worst case scenario—the DA is really pissed and charges you with Tampering with Physical Evidence, arguing that you tampered with the syringe. That would make it a third degree felony which opens you up to prison time or a lengthy probation and a lifelong felony conviction after your name."

"There's no way Colt would let them put Kate behind bars," Lainey said, emphatically.

"He may not have a choice," Maddy explained. "If that's the direction the DA decides to go in, there's nothing your husband can do about it. And Miranda Walters told both Kate and me yesterday that Frank Dempsey's term as DA is almost up. Although she didn't come right out and say he'd be looking for ways to drive up votes in the election year, she implied that it was how the political game is played."

"You think he'd use this case for his own career advancement? Heavens, I need another drink." Deena reached for the pitcher of swirls. "Surely, there's a bigger case than this that can get him votes."

"This is Vineyard, Deena," Maddy said. "Right now tampering with evidence is at the top of the arrest warrant list. Nobody gets excited about a domestic call where some redneck gets a little too drunk and threatens to hit his buddy or a neighbor's dog is barking too loud." She shook her head. "We can always hope that someone robs the 7-Eleven on Main Street before charges are made in Kate's case."

"You've told us the worst case scenario, Maddy. The best case scenario?"

Maddy rubbed her chin. "Probably abusing a corpse." She thought for a moment. "They could also charge you with a misdemeanor instead of a felony for tampering with physical evidence."

"What would happen to me then?"

"A good attorney could probably get the DA to offer you a pretrial diversion."

"A what?"

Maddie had everyone's attention now. "Basically, Kate, you'd sign the equivalent of a contract that admits to the offense, and then you'd be put on unofficial probation."

"And that's it? I get no jail time?"

"Not if it's done right. They sometimes call this a pocket probation because the document is never filed—just put in somebody's pocket or file drawer somewhere. You'd have to report every month to the probation department, pay them sixty bucks each time, and do 120 hours of community service."

Kate's eyes lit up. "I can do all that. Where do I sign?"

"Not so fast, kiddo. The DA will usually offer it before any other legal paperwork is filed in this case, so he can save himself some time. But like all other probations, if you violate it in any way, it all goes bye-bye. Then you *will* do jail time."

"Maddy, I've never even had a speeding ticket. There's no way I would violate it."

"And that's precisely why you have a shot at getting it. Having never been in trouble with the law—unlike someone else we know and love—will go a long way toward leniency." She glanced around the table. "Where is Tessa, anyway?"

Tell Maddy I'm right here. Then let her know that while she was at home swooning over Robbie Castillo and not breaking any laws, I was having all the fun soaping car windows on Halloween and trespassing on old man Yeager's farm to make out with Tommy Weston.

"I totally forgot about you and Tommy Weston." Kate pointed to the chair between Lainey and Deena. "Tessa's right there and wants to remind you that she had fun earning that rap sheet, Maddy."

"I'll bet she did. I can't believe she's bringing up Tommy Weston. That kid was an absolute zero."

Tessa shrugged. **A zero whose father made a couple of million in the computer software business.**

"You always did go for the rich ones." Kate reached for one of the chocolate chip cookies Deena had placed on the table.

"Hey, you never did tell us about your date with Ryan the other night," Lainey said. "Was there a spark between you two?"

Kate tsked. "Maybe. He seems like a nice guy, and he did pick me up in a Ferrari Spider."

Oh God! I hate being dead, Tessa commented. **That's my all-time favorite car ever.** She paused and crinkled her eyes. **Did you know that the medium income for a dentist in a small town in Texas is about one-hundred-and seventy grand, not counting what they have to cough up for the overhead running an office. So how did this Ryan dude afford a two-hundred-and-fifty-thousand dollar car?"**

"I never asked, but he did mention that he'd come into some money recently." Kate narrowed her eyes at the ghost. "Since when did you become such an expert on a dentist's salary?"

Like any other female intent on having the finer things in life, I researched it when a good-looking dentist asked me out once. Since I was only interested in half-mil and above guys, the date never happened. She chuckled. **You know what they say, Katie. Men are like bank accounts. Without a lot of money, they don't generate much interest.**

"You are so shallow, Tessa." Kate repeated the conversation for her sisters, and they all had a good chuckle.

"Aren't you just a little curious how he got that money, Kate?" Deena asked.

"I'd be lying if I said I wasn't. I figured he either inherited it or earned it on some investment or another."

"Enough about your dentist friend. I need to get back to work before Colt blows a gasket," Maddy said.

"He has been a little irritable lately," Lainey commented.

I used to say he had PMS when he acted that way, Tessa said with a grin. **Piss and Moan Syndrome. It always pissed him off more, but he'd go out of his way not to moan around me anymore.**

Kate couldn't help it and laughed out loud. "Well, I, for one, have to be nice to him so that I can get one of those 'pocket probation' things." She gathered up her notes and shoved them into her purse. "I have to get back to work, too. We block out Monday afternoons for surgeries, and thankfully, there are none scheduled today. I'm not sure I could do a C-Section right now 'cause that one drink has me yearning for a nap."

"Isn't tonight the night you're having a drink with Miranda?" Maddy asked. When Kate nodded, she warned, "Don't let her get you talking about Emily. I have a feeling our newest ADA can be a tricky one."

"Trust me. I'm only going for the brownie points. Miranda has a lot of influence on how my case plays out." She made a zipping motion across her lips. "No Emily talk."

After saying her goodbyes, Kate piled into her car and headed for her office. On the way she couldn't quit thinking about all the things she and her sisters had discussed. Ryan Kowalski and his Ferrari Spider kept popping into her head. She had no idea a car like his cost that much money and wondered again, how he'd come up with the money to pay for it. Since she was never one to beat around the bush, she'd simply ask him the next time she saw him, even though she knew it was none of her business.

She pulled into her slot at the clinic and hopped out of her car. With a little luck, in a few hours she'd finish the paperwork piled high on her desk and could head home for that nap she so desperately craved.

*****

Danny Landers stared at the security footage of the carjacking. Even though the quality of the film wasn't the greatest, he could make out Jerome Woodson's wife very clearly as she exited Save Right and pushed the grocery cart to her car. Dressed in cutoffs and a halter top that showed off her petite figure, Ana Maria Woodson would definitely turn heads. Her long dark hair was pulled back into what his sisters would call a French braid, and when the camera caught her face, he could see that her eyes were dark and sensual.

There was no doubt about it. This woman was a knockout, and he couldn't help thinking that she was way out of Jerome Woodson's league. Mentally, Danny scolded himself for jumping to that conclusion so quickly, since normally, he wasn't the judgmental type. But most women who ended up as token wives were either married to rich or famous guys, or men with great personalities. To his knowledge, Woodson was none of the above. Still, it wasn't fair to brand her that way.

The entire carjacking from the time Ana Maria walked out of the grocery store to the time the abductors drove off with her in the car had taken approximately six minutes—not nearly long enough to leave many clues. He debated running through it one more time, but he'd already spent well over thirty minutes looking at it, and he still had to go over the interviews with both Benny and Kate before Colt returned from his meeting with the medical examiner.

The toxicology report from Ernie Jackson's autopsy had come back, and Colt had rushed to the morgue to discuss it with Mark Lowell. Danny had stayed behind to work on the carjacking, which he suspected was actually a kidnapping.

He gave in and played the footage one last time before moving on. This time, something caught his eye, and he paused for a better look. Leaning in closer to the computer, he zoomed in on Ana Maria's face just as the two men approached her.

What was it about her face that had caught his attention? He pulled out a magnifying lens from the drawer desk drawer and placed it against the computer screen.

And then he saw it. Even before the men were close enough to grab her, she made eye contact with one of them, and the look of terror that crossed her face was unmistakable. Danny tried to reason with himself that any single woman in that situation would be fearful if she saw two men approaching, but Ana Maria's expression wasn't just fearful. It was unadulterated terror.

The woman knew her abductors! He was as sure of that as he was that she'd been the intended target all along.

After picking up his cell phone to call Colt, he reconsidered and laid it back down, intending to do a little more research before telling his boss what he suspected. Maybe there was something in the woman's past that might give them some clue as to why anyone would want to snatch her.

He started with the marriage certificate between Jerome and Ana Maria, which was easy enough since they'd been married at the Vineyard County Court House. Nothing particularly unusual there. Jerome Woodson and Ana Maria Arroyo had been married by Judge Walter O'Brien six months earlier with Ryan Kowalski and an unknown woman as witnesses.

Disappointed that he hadn't picked up any new information from that, Danny decided to Google Jerome Woodson, only to find out that he'd graduated from dental school in Austin, spent a few years in Africa with Dentists International, and then had landed in Vineyard in practice with his college roommate a little over nine months ago.

Looking at Ryan Kowalski's name on the screen reminded him that this was Kate's new love interest, and he frowned. He'd known the minute he'd seen her in her office a few weeks back that he still had feelings for her. At the time he decided to let things play out, and if she ever gave him the slightest hint that she might also be interested in pursuing a relationship, he'd act on it.

But after seeing her so scared last night, he'd made a decision not to wait any longer. He planned to drive over to her house after work and tell her exactly how he felt—something he should have done a long time ago. He knew he stood a good chance of being rejected, just like when they were in high school, but she was worth that risk. Regardless of how she responded, it was time for him to end the relationship with Miranda Walters, anyway. It had been fun while it lasted, but both of them knew it would never be anything permanent. He found himself finding ways to avoid her and figured she was doing the same. She'd even mentioned that she was thinking about trying to get her old job back in Laredo.

He looked up as Jeannie tapped on his desk with her pencil.

"Anybody home or should I come back later?" she asked in a teasing voice. "I have no idea what you're thinking about, but your eyebrows are scrunched so low, I can hardly see your eyes. Whatever it is, it must be intense."

He waved her off, embarrassed that she'd caught him daydreaming. "What do you need, Jeannie?"

"Colt called. Said to be ready to head out when he gets back in about an hour. He's apparently got some new information about Ernie Jackson."

"Thanks." After she walked away, he continued to stare at the information on the screen, then switched gears and plugged Ana Maria Arroyo into the Google search bar.

Strangely enough, there were no photos of the woman, and only one article that had appeared in the *Tulsa Register*. It mentioned a lawsuit that had been settled out of court when she'd sued a prominent Oklahoma lawyer who had sexually abused her while she was in his foster care. Other than that, there was nothing.

He decided to play a hunch and checked to see if Ana Maria had ever been in trouble with the law. He was surprised when a page full of offenses appeared on the screen, mostly drug, petty theft, and prostitution charges.

He leaned back into the chair and rubbed his forehead, wondering how a woman who looked like Ana Maria Woodson could have been so addicted to drugs that she'd sold her body on the Tulsa streets for a quick fix.

He clicked onto her mug shot and immediately knew the answer to that question.

After printing the picture and the rap sheet, he grabbed them, then rushed past Jeannie's desk. "I've got to run out and check on something. Would you get ahold of Colt and tell him to call me immediately," he said. "There's been a major development in our carjacking case."

Chapter Eighteen

The parking lot at Vineyard Dental Clinic was nearly deserted when Danny pulled up, making him question whether he should've called first and asked Woodson to come down to the station instead. He'd been so excited when he'd seen the picture of Ana Maria Arroyo from the Tulsa police files that he hadn't even waited for Colt to return from his meeting with the ME and go with him.

He pulled into a spot next to the door and got out. Once inside, he walked over to the receptionist's desk where a slightly overweight, middle-aged woman was on the phone. She motioned with her hand that she was aware of him standing there, then raised one finger—a gesture he took to mean that she'd be with him in just a minute.

He glanced at the coffee machine in the corner, thinking a cup of java would taste really good right about now, but he wasn't looking forward to the strong, day-old coffee back at the station. He'd stop at Starbuck's on the way back to the office and pick one up. Maybe he'd even grab one for his boss.

When the receptionist finally disconnected, she looked up at him—and he would swear that she'd just batted her eyelashes at him—and asked, "What can I do for you, Detective?"

Detective? He wished. He didn't recognize this woman and figured she must be new to Vineyard. "I'm Officer Landers from the Vineyard Police Department, and I'd like to talk with Dr. Woodson if I could. Is he around?"

She nodded. "I'll let him know you're here."

"The parking lot's empty. Is this office closed today?"

The receptionist frowned. "Not normally, but there's a glitch in the interoffice computer program. We had to cancel all the afternoon appointments. You caught us right before we closed up shop." She picked up the phone, hit a button, and announced that he was there. When she looked up again, she said, "Dr. Woodson's in the conference room, but he'll be right with you. He said for you to wait in his office. It's the last one on the left." She pointed down the hallway before giving him another smile. "I'm Dale Yeager, and I'm new in town. I love meeting new people, especially when they're as handsome as you."

He couldn't think how to respond, so he simply nodded, thinking that women were getting braver every day. Quickly, he thanked her and opened the door to the inner hallway. Halfway to the office, he stopped to glance at a picture of both Woodson and Ryan Kowalski, surrounded by a group of African children. He knew from his Internet search that Woodson has served over there with an international traveling dental team, but he had no idea Kowalski had been there as well.

"Ryan and I probably saw twenty-five patients a day in Zimbabwe," Woodson said, coming up behind him unnoticed. "We'd be so exhausted at the end of the day, we didn't even want to stop and eat before we crashed in our cabins. I lost fifteen pounds in the month we were there." He stopped to sigh. "Unfortunately, it only took a few weeks of McDonalds and DiCarlo's Pizza, both of which we craved the entire time we were over there, to pack those pounds right back on."

"I totally get that," Danny remarked, thinking it had been too long since he'd had DiCarlo's Pizza. He glanced back at the picture. "From the smiles on these kids' faces, I'd say they loved you." Danny turned to Woodson with a grin. "I'm still terrified of going to my dentist, even when it's only to get my teeth cleaned."

"And I hate that we're perceived that way. But when you have so little like these Africans do, even something as simple as preventative dental care can seem like a treasure. Unfortunately, most of our time was spent trying to repair years of neglect." He nodded his head toward the room at the end of the hallway and then started that way. "Dale tells me you want to talk to me, Officer Landers. Have you brought some news about my wife?"

Danny followed him into the office and waited for him to sit behind his desk before settling in the chair across from him. "I'll get right to the point. I was following up on your wife's carjacking, and I saw something I hadn't noticed before."

The dentist's face paled. "And what was that, may I ask?"

"After a closer look at the exact moment when your wife actually saw the two men approaching, I got the impression that she knew them."

"And why would you think that?"

"Ana Maria took one look at the older of the two, and her face reflected an intense fear—like she knew her attacker and was terrified of him."

Woodson tsked. "You don't think any woman would have been fearful of two men approaching her at that time of night?"

Danny shrugged. "Maybe so, but the parking area was well lit, and there were at least four other people in the lot."

"And this is why you came to see me today? I've already told you I've never seen these men before. I seriously doubt that my wife knew them, either."

"How much do you really know about your wife, Dr. Woodson?"

"As much as one can know about the woman he's been married to for half a year. I didn't have her investigated, if that's what you're asking."

"Did you know she had a rap sheet?"

Woodson's expression turned to anger. "I don't believe that."

Danny shoved the paper in his hand across the desk for the dentist to see. "Looks like your wife was a junkie, and stealing and hooking to pay for her drugs."

"Now wait just a minute, Landers." Woodson's face was scarlet now, and he looked like he was about to erupt. "My wife would never do drugs. She doesn't even take aspirin."

Danny leaned back in the chair, trying to figure out if Woodson was covering for his wife or if he'd been completely duped by the woman. "That's exactly what I thought. So I pulled up her mug shot." He slid the photo across the table.

Woodson stared at it, then shook his head. "I think you'll agree this is not my wife. And I have to say, Officer, I don't appreciate you coming here with this preposterous story that suggests the carjacking might have been my wife's fault."

"I never said that nor did I mean to infer it, Dr. Woodson. I'm just saying that this is the only Ana Maria Arroyo in the entire state of Oklahoma."

Woodson stared at Danny for a few seconds before responding. "Have you ever seen the movie *Sleeping With the Enemy* starring Julia Roberts?

"What does that have to do with anything?"

Woodson looked away for just a moment before reestablishing eye contact with Danny. "In the movie, a woman fakes her own death to run away from an abusive husband. She resumes her life under an alias so that he can't find her. Is it too hard to fathom that maybe that's what my wife was doing, even though I still don't buy that she knew those two men?"

"That's possible," Danny conceded. "She could have—"

"So she lied about her name," Woodson interrupted. "Like I've told you before, I married her without really knowing her. I'm sure that once we find her, she'll be able to clear this all up."

Danny studied his face, trying to decide if the man was lying or just ignorant about the woman he married. Right now, his gut told him to put his money on lying, but he had no proof. He stood up. "I hope so. In the meantime, is there anything you can tell me that might help us find out who she really is?"

"Like what?"

"Like something she said about another city other than Tulsa that might give us a hint as to where she grew up. Or maybe a lock of hair from her brush for a DNA check."

Woodson stood, walked to the door, and opened it. "I have a couple hours of paperwork to finish up before I can go home. I'll check for anything that might prove useful once I get there." When Danny walked past him into the hallway, Woodson added, "You'll let me know the minute you find out anything more about my wife?"

"Absolutely." Danny walked up the hallway, glancing once again at the picture of the two dentists in Africa.

Something wasn't right about the picture, but he just couldn't put his finger on it. After thanking the receptionist— and getting another round of her ridiculous eyelash batting thing—he walked to his car and got in. But he didn't start the engine.

He was missing something very important. He could feel it. But what was it?

*****

Even as Kate climbed into Miranda Walter's car, she was still mentally slapping herself for agreeing to have drinks with the woman. She'd been Lainey's friend in high school and hadn't given Kate the time of day. So, why was she acting all buddy-buddy now?

"You look great, Kate. That is definitely your color," Miranda said, leaning over for an air kiss when Kate was strapped in. "I always wished I could wear bright yellow, but for some reason, it made me feel like Chiquita banana."

"Who?"

Miranda laughed as she pulled the Mercedes away from the curb and headed down the road. "I guess I'm showing my age. When I was a little girl, my grandmother used to sing a little ditty about a banana woman named Chiquita. Said it was a popular advertisement for the fruit. I would always draw her picture with a big hat and of course, a bright yellow body. "

"Now you're making me self-conscious. I'll be thinking everyone is looking at me and comparing me to a banana," Kate teased before she got serious. "So why did you want to have a drink with me tonight?"

"No reason," Miranda responded. "I just thought we could catch up, and I wanted to see how things are going with you and Ryan."

Kate laughed "Not well. Seems like every time we're on a date, Danny pulls me away for one reason or another." When she realized how that must've sounded, she explained herself. "On our first date, he whisked me off to the morgue to tell Colt something I remembered about Benny, and then last Saturday night while Ryan and I were having dinner at a friend's house, he dragged me away so that Colt could interrogate me."

"Bet that was fun." When Miranda's phone rang, she pulled it from her purse. After glancing down at it, she clicked it off. "Do you have any thoughts about all the things that are happening in Vineyard lately?"

Kate shook her head. "Things are getting weird, but I don't know what to make of them. So far we've had a homeless man die of what they believe may have been ricin poisoning, and it just so happens that his long-lost sister has been in Vineyard looking for him. Then an El Paso cop, who's in town to investigate a double identity thing, ends up dead in his hotel room, and now a young woman is kidnapped. I'm getting a little nervous."

"You think Woodson's wife was kidnapped?"

"Don't you? Maddy said the thugs had plenty of time to grab her purse and make off with just her car, but instead, they shoved her into the back seat and then took off."

"I see what you mean." Again, Miranda's phone rang, and she glanced down at it. "Please excuse me, Kate, but this is the second time the office has called. Give me a minute to make sure it's not an emergency." She picked up the phone. "Yes?"

Kate stared out the window, trying to give Miranda as much privacy as one could while sitting in the car with someone on the phone. It was easier than she expected, since the person on the other end was apparently doing all of the talking. Miranda simply responded with a yes or a no.

After a few minutes she hung up and turned to Kate. "Work. They can never let a girl have a night off without at least one interruption."

"I know that feeling. We'll be lucky to make it through one Cosmo without one of us getting a call." Miranda turned off Main Street into the parking lot at Vineyard Dental Depot. "Hey, Kate, I forgot that I need to ask Woodson one more question about his wife. Do you mind waiting out here? I promise I won't be long."

Kate shrugged. "I'm good. After the day I've had, I can use a little doing-absolutely- nothing time."

"I'll be back in a flash." Miranda exited the car and practically sprinted to the front door. No sooner had she disappeared, when her phone began to ring again.

Kate looked over and saw that Miranda had left her purse on the floor by her seat, forgotten in her haste to talk to Woodson. She worried that her office was calling back but had no intentions of answering it to find out. Then the phone rang again—and again—and on the fourth time, she bent down and retrieved it from the purse. Her breath caught in her throat when she saw Danny's face light up the screen.

Sure she was violating every friend rule in the book by answering, she hit talk, anyway. "Hello, Danny." There was silence on the other end before she announced herself. "I'm on my way to have a drink with Miranda, and right now I'm waiting for her to finish an errand at the dental clinic. She forgot her purse in the car, so I answered it. Can I give her a message?"

"What dental clinic?"

"Vineyard Dental Depot. Miranda needed to ask Jerome Woodson one more question."

"Oh God!"

"What?"

"I just got a call from Colt. He thinks something fishy is going on, and right now, the signs point to those two dentists being involved in more than just root canals."

"Oh no!" Kate glanced at her watch. "Miranda's been in there longer than she said she would. I need to warn her."

"No!" Danny shouted. "Stay right where you are. I'm on my way."

She hung up the phone and deliberated whether to wait on Danny to arrive as he'd said or to go in and somehow warn Miranda about the two dentists. On the one hand, Danny only said Colt *thought* something fishy was going on. That could mean a lot of things and be as innocent as Jerome and his wife having an argument. Maybe Ana Maria had staged her own kidnapping to teach him a lesson. Maybe Jerome had staged it for that very same reason.

On the other hand, warning Miranda would mean she'd have to 'fess up to answering the woman's phone. It might make her wonder if Kate had been rifling through her purse. With the assistant district attorney's power to bring harsher charges down on both her and Benny if she so chose, having Miranda think she'd been snooping in her purse might not be the smartest way to go.

Kate glanced at her watch. It had now been fifteen minutes since Miranda had gone into the dental office. She decided she couldn't wait any longer and grabbed Miranda's purse as well as her own before getting out of the car. If this ended badly with Miranda furious at her, then so be it. She had to at least warn her that Danny was on his way.

As she stepped into the office, the first thing she noticed was that she was the only person in the room. Where was everyone?

She leaned into the receptionist window, barely able to hear the voices coming from the back room. After a few minutes, she figured out the voices belonged to Miranda and Jerome—and they were arguing.

She opened the door to the inner office area and laid the purses on the counter so she could carry out her plan to let Miranda know she might be in danger. The problem was— she had no plan. She scolded herself for not thinking up some logical reason for coming into the building. She'd have to wing it and hope Danny arrived before she got herself into too much trouble.

Creeping down the hall, her attention was diverted to a picture on the wall with both Ryan Kowalski and Jerome Woodson in the center of the group of smiling kids somewhere in Africa. From the looks of things, it was obvious that both dentists had done some kind of missionary work there, which was not odd, in itself—except for the fact that Ryan hadn't mentioned it. There had been plenty of opportunity to share that information with her, especially when he'd told her so much about how he and Jerome had met in college and had been best friends ever since.

As she stared at the picture, something else caught her eye, and she took a step closer. There it was—that thing that was right there begging for her to notice. Both Ryan and Jerome were wearing red rosary bead bracelets, probably a gift from the children. Normally, this wouldn't be unusual, but she couldn't help thinking that it was pretty coincidental that these men had the exact same bead that was the source of ricin circling their wrists.

And ricin was the suspected poison that had killed Ernie Jackson, according to Colt and the ME. Okay, maybe it was just a coincidence and meant nothing at all, but then again, maybe that's what had Danny all excited and racing to the clinic. She made a mental note to bring it to his attention when he got there in case it wasn't.

As she walked further down the hall, the voices grew louder. Stopping in front of the door at the far end, she stood perfectly still and listened as Miranda and Jerome shouted at each other.

"You're going to go to jail, Woodson, and you have your wife to thank for it," she heard Miranda say.

"It wasn't my idea to marry the woman in the first place. Not only was she stupid, she was the absolute ice queen. The only thing I got out of this marriage was a live-in diva, who thought that cooking and cleaning were beneath her, and a cold shoulder every time I tried to touch her."

"Your inability to satisfy your wife has nothing to do with how much trouble you've gotten yourself into," Miranda responded.

"The woman was a goddamn curse, and I'm glad that maniac is stuck with her now," Jerome shouted at her.

Kate covered her mouth with her hand to stop the gasp. She couldn't believe what she was hearing. When she'd first met Ana Maria Woodson with Jerome at his office a few weeks before, it had seemed like the man was overly protective of her. And then there was the ring twirling thing back at the Mission, which she'd interpreted as his way of letting them know he was married and off the market—like anyone cared after they'd gotten one look at his partner, Ryan. It baffled her. How could Jerome harbor those kinds of feelings for his wife and then talk about her in such a negative way like he was doing right now?

She inched closer to the door and was so intent on listening, she didn't hear footsteps come up behind her. When she felt a tap on her shoulder, she turned directly into the body of Ryan Kowalski, who was standing so close, she bumped his chest.

One look at his face, and she screamed at the top of her lungs.

Chapter Nineteen

Ryan's face morphed into utter confusion. "Sorry. I didn't mean to scare you like that."

Kate eyed him suspiciously, not sure what to do next. Before she could say a word, Miranda and Jerome rushed out into the hallway.

"What's going on?" Miranda asked, zeroing in on Kate. "Why didn't you stay in the car? I told you I'd be back in a few minutes."

Kate slid her tongue across her lower lip, a maneuver to give her a few more seconds to come up with a good answer without alarming the two men. "You left your phone and your purse, and Danny called. Said he needed to talk to you."

"You answered my phone?" The accusatory tone was not lost on Kate, reminding her that this reaction was exactly what she'd worried about.

She swallowed hard. "I wasn't going to, but it kept ringing. I thought it might be your office calling with an emergency."

Miranda looked first at Ryan, then at Jerome, before turning back to Kate. "How long have you been out here in the hallway?"

"Not long," Kate said, a little too quickly. "I was so engrossed with this picture of the guys in Africa that I didn't hear Ryan come up behind me. And thus, the scream. I'm sorry if I interrupted your conversation." The minute the words were out of her mouth, she wished she could suck them back in. She'd just let both Ryan and Jerome know that she might have overheard what Jerome had been saying about his wife.

"Well, I, for one, am glad to see you, Kate. I was just coming back to take care of a few things in my office before I drove home. But now that you're here, I'm thinking a nice cold margarita might be just what the doctor ordered. And if a certain female doctor agreed to share one with me, it would really make my day." Ryan reached for her hand. "Maybe this time Landers won't interrupt us."

She tried to act normal, then remembered her earlier conversation with Danny. She had no idea what "something fishy" meant, but now, after seeing both Ryan and Jerome each wearing a red rosary bracelet in the picture, her senses jumped to high alert.

She turned to Miranda. "Can I talk to you for a minute?"

"Sure." The ADA moved closer to her.

"I mean in private."

"What do you need to say to her that can't be said right here?" Jerome asked, the annoyance in his voice unmistakable.

"None of your business, Woodson," Miranda said, before guiding Kate down to the other end of the hall. "What's up?"

Kate leaned in to whisper. "Colt thinks there's something going on here, and Danny's on his way right now to find out what that might be."

Miranda's eyes widened. "When did he tell you he was coming?"

"About ten minutes ago, but the only way here is through downtown, and you know what a parking lot that can be at this time a day. Even with sirens blaring, it would be hard to get past that kind of gridlock quickly." Kate stole a peek over Miranda's shoulder. The two dentists looked to be in a heated conversation. "We can't wait on Danny. We need to get out of here and fast."

Miranda took a deep breath and grabbed her purse from the counter where Kate had laid it. "You're right. Walk back with me, and we'll make our excuses."

Kate nodded, then followed Miranda down the hall. As soon as they reached the two men, Miranda dug into her purse, pulled out a gun, and coldcocked Ryan with the handle before he could even turn around.

When Kate screamed, Miranda whirled around and hit her in the face with her fist. "Shut up! If you hadn't been such a snoop, none of this would have happened."

Kate fought to hold back the tears, but the impact had jarred her, and her cheek where Miranda's fist had connected, was throbbing. "I swear I didn't hear anything," was all she could think to say.

"You're a lousy liar," Jerome said. "I can see it in your eyes. You heard every word I said about my wife. Now, you're going to find out what happens to people who stick their noses where they shouldn't."

Miranda poked the barrel of a gun into her chest and shoved her backward into an empty treatment room. "Sit down, Kate." When Kate hesitated, Miranda smiled. "I don't want to hurt you again, but I will. If you cooperate, you might live through this ordeal."

Kate knew that was an outright lie. Whatever Miranda was mixed up in with Jerome— and she couldn't rule out Ryan being involved as well, even though he was still unconscious in the hallway—she was smart enough to know that she'd seen too much to walk out of the clinic alive.

She glanced at the clock. Where was Danny?

When she was settled in the dental chair, Jerome reached into the cabinet above the sink and pulled out a roll of wide adhesive tape. In a flash, he ripped off two large pieces and taped first her right, then her left arm to the steel rails on the side of the chair. When she struggled against them and screamed as loud as she could, he tore off another strip and slapped it across her mouth. Then he went back to the cabinet and retrieved a strap of some kind. "This is what we use to restrain children when they're sedated. It should work nicely on you." He placed it across her abdomen and clamped it shut behind the chair before tightening it like a seatbelt.

"Hurry up, Woodson," Miranda commanded. "The cops are on their way."

He ignored her and continued to stare at Kate. "I saw the way you looked at Ana Maria right here in this building a few weeks ago," he said. "I could tell you were wondering how a beautiful woman like her could have ended up with a guy who looks like me." He snickered. "If you'd known that I'd only married her to save her from her overly possessive and jealous husband, you would understand just how far I'd go for money. I could see repulsion in her eyes every time she looked at me, but running away from the head of one of Mexico's biggest cartels didn't leave her with many options. The psychopathic spouse has eyes all over the U. S. If she wanted to stay alive, I was her only chance. Believe me, I was paid handsomely to go along with the charade, and even though I never expected her to fall in love with me, I did think I'd get to enjoy some time in the sack with her, at the very least."

He leaned close enough that Kate could smell his breath. It was sweet like he'd just gargled with one of the product samples he gave out to his patients.

"I know you heard me talking earlier," he said in a low voice. "Apparently, the cold bitch broke the number one rule of being on the run. She called her sister in Mexico City." Jerome blew out a breath. "Although Ana Maria got just what she deserved, it's left me vulnerable since the police now know she wasn't who she said she was. It won't be long before they launch a full investigation into both of us."

Kate had no idea what he was talking about, but his face left no doubt that he was furious now. She wanted to shout that the police were on their way, but what good would it do? Miranda already knew that—plus her mouth was taped shut.

As she followed him with her eyes, Jerome walked over to the cupboard and pulled out a vial of some sort of medication, probably a sedative. Watching him fill a syringe, she shivered, positive that whatever it was would end up in her veins.

Before he finished, Miranda bent over the chair with the gun still in her hands. "I'm sorry Katie. If you just hadn't been so damn nosy." Then she turned around and shot Jerome at point blank range.

As the man fell to the ground, his face registered first surprise, then disbelief while blood flowed from his chest across the white tile floor. In that moment, Kate felt a hot rush of terror consume her body. She'd hoped that Miranda had been coerced into taking part in whatever Jerome was mixed up in, and that she'd come to her senses before things got out of hand and someone else—namely her—got hurt.

But that little bubble of hope exploded like a balloon bursting after a pin prick. She'd just witnessed Miranda Walters killing Jerome Woodson in cold blood. No way would the woman allow her to walk out of there alive, despite what she said. And as the ADA, she'd prosecuted many cases and probably knew every trick in the book to make herself look innocent.

Kate tried to think of a way to keep her talking long enough for Danny to get there, but it was impossible with the tape over her mouth.

"I have to hurry before your cop lover gets here," Miranda said, donning gloves before wiping the gun clean of her prints. Moving to the dental chair, she wrapped Kate's fingers around the barrel, making sure to get the print of the right pointer finger on the trigger. When she made eye contact with Kate, she explained. "This will prove that you killed Woodson. Then I'll say you came at me with the gun, but somehow I managed to get it away from you before you killed me as well. And oops! The gun just went off as we struggled. Then I'll slide your body out of the chair and position you close to Woodson before I call the cops and give them my best hysterical performance. When Ryan comes to, I'll convince him that you hit him from behind before you turned the gun on me and Jerome." She wiggled her eyebrows, almost in a comical way. "Kind of clever, don't you think? Woodson turned out to be a major screw-up, and this is the perfect way to get him out of the picture permanently. I should probably thank you for being so rude and checking out my phone."

She stepped on the foot pedal and tilted the table into a semi-upright position. With only her arms taped to the sidebars and the seatbelt restraint to keep her in the chair, Kate could barely breathe and felt her body sliding down the chair. But she didn't have time to think about that. When she looked up, Miranda was standing a few feet away with the gun pointed directly at her chest.

"Sorry, girlfriend, I didn't want it to end this way."

Just as she was about to pull the trigger, the door burst open and Danny rushed in, his service revolver in his hand. "What the hell is going on in here?"

*****

Miranda dropped the gun on the instrument tray that still held the syringe filled with the medication Woodson had drawn up, then she ran to Danny and threw her arms around his neck. "Oh God, honey! You have no idea how glad I am to see you right now."

His eyes strayed to the body lying face down on the floor. "Is he dead?" When Miranda nodded, he took a step forward and leveled his gun. "Is the killer still here?"

Miranda pointed to the dental chair, but it was turned around and he couldn't see who was strapped in it. Cautiously, he made his way over there, and when he was close enough, spun the chair around. He gasped when he saw who it was.

Turning back to Miranda, he shot her a look of confusion. "And you're telling me that Kate Garcia killed whoever it is on the floor over there?"

She bobbed her head up and down. "It's Jerome Woodson. I have no idea why she killed him, but I heard them arguing when I came in."

Danny glanced back to Kate, who was now blinking furiously. His gut told him there was no way in the world Kate could be a murderer, but it was hard to discount Miranda's eye witness account. "Where'd she get the gun?"

"I suspect it's Woodson's. Kate was screaming at him— something about his wife. When she saw me and took her eyes off him, he lunged at her. That's when she shot him."

Danny rubbed his forehead as if that would help make sense of all this. Why would Kate kill Woodson?

"So, you're the one who strapped her into this chair?"

Miranda nodded. "I knew you were on your way, and I figured I would be safer if she couldn't come at me the way she did with Woodson."

"Why gag her?"

Miranda shrugged. "She started screaming obscenities at me."

Up to this point, Danny had been confused about what was going on, but he would bet his life that Kate Garcia was no more a murderer than he was. So why was Miranda trying so hard to get him to believe she was. His gut told him his girlfriend was more than just an innocent bystander in all this, but he couldn't figure out the connection to Woodson.

While he was contemplating this, Miranda moved closer and leaned her body into his, rubbing her ample chest against his. Then she snaked her arms around his body, but Danny didn't react. He was too busy watching Kate blinking her eyes. Two blinks followed by three. Pause, then two and three more blinks. After the third time, a light bulb went off in his head.

It was their signal for danger from way back when they were kids. Two blinks, then three always meant one of them was in trouble. How could he have forgotten that? He pushed Miranda away and leaned down to pull the tape from Kate's mouth, but she was blinking so fast now, he stopped to stare.

Danger! He knew it—could feel it. He turned toward Miranda just in time to see her grab the gun from the instrument table and aim it directly at him. Without thinking twice, he fired, hitting her arm and causing her to drop the weapon. Screaming in pain, she dove for the weapon, which had clattered across the tile floor, but Danny beat her to it and kicked it away.

He pointed his revolver at her. "I hope to hell you have a really good explanation for all this, Miranda. Now stand up and walk over to the corner where I can see you."

Keeping his gun trained on her, Danny snaked his arm around the dental chair, and in one quick motion, ripped the adhesive tape off Kate's face.

She winced in pain before shouting, "Miranda killed Jerome, Danny. Something about his wife running away from the head of one of Mexico's biggest cartels."

"That's a damn lie," Miranda screamed from the corner as she held up her hand. "You need to get me to the emergency room, Danny, before I bleed out right here in front of you."

Danny glared at her. "You always were a drama queen, Miranda. At the very worst, you have a couple of broken bones in your arm." He picked up the gun from the floor. Then he grabbed a stack of gauze and threw it to her. "Put pressure on it with these," he said as she continued to whimper in the corner. He had no idea how she was involved in all this, but right now, he didn't care. If it hadn't been for Kate and their childhood version of Morris Code, he'd be lying on the floor right next to Woodson and be just as dead.

Just then his phone rang, and he shifted the gun to his other hand so he could answer. "Landers."

"Danny, where are you?" It was Colt, and from the sound of his voice, he was excited about something.

"At the Vineyard Dental Depot with Kate and Miranda. Woodson's dead, and Miranda's been wounded."

"I'm on my way with backup. I'll get Rogers to call for an ambulance right now." Danny waited while Colt instructed his officer. When he came back on the line, he asked, "Do you have any idea where Woodson's dental partner is?"

"In the hallway out cold."

"Keep an eye on him," Colt instructed. "Doc Lowell just discovered what poisoned Ernie Jackson."

"Was it ricin?"

"Abrin. It's a sister to ricin, only much more toxic. I'll tell you more when I get there. In the meantime, try to get cuffs on the other dentist before he comes to."

"Why?"

"Because Doc found the source of the abrin sewn into a cavity where Ernie had recently had a tooth pulled."

Danny glanced toward the door to make sure Kowalski hadn't roused to consciousness. If what Colt said was true—and he had no reason to doubt it—one or both of the dentists were involved in Ernie Jackson's death.

But why?

He cut Kate loose with his pocket knife and helped her to stand. Then he handed her his service gun. "Keep this trained on Miranda at all times," he instructed. "I need to make sure Kowalski isn't going to be a problem if he wakes up." He pushed the door open slowly and inched his way toward the still prone Kowalski. When he was close enough, he jabbed him with his foot, and although the dentist moaned, he didn't move. After pulling the unconscious man's arms behind his back, Danny quickly slipped on the cuffs.

As he headed back to the treatment room, his mind was on the information Colt had just given him. He searched his brain for a reason why the two dentists would want to kill the homeless man, but he came up empty. Although Jackson was about to become a rich man, Kowalski, and Woodson couldn't have known that he'd just inherited a multibillion-dollar pharmaceutical company from a father nobody knew he had. Could the two of them have found out somehow and decided to kill him for the money?

No, that didn't make sense at all since the only people who benefited from Jackson's death were Benny Yates and Rachel Alexander, who now controlled one-hundred percent of her father's company.

With his only set of cuffs on Ryan Kowalski, all he could do was make sure Miranda Walters didn't try anything stupid. Retrieving his weapon from Kate, he decided to see if he could get her to talk.

"What were you and the dentists into, Miranda?"

She looked surprised by the question. "Shouldn't you read me my rights first, Danny?"

"You have the right to remain silent. Anything you say or do can be used against you in a court of law. You—"

"Oh, can it, Landers," she interrupted. "I know all that, and I'm choosing to remain silent." She paused when she heard the front door opening and closing and the sound of footsteps running down the hall.

Within seconds, Colt and three of his officers rushed through the door. When he spotted Kate, he moved quickly to her side. "What are you doing here?" he asked before he saw her face. "Are you okay, honey? What's going on?" His voice was now soft and empathetic.

"She killed Jerome Woodson and was about to kill me," Miranda said, moving slowly toward Colt before Danny motioned with his gun for her to back up against the corner wall again.

Colt looked first at her then back at his sister-in-law. "I have to say I find that truly ridiculous, Miranda, knowing how Kate goes to the trouble of catching spiders in a box so she can release them outside unharmed."

"I'm telling you, Colt. She's involved with Kowalski and Woodson in some sort of identity theft thing," Miranda screamed.

Kate glared at Miranda before walking toward her. "Is that what this is all about? Stealing someone's identify?" She faced her brother-in-law. "Finally, something is making sense. Identity theft could explain the other Emily from El Paso and the reason Ross Perry was killed. But I've had more than enough adventure for one day. From here on out, I'm leaving that up to you and your deputies, Colt." Kate sighed, thinking of the horrible poison-induced way Ernie had died. She faced Miranda. "I hope you burn in hell."

Chapter Twenty

Rogers opened the hall door and pushed a very confused-looking Ryan Kowalski into the exam room. "He woke up and started screaming for his attorney. Says he has no idea why we've got him in handcuffs."

Kate made eye contact with Ryan, trying to decide whether to believe him or not. "Are you saying you know nothing about Jerome's wife?"

"I could've sworn I just heard you say you were through with all this amateur sleuthing, Kate." Colt nailed her with an icy glare. "If you don't mind, I'll take it from here." He tilted his head toward Miranda. "My officers are going to take you and Kate out in the hall for a few minutes while I talk to Ryan."

Kowalski glanced around the room. "Where's Jerome?"

Colt tipped his head toward the floor. "Dead."

Miranda was halfway across the room and shouted, "Kate killed him when he tried to restrain her. Don't say another word, Ryan, or they'll find a way to blame you, like they're doing with me," she managed to say before Rogers nudged her toward the door.

Colt shot her a look that shut her up immediately. "First of all, my sister-in-law, in all likelihood, did not shoot your partner, although for now, she's a suspect." He turned to Kate, and as Flanagan guided her toward the hallway, he smiled at her, something Danny hadn't seen him do since the investigation started.

When it was just him and his boss in the room with Kowalski, Colt asked, "Who extracted a back molar from Ernie Jackson recently? You or your partner?"

"What's that got to do with why you've got me in handcuffs like I'm some common criminal, Sheriff?"

"Why don't you just answer the question, and we'll find out," Danny said, taking a step closer.

"I don't recognize that name, so I'd have to say he was probably Jerome's patient." His eyes lit up with recognition. "Hey, isn't he the guy who died at the Mission a few weeks ago?"

"One and the same," Colt answered. "The ME found a bead from some sort of foreign jewelry in Ernie's mouth, sewn into the cavity where the tooth was."

Ryan's face scrunched with anger. "And you think either me or Jerome put it there? That's preposterous."

"The ME has concluded that Ernie was poisoned with—Colt reached into his shirt pocket for his notepad and flipped it open.—Abrus precatorius, a toxin from the seed of what's commonly called rosary pea, Indian licorice, and John Crowe beads, among others."

"Hell, Sheriff. I don't even know what that is. How would I know where to get it?"

"That's what it is!" Danny interrupted, suddenly realizing why he'd thought there was something odd about the picture of Jerome and Ryan in Africa. "There's a picture in the hallway that says differently. Both you and Jerome are wearing bracelets made of that same kind of bead."

Kowalski blew out a breath. "I gave that bracelet to my girlfriend as soon as I returned to the states." He flicked his head toward his pocket. "Get my phone and call her yourself if you don't believe me. But I still don't get it. They use those beads to make all kinds of jewelry over there. How could that have killed the homeless guy?"

Colt referred to his notes once again. "According to Dr. Lowell, the bead he found in Ernie's mouth had a puncture hole on one side that allowed the toxin—which is more potent than ricin, by the way—to seep out slowly into his bloodstream. This guaranteed that his death would occur three or four days after insertion and wouldn't be connected to the tooth extraction."

"That doesn't make sense," Ryan argued. "Why would we do that, knowing you'd find it in an autopsy?"

"Because in most homeless deaths, there is no autopsy. And given Jackson's proclivity for eating out of dumpsters, of course, we'd think he died of food poisoning." Danny shook his head. "It actually was the perfect crime until we discovered a life insurance policy naming Benny Yates as the benefactor. It was too much of a coincidence that Ernie and Emily had died suddenly, both leaving Benny most of their money. We decided to dig deeper and ordered an autopsy. That's when the ME found the bead in Ernie's mouth."

Ryan shook his head. "I swear I had nothing to do with his death, Sheriff, and for the life of me, I can't come up with a good reason why Jerome would want him dead, either."

"I can't answer your question right now, Kowalski, but I promise it won't take me long before I can. Officer Rogers will read you your rights and transport you to the station where you'll be booked for suspicion of murder."

"What about the cuffs?"

"For now, they stay on until we can get you into a room to see how you fit into all of this."

Before the dentist could protest, Mark Lowell and the CSI team showed up to examine the body and bag the evidence. Colt acknowledged the ME before he pushed Kowalski toward the entrance and out the door.

As soon as Miranda saw him and Danny, she became belligerent. "I'm the assistant DA, Colt. I'll have your job if you don't take me to the hospital immediately."

"You do that, Miranda. Right now I have an eyewitness who says you killed Woodson and—"

"Yeah, but not only is your eyewitness a family member, she's also a killer," Miranda protested.

"Maybe she is. But for now, I'll need both of you at the station until we can get to the bottom of this." Colt turned to Flanagan. "You and Rogers take her to the ER and get her arm checked. Then bring her back to the station. Landers, you take Ryan in your car, and I'll take Kate. We'll meet you back there."

Danny opened his mouth to argue, but Colt held up his hand. "Just do what I asked."

Danny nodded and marched Ryan out of the dental clinic in much the same fashion as Flanagan had done with Miranda only minutes before.

When it was just Colt and Kate in the hallway, he stared at her. "You know I love you, right?" When she nodded, he continued, "I've been so hard on you because I was afraid something like this would happen. You're like a little sister to me, Kate. I had to try to stop you from doing something stupid."

Kate smiled up at him. "I love you, too, Colt, but honestly, I was just supposed to have a drink with Miranda tonight. I never dreamed I'd end up strapped in a dental chair waiting to die." She felt tears threatening as she realized just how close she *had* come to that end. If it hadn't been for Danny barging through the door seconds before Miranda fired the gun...

"Is your other sister here with you?" Colt asked. "She always seems to show up when one of you is in trouble."

"Tessa?"

"Yes. Wish the hell she'd stay in the afterworld and leave the police investigations to me."

Kate looked around and was surprised to see her sister's ghost at the door, an amused grin on her face.

Holy crap! I almost missed the party. But you have to know I would never have let that beotch kill you. Tessa smirked. **Tell Colt to bite me.**

*****

The ten minute ride to the police station was spent in silence before Kate turned to her brother-in-law. "Colt, do you think Benny and I will go to jail for moving Emily's body?"

"I have no way of knowing how the district attorney will handle this. It's my job to give him all the facts and let *him* decide if there's enough to proceed to trial. I'm hoping he'll be lenient, especially since you have no prior record, but I can't make any promises. You did break the law, you know."

She hung her head. "I know, but we were only trying to save the Mission, and we had no idea what we did was a felony."

"Doesn't matter. Ignorance is not a defense." He sighed. "I shouldn't tell you this because I don't want to get your hopes up in case it doesn't play out this way, but I'm thinking that Frank Dempsey will have enough on his plate trying to explain how one of his ADAs was involved in a murder— assuming she is."

"Assuming she is? I saw her shoot Woodson in cold blood."

"I know, Kate, but the burden of proof lies with the prosecutor. And Dempsey's going to be busy making his case."

"So you think he might let me slide?"

Colt laughed. "That's unlikely, but I do think he might be coerced into making a deal that is favorable to you, since he now has three murders on his calendar." He pulled into his spot at the police station and killed the engine. "You need to give that guy in Colleyville a call. I guarantee he'll get the best deal for you, Kate." After exiting the car, he walked around to the other side to let her out.

She smiled at him as she slid out. No matter how much he fussed, she knew he would always have her best interests at heart. He opened the door to the police station and allowed her to go in first. Before the door closed behind her, Maddy, Deena, and Lainey rushed up, all talking at the same time as they group-hugged.

"Give the girl a chance to breathe," Colt said. "You'll get an opportunity to talk to Kate once we're through processing her. I need to speak with Kowalski and then Miranda as soon as she gets back from the ER, so it'll be a while before we get your sister into the interrogation room. You might as well make yourself comfortable." He nodded to Danny, who looked up from his desk where he was filling out forms with Ryan sitting across from him, still in cuffs.

"Rogers, will you take Kowalski back to the interrogation room?"

Danny waited until Ryan was gone before he got up and walked over, his eyes on Kate the entire way. "You okay? You want some coffee or something?"

She shook her head. "I'm good, thanks, although I could use an adult beverage about now."

His eyes wrinkled with mischief. "That can be arranged but not right this minute. Seems to me, I do owe you at least one drink for saving my life back there."

"I could say the same thing about you. And I'll take you up on that offer for something stronger than coffee—after I convince both you and Colt that I had nothing to do with any of this."

"I think there's a good chance of that happening." He looked back as Colt called his name and motioned for him to come over. "Gotta go see what Kowalski has to say for himself. Try not to worry too much." He turned and headed toward the interrogation room.

That boy does fill out that uniform nicely, Tessa said, appearing suddenly, watching Danny walking away. **And he definitely has a thing for you, Katie. That can't hurt when he gets you in that room with Colt.**

"Tessa's here," Kate announced, giving her sister an imaginary high five. "With all five Garcia sisters standing together, these cops don't stand a chance.

*****

Ryan Kowalski tapped nervously on the table while Colt and Danny sat down in the chairs across from him. For a few minutes, nothing was said, and the nervous tapping increased. Danny had been in this room with his boss enough times to know that this was exactly the reaction he had intended.

Finally, Colt broke the silence. "Your ex confirmed that she does have the bracelet in the photo, Kowalski. But that doesn't prove you didn't bring back another piece of jewelry made from the same castor beans."

"I didn't, Sheriff. I swear."

"We've also confirmed after looking at your appointment book that your partner was the one who extracted Ernie

Jackson's molar exactly three days before the man died. From his patient notes, he inserted an antibiotic bead for something called PJI. Can you tell me what that is?"

Ryan looked confused. "That's Periprosthetic Joint Infection. It's an inflammatory process around a tooth implant. Although I don't know if the man who died had one, it's odd that Jerome never told me about it. We have a weekly pow-wow about all our patients to discuss things like that and the best way to treat them."

Colt opened the folder and read the autopsy report. "The ME didn't mention a tooth implant." He looked up when Jeannie opened the door and handed him a file folder. After glancing through it quickly, he confronted the dentist. "You've been seen driving a Ferrari Spider around town recently—one you paid cash for, according to the dealer. A little out of reach with a dentist's salary range, don't you think?" Kowalski continued to stare, and Colt pressed further. "We thought so, too, and took a peek at your financials. Looks like your bank account got a lot fatter exactly one month ago—to the tune of a mil-two."

Kowalski leaned back in the chair, a half smile crossing his face. "That's all legit. My dad was also a dentist and owned a small strip mall in Abilene where he practiced. When he got sick he refused to sell the property. I think he always thought he'd beat the cancer and resume his practice." He stopped to swallow back his emotions. "But that never happened. He died and left the property to me. Last year, I was approached by a major Japanese car manufacturer who wanted that property to build a United States headquarters, complete with production and distribution capabilities. My property was the last piece of their project puzzle. So I held out— played hardball. It worked."

Although Danny had been prepared to believe the worst about Ryan Kowalski, his gut told him that the man had nothing to do with Ernie Jackson's murder. And you couldn't lock a man up just for going out with the girl you loved…

Oh my God! He nearly choked on his own spit. Did he just admit to himself that he loved Kate? Could it be possible or was he still trying to be that scrawny teenager protecting his best friend? He was so caught up in his own thoughts that he tuned out the conversation in the room until he saw Kowalski stand.

"We'll need to keep you here while we corroborate your story. Officer Rogers will take you to the holding area." Colt stood and walked the dentist to the door where Rogers was waiting.

When he was gone, Colt looked at Danny. "He's not our guy. We need to talk to Miranda. See if Jeannie can get Frank Dempsey over here to sit in on that interview."

Danny grinned. "Are you thinking you can turn Miranda if the DA offers her a deal?"

Colt nodded. "Miranda Walters was never loyal to anyone, not even to her best friends in high school. If she reacts to the charges like I think she will, she'll jump at any offer that limits her jail time. No DA wants to share a cell with people she put away."

Danny smiled to himself as he relayed Colt's message to the secretary. If all went the way Colt hoped it would, Kate would be cleared of any charges and free to go home. If it wasn't too late, maybe he could take her out for that drink and see what happened.

Waiting for Rogers to bring Miranda to the interrogation room, Danny let his mind wander about the woman he'd been dating for the past two months. She'd mentioned identity theft back at the dental clinic. Could she really be mixed up in something like that? And if so, how could he have not suspected something was going on?

He didn't have to wait long to ask the questions that were burning in his brain. With her right arm in a cast, Miranda walked into the room, glanced his way, then sat down across from him.

Colt looked first at her, then Rogers. "What's the diagnosis?"

"Broken radius and ulna," Rogers responded. "The ER doc said she'll need six weeks to heal."

"I could use a Vicodin about now," Miranda said, defiantly. "But I guess that's not one of my rights."

"No, but you do have the right to have an attorney present, you know," Colt began.

She stared at him before shaking her head. "I'm the best attorney I know."

Danny wanted to remind her that a person who represented herself had a fool for a client, but he figured her arrogance might be to their advantage. "Tell us how you were involved, Miranda."

Her eyes turned angry. "How many times do I have to tell you I wasn't involved? I only know what I heard Jerome and Kate talking about when I walked in."

"And that was?"

She shrugged. "Something about him getting a lot of money for marrying Ana Maria. Seems she was running from her ex, some bigwig in one of the most brutal cartels in Mexico."

"Who paid Woodson?"

"I have no idea."

Colt pulled out a sheet from the file folder and slid it across the table. "This is the real Ana Maria Arroyo. We were surprised to find her name on Woodson's dental client list, so we did a little investigating. Seems she lives under the bridge on Bell Street, just like both Emily Ruiz Santiago and Ernie Jackson did." He nailed her with a glare. "Are you seeing a pattern here, Miranda?"

Again she shrugged and looked so arrogant and sure of herself that Danny wanted to remind her of the seriousness of the charges against her.

"Like I said, I only know what I heard Woodson say to Kate. You might want to ask her about all this."

Just then Frank Dempsey walked in, and Miranda jumped up to greet him. Instead of going to her, the DA made his way over to Colt and pulled up a chair beside him. Miranda's smile evaporated when she realized her boss was not there to defend her.

"We asked Frank to sit in on this because we hoped we could work out a deal with you," Colt said.

"I don't need a deal." Her voice dripped with confidence. "I'm not the bad guy here. You apparently haven't heard a word I've said about your sister-in-law and Woodson."

Colt flipped on the recorder in front of him. "You might want to rethink your position, Miranda."

Danny watched her expression as a conversation between Woodson and what was clearly her voice played on the recorder.

Don't screw this up or we'll both feel the wrath of the big guy, she was heard saying. *He's pleased with your idea about using the homeless. Says he'll be able to double our fee if you can up the number of new identities.*

Her face went from curious, to surprise, then anger in a matter of a few seconds when she realized what Woodson had done to her.

When it was finished, Colt turned it off and confronted her. "Apparently, Woodson taped *all* your conversations. He must've been worried that you'd try to double cross him down the road." He locked his hands behind his head and leaned back in the chair. "Are you ready to help us out now?"

Miranda stole a glance toward her boss. "Frank, what kind of deal are you offering?"

The look on his face implied that he would have preferred not to deal, but to his credit, he kept his voice calm. "I'll take the needle off the table and allow you to serve both murder convictions concurrently."

Miranda slammed her hand on the table. "I had no idea Woodson was going to kill anyone," she screamed.

Colt pressed the start button on the recorder again, and this time, Miranda was heard instructing Woodson to take care of Ross Perry. When it was over, he looked across the table. "Care to comment, Miranda? I don't have to tell you that killing a police officer is a capital offense, punishable by death here in Texas. Your boss is offering you a pretty decent deal."

"Perry might have been a police officer, but he was just as much of a criminal as Jerome was," she said before clamping her mouth shut. "That's all I'm going to say."

Dempsey leaned across the table, his eyes narrowed and angry. "You've got exactly five minutes to take my offer before it goes away." Reaching down, he clicked the timer on his watch.

It only took a minute and a half before Miranda leaned forward. "Okay, but I want to serve my time in a minimum security prison away from all the scumbags I sent away, and I want time off for good behavior."

"You'll be isolated, but no minimum security." the DA countered. "Now tell us about the identity theft."

"What about if I give you the name of the Mexican smuggler who arranges the transactions. He's really the one who's behind all this."

Frank looked at Colt before nodding. "If the Mexican authorities catch this guy with the information you've provided, then yes, we'll consider minimum security."

After a few seconds, she spoke directly to her old boss. "I guess I don't have a choice."

She looked across at Danny. "Could you ask Jeannie to bring me some water, please?"

He nodded. Nobody spoke as they waited until the secretary returned with a bottle.

Miranda took a big gulp then began to speak. "I met a human smuggler from Mexico about a year ago while I was clerking for a judge in Houston. Before long, I was helping him bring high-level, wealthy immigrants into the country, using a forger for the fake IDs." She paused to take another sip of the water. "On a trip to Vineyard to visit my family, I ran into you, Frank. After you offered me a job and I moved back, my contact in Mexico saw it as the perfect opportunity to make even more money together. He had a client waiting in the wings who was willing to pay three times the asking price. All we had to do was guarantee that she'd never be found."

"And that was Ana Maria?" Danny asked.

Miranda nodded. "I'd met both Ryan and Jerome once at a party when I was visiting my cousin in Abilene and was excited to see that they'd also moved to Vineyard. Knowing they were both single, I saw it as the perfect opportunity to hide this woman with a husband and a new name."

"And Woodson went along with this plan?" Danny pressed.

"Not at first. I actually thought Ryan would be the best one to marry her and even went out with him a few times to feel him out. In the end, I decided he'd never go for it and concentrated on Jerome." She took another drink and slid her tongue over her dry lips. "Not only was he interested, but he had this great idea about checking out some of his clients. He thought he could use their identity for the immigrants crossing the border and then relocate them to other cities in the US. When this pro bono dental gig fell into his lap, he started making a huge amount of money just by providing the names of members of the homeless community who weren't using their own Social Security numbers and seemingly had no family ties."

"Seemingly?" She had Colt's full attention now.

"Yes, but he didn't vet them as well as he should have, and it came back to bite us in the ass."

"Emily Ruiz Santiago?" Colt probed.

Miranda nodded. "She was the first of Jerome's screw ups."

"Did he kill her?"

"No," she said emphatically. "Emily did that all by herself. But we didn't know she wasn't using her given name since Jerome checked out Emily Ruiz, not Emily Santiago. We had no idea she was an heiress until after the fake Emily was killed."

"What happened with that?"

"Apparently, the El Paso Emily started dating a cop there."

"Ross Perry?" Danny asked.

"Yes, when she confided in him about her true background, he did a little digging around about her namesake and discovered the real Emily Santiago was rich. That's when he hatched a plan for his new girlfriend to collect monthly stipends from the estate."

"Why did you want Perry to disappear?" Danny asked, carefully avoiding the word killed so as not to put Miranda on alert.

"Because when Perry's lover was killed and it all blew up in his face, he came to Vineyard and approached Jerome with a blackmail offer to keep the cash flowing. Threatened to expose all of us if he didn't keep receiving a check every month"

Colt rubbed his chin. "Why would he do that? He'd go down with the rest of you."

"Not necessarily. He'd been careful, and there was nothing to connect him to the fake Emily or her money. He also wanted in on the deal with the smugglers. That's why he went to see Ernie Jackson's sister. He wanted to see if somehow he and she could connect both murders to Benny Yates."

"So how does Ernie play in all this?" Colt asked. "Was someone using his identity, too?"

She shook her head. "Unbeknownst to Jerome, Ernie was in the office when he was on the phone with me about Emily and Ross Perry. When he asked a couple of questions about Emily, Jerome suspected he might have overheard and came up with the idea to use the castor bean implant after he pulled his tooth. Said it only took enough of the poison to fit in the head of a pin to be lethal." She looked at all three men across the table, her eyes devoid of any emotion. "It would've worked, too, if the Emily ordeal hadn't happened. Ernie was just a homeless schizophreniac with no one who cared about him—or so we thought. Then his sister came to town, and we learned Ernie had left his insurance to Benny. That's when you guys got involved and ordered the autopsy."

Colt bit his lower lip, apparently thinking about all that she'd said and probably trying to decide if he believed her. "Was Ryan involved?"

She shook her head.

"What about Kate?" Danny asked.

Miranda met his stare and gave him a half smile. "Your girlfriend's only crime was sticking her nose in all this."

Danny's heart took off in triple time, hearing Miranda assure them that Kate was definitely not involved. Maybe he would get to take her out for that drink, after all.

Miranda's gaze softened. "You don't think I noticed how you looked at her, Danny?"

He ignored her question and pressed on. "How did Kate end up at the dental clinic with you?"

"When I found out Kate and her sister were the ones who discovered Perry's body, I realized I had to find out how much she knew. Woodson called while we were on our way to have a drink and said he needed to talk to me right away. I should have known she wouldn't wait outside."

A pang of guilt struck Danny. He'd been the one to call, sending her running into the clinic to save Miranda. He had a lot to make up to her. And just maybe he'd get up enough courage to tell her how he felt about her.

Chapter Twenty-one

Kate glanced around Deena's dining room table, and her heart swelled with pride. She didn't need anyone to tell her that she had a great family, but after coming so close to having it all taken away from her, she was more appreciative than ever. She loved these people with all her heart, and what was even better, they all loved her back.

"Earth to Kate," Maddy said.

Kate glanced up and was surprised to see everyone staring at her. "What?"

"I don't know what you were thinking about just then, but the smile on your face nearly split the corners of your lips," Lainey said. "Where were you, anyway?"

Kate moved her eyebrows up and down. "Wouldn't you like to know?"

Make up something really mind-blowing, Tessa said from behind her. **See if you can make Colt blush.**

She ignored her sister's ghost and leaned forward. "I was thinking about how much you all mean to me. I don't think I could've gotten through all this without your love and support."

"Your sisters definitely stepped up," Colt said, taking a swig of his Corona. "The look on Frank Dempsey's face when you all marched into his office was priceless. He didn't know what hit him."

"It was a Garcia frontal attack," Lainey said. "I'm not sure if all of us pleading for leniency had anything to do with his decision to go easy on you and Benny or not, but it's the only thing we could think of."

"Hell, no, it didn't," Maddy said. "After one phone call from that lawyer in Colleyville, Dempsey decided he didn't want to go through another courtroom war that he probably wouldn't win." She snickered. "You gotta love a fast-talking lawyer."

You know what they say. A bad lawyer drags your case on for years. A great one—even longer.

"Tessa said a good lawyer can extend your case for an eternity," Kate repeated. "Guess that's why I got one of those 'pocket probation' things you were talking about, Maddy."

"Yeah, but I hope you remember what I said about them, kiddo. One slip, and you'll be pretty in orange."

Everyone was still laughing when Deena brought in her famous jalapeno popper dip and another pitcher of margaritas. "Colt, do you know what ever happened to Ana Maria Woodson?" she asked.

"Only that when they arrested the Mexican smuggler, he mentioned that she was with her husband again. According to him, the man has the local police in his back pocket, and no one can do a thing to help her."

"Oh no. Poor woman," Deena said, refilling Kate's glass. "So, what about you? How are you and Benny going to use the inheritance money?"

Kate shrugged. "Not sure how much will be left after Uncle Sam takes his share, but Emily wanted fifty percent to go to the homeless community. Benny and I decided to use some of it to expand the Mission with a business office to help them explore avenues to gain access to income they're entitled to."

"Like what?"

"Social Security and Disability checks, for starters. If families wanted to help their loved ones, knowing they'd have a safe place to mail checks would be really helpful." She sighed. "Of course, the Mission will get the lion's share of the inheritance. Hopefully, we'll be able to feed more people. And we've got our sights set on that empty warehouse on Bell Street to eventually convert into a shelter. Maybe a halfway house for the few who can transition back into a normal life."

"Did Benny ever tell his wife the real story about Emily?" Lainey asked.

Kate nodded. "I was there when he did. Wendy cried, but after a while, agreed to go to counseling to try to get past it all. And I forgot to tell you that Benny's going to look into purchasing a mobile food wagon with Ernie's insurance money. That way we can stock it with sandwiches to take to the homeless people who can't or won't come to the Mission. "

"That's terrific. Will you have any of Emily's money left to use on yourself?" Deena asked.

Kate grinned. "After I pay back my student loans, there should be a little left for some family fun."

"Yay for family fun," Deena said as the doorbell rang, "I so need a vacation."

"Expecting someone?" Maddy asked.

She shook her head, then went out into the foyer to see who was at the door. She walked back into the dining room with Danny Landers, looking very hot in shorts and a t-shirt. "Look who I found outside my door," she said, ushering him to the chair across from Kate.

"I called him," Colt said. "Since he was responsible for Kate being here today, I thought he should celebrate with us."

Kate felt a rush of warmth travel from her neck to her cheeks. "Who's minding the store?" she asked, mentally slapping herself for the dumb question.

"Flanagan and Rogers are running the show," Colt said. "Hopefully, now that we have the killers off the street, Vineyard will go back to being the laid back, neighborly city it's always been."

"Yeah. Who would have thought our own assistant district attorney would be the one behind all this," Deena said as she handed Danny a beer and a plate for the popper appetizer.

"Did Miranda give you any clue when you went out with her that she was up to her eyeballs in crime?" Lainey asked.

Danny's face pinked before he smiled. "Boy, wish I could say I knew all along and was just going out with her to get information." He filled his plate with a generous portion of the dip and tortilla chips before adding, "Truthfully, I never suspected anything until she pointed a gun at me."

"Don't feel bad, Danny. She had us all fooled," Colt said. "She's a lawyer, and they know all the tricks."

Yeah, the only difference between a lady lawyer and a pitbull is lipstick, Tessa wise-cracked. **I could go on for hours with lawyer jokes, Kate.**

Kate threw her arms in the air. "Please don't. I want to enjoy today without your twisted sense of humor."

Everyone at the table knew who she was talking to— everyone, that is, except Danny who was looking at her like she had grown a second head.

"I do have a twisted since of humor," Lainey said attempting to make Kate's statement less off-the-wall. "And I so love to make you laugh."

That seemed to appease Danny, and he reached for another helping of chips and dip.

"What will happen to Miranda now?" Deena asked.

Colt shrugged. "It's all up to Frank Dempsey if he gives her any more of a break, but my guess is, he wants the bigger fish more than he wants to punish his ex-employee for embarrassing him and his department." He drained the beer and placed the empty bottle on his table. "Don't forget this is an election year, and the arrest of a big time Mexican smuggler will go a long way in erasing the Miranda Walters debacle from the voting public's mind. That said, there's no way he lets her off without a life sentence."

"What about Rachel Alexander? And Ryan?" Kate asked. "Are you charging him with anything?" She glanced toward Danny, noticing the frown that crossed his face when she'd mentioned Ryan's name. Judging from his reaction, she decided Tessa had been right about dangling another man in front of Danny.

"Ernie's share of Alexander Pharmaceuticals reverted back to his sister when she presented his death certificate to the executor of her father's will. As for Kowalski, he had no idea Woodson was using the homeless patients in his very lucrative scheme to smuggle rich immigrants into the country." Colt checked his watch before continuing. "Last I heard he was moving back to Abilene to join a practice there with some college friends. Said Vineyard held too many bad memories for him."

Kate had to bite back her own glee as she glanced again at Danny. He was now smiling like the proverbial Cheshire cat.

Colt stood and took his plate and empty beer bottle to the kitchen. When he returned, he said his goodbyes. "Lainey and I are having a date night tonight, and I have a lot of things to do before then."

"What time are you bringing Gracie over?" Maddy asked. "Abby's got a fun night planned for the sleepover." She turned to her sister. "Show this man how much we appreciate him not lecturing us for interfering in his case—yet again."

"Oh, I'm not through with you sisters, yet." Colt tried to be serious but was unable to stop his eyes from crinkling with mischief. "I'm just organizing my bullet points. Trust me, you guys are still on my lecture circuit."

That man can be so damn cute when he wants to be, Tessa said. **Too bad I gave him to Lainey.**

Kate wanted to remind her dead sister that she had nothing to do with Colt and Lainey connecting— unless you considered the fact that her death forced them to work together. But she clamped her mouth shut since the last time she said something back to her sister, Danny freaked out. One more conversation to "herself" would send Danny running.

After Lainey and Colt left, Danny and Kate helped Deanna clear the table and load the dishwasher. Kate said goodbye to her sister and walked out to her car with Danny right beside her. When she slid into the driver side, he leaned in close enough that she could touch his lips. She resisted the temptation and waited for him to make the first move, already deciding that if he didn't, she would.

"Have you given any more thought to me taking you out for that drink, Kate?" His eyes looked hopeful.

She wanted to say something funny, but now was not the time. All she could think about was finally being alone with him. "How about tonight?"

His eyes lit up. "You'll have to settle for my pickup instead of a Ferrari," he said, staring into her eyes.

She couldn't hold off any longer and touched her finger to his lips. "I don't care about stuff like that, Danny. I've missed you."

"Me too." He bent lower and kissed her lightly. "Let's see where this takes us." His eyes turned mischievous again. "I'll pick you up at six. We can swing by Emilio's for dinner to go along with that drink. I've been told a woman with her favorite Italian food and a few glasses of wine on board is easier to seduce." He straightened up and started to walk away, before saying over his shoulder, "Be sure and wear that sexy, red blouse you had on when you went to dinner with Kowalski at your coworker's house."

She couldn't help but grin. "Tessa, did you hear that?" But there was no answer.

She poked her head out the window and looked up. She could have sworn she saw Tessa walking through the pearly gates. Before the gates closed, Tessa turned and blew her a kiss.

A sense of sadness washed through her as she wondered when or if she would ever see her dead sister again. In her heart, she hoped she would, but that would mean she'd have to get into trouble again. And that would come with a DOC jumpsuit.

No, for the time being, she had to walk a straight line.

She'd worry about that later. Right now, she had to get home and get ready for her date with Danny. After waiting all this time, she didn't need food and drinks at Emilio's. She was ready to find out if her best friend snored.

The End

About the Author

Photo by: Jane Harbin Helms

Liz Lipperman started writing many years ago, even before she retired from the medical field. Wasting many years thinking she was a romance writer but always having to deal with the pesky villains who kept popping up in all her stories, she finally gave up and decided since she read mysteries and obviously wrote them, why fight it? She's currently working on two mystery series--the Jordan McAllister Mysteries and The Garcia Girls Mysteries. You might also want to check out her romantic thrillers, Mortal Deception and Shattered. She wants readers to know that her G rated cozies are written as Liz Lippmann and her R rated, grittier mysteries as Lizbeth Lipperman.

She lives north of Dallas with her HS sweetheart hubby. When she's not writing she spends her time doting on her four wonderful grandchildren.

Other Books by Author

Writing as **Liz Lipperman**:

Clueless Cook Mysteries:
LIVER LET DIE
BEEF STOLEN-OFF
MURDER FOR THE HALIBUT

Jordan McAllister Mysteries:
CHICKEN CACCIA-KILLER
SMOTHERED, COVERED & DEAD - *novella*

Shorts:
CAN'T BUY ME LOVE - *short story*

Writing as **Lizbeth Lipperman**:

Dead Sister Talking Mysteries:
HEARD IT THROUGH THE GRAPEVINE
JAIL HOUSE GLOCK

A Garcia Girls Mystery
MISSION TO KILL

Romance:
MORTAL DECEPTION (a Romantic Mystery)
SHATTERED (a Romantic Thriller)

74033496R00159

Made in the USA
Middletown, DE
19 May 2018